"Rebecca Mahoney?" The voice on the phone dragged out my name in a velvety, almost amused voice. "I'm Jeanette Sheldon. Perhaps you've heard of me."

I drew a blank. In which of my temporary jobs had I offended this woman? And when? Perhaps the Saturday I was hired to make snow cones in the park? The week I tried to hang wallpaper?

"I've never heard of you," I said.

"I forget how young you are. You must have bypassed the rumors. I want to talk to you about the president. President Remington."

A dead former president. So Remington's death today was the reason I was letting my beer go flat beside me. "I'm just a temp. I'm with a photographer for the newspaper, but we're only covering the St. Patrick's Day pub crawl today. I'm sure the paper will be running a number of stories about Michael Remington tomorrow, but I don't have anything to do with that."

I felt as much as heard her clear her throat. "They'll print interviews with his son, and of course his wife."

"That's right. I'm sure they will."

"But you'll be the one talking to the president's mistress."

I shook my computer mouse to life to do a Web search for Jeanette Sheldon. Maybe she was just a nut. She had to be if, out of everyone in the Bay Area, she'd picked me to confess to.

"*You* were President Remington's mistress? How did you get my name anyway—" I couldn't finish. A photograph of her on the computer screen choked off my words.

"What is it?" The imperious voice sank to a mur~~~ now.

I stared at the dates b
"You're supposed to l

Also by BONNIE HEARN HILL

KILLER BODY
INTERN

DOUBLE
EXPOSURE

BONNIE HEARN HILL

MIRA

ISBN 0-7783-2145-2

DOUBLE EXPOSURE

Copyright © 2005 by Bonnie Hearn Hill.

www.MIRABooks.com

Printed in U.S.A.

To Linda Nielsen and Sheree Petree
for the good ideas and the roadies along the way.

ACKNOWLEDGMENTS

I'm grateful to the following for their assistance and support during the writing of this book:

Dianne Moggy, Amy Moore-Benson, Valerie Gray and Susan Pezzack.

The one and only Laura Dail.

The sales team: Donna Hayes, Loriana Sacilotto, Alex Osuszek, Gordy Goihl, Ken Foy and Fritz Servatius.

Tania Charzewski, Megan Underwood, Chere Coen, Genevieve Choate, John Searles, for spreading the word.

Sheree Petree and Meg Bertini, for the inspiration and feedback. Ditto Nené Casares, Barbara Parnell, Jonni Pettit and The Tuesday Night Writers.

Hazel Dixon-Cooper for the title stuff; Debra Winegarden for the art stuff and the protein drinks; Pat Smith, Jodi Fitzpatrick, Cindy Wathen, Nancy Walker (Kunde Estate Winery) and Bob and Carol O'Hanneson, for the winery stuff; Francine and Hershey Conae for the dog stuff; Jay Crosby for the photo stuff (and the laughs); Auntie Jette for the Palm Springs stuff; Larry Hill for the Sheherazade stuff; Darla Fine for the Whidbey Island stuff.

Darrel Wong for the photo.

Jack Scow and Reneé McCallum for keeping me accountable, even when I was on deadline.

Valley Public Radio, KVPI, for auctioning off a name in this book—and to the mystery person with the high bid; Friends of Fresno City College Library, especially Jannett Jackson and the Simbas.

Noeline Morrison, Rochelle Petroni Kaye, Jennifer Badasci, Jacob Procell, Jimmy, Jared and Thori Hinson. They know why.

Finally, thanks to the Sacramento SPCA and those responsible for placing Parker, the SPCA Cat of the Week, ahead of me on a television news broadcast during my book tour in 2004. He's an amazing addition to my life.

One

Reebie

Everyone in San Francisco was drunk that night, so drunk that I had to drive the taxi.

Saint Patrick's Day. I was raised to be proud of my heritage, proud to be Rebecca Mahoney, otherwise known as Reebie. Still, I was always amused, in a smug kind of way, to see this entire, mismatched city pretending, for twenty-four hours, to be as Irish as I am all year long.

I was working a temp job. After the fiasco with my ex and losing the winery I loved, I couldn't settle. Instead I bounced from cosmetic saleswoman to various temp jobs, to my newest assignment, working through my temp agency, this time for the local newspaper. My job? Coordinate the food at this St. Patrick's Day pub crawl. I'd coordinated

dozens of events at the winery, so this would be no
problem.

The eclectic Celtic wannabes at the pub were already in their cups, as my dad would say. I should
have been, too, crooning "Danny Boy" and forget-
ting about the laptop I'd lugged in like a bad date, at
the insistence of my panties-in-a-wedge supervisor,
who had insisted I keep her posted, via e-mail, re-
garding my whereabouts.

Alberta, the newspaper's HR director who'd
interviewed me, had explained to me that the paper
was trying to drive down its demographics—trans-
lated, get more young readers—by sponsoring the
event. *Dumb* down sounded more like it, but I
needed Alberta's approval for only a short time.

Since I'd lost the winery, I didn't care what I was
or what I did. I had a second part-time job at a cosmetics counter, but this one at the paper would give
me a little extra money and an excuse to hang out
with my photographer friend Daphne Teng.

The television above the bar was broadcasting
footage of former President Remington, who'd died
this morning. The revelers seemed to be paying little attention. Daphne and I snagged the coveted corner booth, the only one with a good-size square table
just large enough for our two pints. Daph snuggled
in against the wall and lifted her glass.

"Cheers," she said in the clipped accent of one
who had been taught English somewhere other than
America. "We don't have to start for thirty minutes.

Let's get a nice little buzz on and check out the guys."

I should have left it at that, focused on the pub crawl, a little beer, another easy temp job. Just hand out the corned beef, make the drunks think they were having fun, collect my money and go home. But, no. Instead of joining Daph in the consumption of a Harp Lager, I had to unfold the laptop on the edge of that tiny table, e-mail Alberta that I'd arrived early, then pull out my cell phone and check my answering machine. When I heard the commanding yet strangely familiar voice of a woman named Jeanette Sheldon on my voice mail, without weighing the wisdom of the move, I called her back.

Clearly disgusted, Daph sighed, picked up her glass and headed for the bar where, if the noise level was any indication, most of the fun was taking place. I didn't blame her.

Jeanette answered. I introduced myself.

"Rebecca Mahoney?" She dragged it out, in a velvety, almost-amused voice. "And I'm Jeanette Sheldon. Perhaps you've heard of me."

I drew a blank. In which of my many temporary situations had I offended this woman? And when? Perhaps the Saturday I was hired to make snow cones in the park? The week I tried to hang wallpaper?

"I've never heard of you," I said.

"I forget how young you are. You must have by-passed the rumors. I want to talk to you about the president. President Remington."

A dead former president. So Remington's death today was the reason I was letting my Harp go flat beside me. I took a bitter swallow and smacked my lips, half-hoping she heard.

"I'm here with a photographer for the newspaper, but we're only covering the pub crawl today. I'm sure the paper will be running a number of stories about Michael Remington tomorrow, but I don't have anything to do with that. I'm just a temp."

I felt as much as heard her clear her throat. "They'll print interviews with his son, his son's wife, and of course, June."

"That's right. I'm sure they will."

"But you'll be the one talking to the president's mistress."

I shook my computer mouse to life, nearly tipping over my pint. I Googled as fast as I could, doing a Web search for Jeanette Sheldon. Maybe she was just a nut. She had to be if, out of everyone in the Bay Area, she'd picked me to confess to.

"*You* were President Remington's mistress?"

"You heard me. The old rumors are true. I'm telling you this only so you'll agree to talk to me."

I hadn't heard the old rumors, but if there were any, I'd find them online. "Why are you coming forward now?" I asked.

"That's part of what I want to talk to you about."

The revelers at the bar launched into "An Irish Lullaby," Daphne's lilting accent soaring over the others. My laptop screen filled with several promising links. This woman might be for real, after all.

Too-ra-loo-ra-loo-ral, too-ra-loo-ra-li,
Too-ra-loo-ra-loo-ral, hush now, don't you cry.

"Leo Kersikovski works in the newsroom at the paper, and I'm sure he'd be interested in talking to you," I said over the song, which seemed to grow in volume by the moment. It would be a good break for hunky Kersikovski. If Jeanette were on the level, he might even scoop the *Chronicle*. Of course, if she were on the level, wouldn't she be calling the *Chronicle*, anyway? "Mr. Kersikovski might still be at work. If you hang on a minute, I can get his direct extension from the photographer."

Too-ra-loo-ra-loo-ral, too-ra-loo-ra-li,
Too-ra-loo-ra-loo-ral, that's an Irish lullaby.

"I said I want to talk to *you*."

The certainty in her tone sent a tiny chill through me. Again, I had a feeling that I'd heard that voice before.

"And I told you I'm just a temp," I said. "My only connection with the newspaper is setting up the Saint Patrick's Day pub crawl. How did you get my name, anyway? Why—?" I couldn't finish. A photograph of her on the computer screen choked off my words.

Beautiful, so amazingly beautiful, but it wasn't her arresting eyes, her flawlessly sculpted features that stopped me; it was those dates beneath her photograph, the second one in particular. *Jeanette Sheldon, 1945-1976.*

"What is it?" The imperious voice lowered to a murmur now.

I stared at the screen of my laptop. "You're supposed to be dead."

"Things are not what they seem. Do you know that poem?"

"What poem?" I sat frozen to the photograph of her on the laptop. Why was this happening to me, and why couldn't I shake free of it?

"*The Emperor of Ice Cream.* A marvelous poem by Wallace Stevens, one of the president's favorites." I could hear the wistful smile in her voice, the softening. "It's time, Reebie Mahoney, for us to talk, and I have something very important to tell you. Now, how soon can you get over here?"

Two

I hadn't wanted to take the cab, but when the driver confessed that his last patron had just shared a pint of Irish whiskey with him, I had no choice but to get him out of the driver's seat.

"The first time, the first," the driver kept repeating, as if he had to answer to somebody. "I have never tasted whiskey, and I will never do that again. Never."

I told him I had an emergency and talked him into moving over. Before either of us was exactly certain what I was doing, I'd slid behind the wheel as Daphne jumped into the back with her camera. Now I feared the driver was beginning to have second thoughts—and so was Daph.

"Reebie," she ventured, "are you sure this is a good idea?"

Through the rearview, I could see most of her

face, the tiny dark glasses, the short sweep of hair for which she forked over more than my car payment to have bobbed in London every couple of months. Its obsidian shine stood out in contrast to the bold, blue streak where it curved against her left cheek.

"We don't have any choice. It's a Nob Hill address. I can get us there in a couple of minutes."

I still knew the streets of this city I loved, where Geoff and I used to come whenever he could talk me into taking a break from the winery. I shot down Howard to Fourth, crossed Geary, Post, Sutter.

"Who'd you call back there, Reebie? Why are we doing this?" English might be her second language, but next to her version of it, my flat California vowels always sounded one-dimensional and limited.

"We're going to meet a woman," I said. "If she's for real, you're going to need photos for Leo Kersikovski."

"I know you kind of like LK. Who doesn't? But do you really think there's a story there?"

Liking his looks didn't mean *liking*. "I barely know him," I said. "It's about her. Jeanette. She said she had something to tell me, and I have to check it out. If she really is who she says she is, it will be Kersikovski's lucky day."

Beside me, the cabdriver adjusted his turban. I could feel his embarrassment in the gesture. I also believed what he told me earlier, that this momentary lapse was a first and a last. I understood firsthand about mistakes and the motivation they could provide.

I glanced up at his photo ID clipped to the visor. Pargat Singh.

"You'd better take the rest of the night off, Pargat," I said. Rebecca Mahoney, great fixer of everyone else's lives. Not so hot when it comes to her own.

"Is against the law." The driver gestured toward the ID.

"So's drunk driving."

Just then, I had to take a sharp corner on Powell I hadn't seen coming. Pargat and Daphne gasped in unison. Then, stark silence.

Pargat had a point. One look at my gender, not to mention the hair I like to think of as strawberry blond, but which is probably closer to faded auburn, and the lamest cop would ascertain that I was not the licensed driver in the photo. What would be the fine for illegally driving this Yellow Taxi that for some ungodly reason was painted putrid green?

"Reebie, this is crazy." Daph's voice had lost its lilt. "You don't need any more trouble."

"I know." Oh, did I know.

"Then, let's go back to the bar, finish the pub-crawl photos, and call LK about this other thing. That will make you look good. He's tight with Alberta. Maybe he can get you more assignments. The community-relations department hires temp help for all of its events."

The voice of reason, but I wasn't listening.

"Jeanette Sheldon claims she was President Remington's mistress back in the sixties and early seventies," I said.

I could feel Daph process, the way a computer does—pausing, processing, pausing, recording. "No one taught us that in American History back in Singapore."

"No one taught it here, either." Adrenaline fueled my climb up to the fancy address. "The media covered up for the president, but the stories leaked out over the years. I did a Google search for Jeanette on the computer. You ready for this? She was supposed to have died in seventy-six."

Daph leaned forward in the seat, and I glanced up at the askew mirror in order to see her better. Her skin was the color of French toast when it's done right, which is seldom. Wonderful—I'd even started thinking like a caterer. "That proves that the woman who called you isn't the real Jeanette. Probably another San Francisco nutcase. Let's not go there."

"We have to. Something about her voice. I think she's on the level."

I didn't say the rest. I couldn't even bring myself to tell Daph—who'd helped me land this assignment—that I had a feeling about Jeanette Sheldon, a link that went beyond our conversation. I was certain I'd heard her voice before. I wasn't sure where. I just needed to do this one thing before I returned to my anonymous life.

The moment we crossed Jones Street, I recognized the building to our right from Jeanette's description. Seven stories laced with ascending fire-escape ladders, an awning shading its entrance—this was the place.

"High-rent district," Daphne said. "Piss-elegant, isn't it?" She loved to use words she considered *American*. I'd often thought she was more of this country than I. She embraced it with much more passion, celebrated every aspect of it, including its tackier ones.

"Bring your camera," I said.

"Are you sure it's worth it, even if this lady really was President Remington's mistress? Everyone at the paper who's worked with you, even that bitch Alberta, likes you. You might have a chance to go full-time in community relations."

Just what I wanted—a full-time job organizing pub crawls, fund-raisers, and let's not forget wine tastings, like many of those I had attended when I was a legitimate vintner.

"Bring your camera," I repeated.

Jeanette Sheldon had told me to ask for Nora McFarland. "I no longer use my own name, for obvious reasons," she had explained.

After an unpleasant exchange with a doorman whose accent seemed a cheap imitation of Daph's, we took the elevator, musty and claustrophobic as a closet.

Daph crossed her arms over her black jacket.

"That asshole needs to brush up on his customer-service skills."

"Never trust a man with lifts in his shoes."

"Really? How can you tell?"

"I'll show you when we leave, and I hope it's soon."

The fourth floor had the hushed, carpeted feeling that was more hotel than apartment. We found the right door at the end of the hall. I stood looking at its large pewter knocker. I'd never used a door knocker in my life. With a sigh, Daph reached across me and pressed the bell hidden along the carving of the door frame.

No one answered. She rang again.

"Well, that solves that problem," I said, disappointed. "I don't know about you, but I'm ready to leave."

She paused, eyeing the doorbell again, as if trying to make up her mind. "But why would she call you, insist that you come over here, and then not open the door?"

"Not my problem." This was my new, post-winery, post-Geoff attitude. I needed to stick with it.

"What if there's something wrong?" The concern in Daph's eyes reminded me—surface flippancy and spoiled-brat lifestyle aside—how deep the vein of decency ran in her.

"You want me to try the knob? Is that what you're saying?"

"If you don't, I will. We can't just walk away."

Why had I come here? Why couldn't I ever learn? I shrugged. "Then do it, if it makes you feel any better."

She twisted the knob, and I half expected it to open, if only because she commanded it to. Nothing. I breathed relief.

"It's locked," she said.

"Good." Whatever game Jeanette Sheldon had been playing no longer involved me. "Now, let's get out of here."

Daphne brushed the blue strand from her eye. It looked eerie in the dim light of the hall. "Maybe we ought to talk to the doorman," she said. "Just be sure everything is okay."

"You really want to tangle with him again?"

She toyed with the diamond at her throat, the only embellishment to her understated attire. "We can just ask him to ring up the apartment. The woman sounded serious about seeing you, didn't she?"

"Very." I had no choice. "Okay," I said. "Let's try talking to that asshole of a doorman."

We'd barely turned toward the elevator when we heard it. A woman's scream, a single, piercing scream, coming from inside. And then, what could only be a gunshot.

Doors opened. Heads poked out. The previously silent sanctuary of wealth immediately filled with activity.

Daphne turned to me. "I knew something was wrong," she said. "Do you think—?" She swallowed the rest of the sentence, but I knew what she was imagining, knew as surely as I could still feel that scream in my gut what we would find inside.

The doorman arrived holding his circle of keys.

"What happened?" he demanded with a look so caustic with suspicion that I felt compelled to defend myself.

"I don't know. She never answered the door."

"Step back, please." He moved ahead of Daph, rapped his knuckles against the door, then unlocked it.

"Mrs. McFarland," he called. "Is everything all right, ma'am?"

He went inside, and so did we.

"Holy shit." The haughty doorman demeanor had vanished. In its place was a scared, speechless little man in a uniform a size too big for him.

I wanted to turn around, leave, run away from this, but it was too late for that. Instead, I stepped beside him, steeling myself.

A woman sprawled across the once-white sofa, now splashed with the same blood that leaked from the hole in her head. She'd been shot as Daph and I stood outside her door, debating which steps to take next.

I stepped back from this surreal scene. The paintings on every wall were smoke-wrapped images of women's faces and torsos, black and white except for the vivid reddish-purple lips. They would have struck me as disturbing in a different setting. Now, they seemed mild compared to what I was witnessing. Cold air whipped into the room. I motioned toward the opened louvered doors.

"In there," I said to Daph. "Someone was in here."

She headed through the doors. I tried to follow, but the doorman stopped me, firmly gripping my arm. "No one's been in here but you."

"That's ridiculous." I shook myself free of the twerp. "I told you we never came in here."

"So you say."

"Of course I say. That's how it happened. Shouldn't you be calling the police?"

"I did, from downstairs. You and your Japanese buddy aren't leaving until they get here, either."

"Chinese, and we'll leave when we feel like it."

A woman screamed from the hall. A man in a suit crowded into the room. When he saw the sofa and the woman on it, he said, "Oh, my God," and left as rapidly as he entered.

Another scream. The same woman.

Daphne shouted from the next room. "The window's open. Someone could have gone down there."

I moved closer to the murdered woman, as if pulled to her by an invisible chain. She was fifty, possibly older, one of the most beautiful women I'd ever seen, caramel-colored hair pulled back from her smooth forehead, eyes full of the same fear that had filled her final scream. Horrified, I stood there, unable to turn away.

I tried to swallow, to breathe through the dizziness that overtook me.

"Reebie." Daph touched my arm. "What is it?"

"I know her," I said. "I mean I've seen her."

"You have? Are you sure?"

I nodded. "I talked to her just last week."

Three

The Mistress

Cabo San Lucas
1975

They called it Mistress Eve. Jeanette had coined the term when the four of them had decided to gather, dateless that Christmas Eve, at what Marcus called his *hideaway* in Cabo San Lucas. Not much of a hideaway with the likes of his actor buddies flying in, demanding everything from margaritas to women in the local bars. Eddie Palacios, her old lover and good friend, was on his way from New York and would be there in time for dinner.

Jeanette and Kim had worked all day in the beach house on her new idea for what she wanted to call the Scheherazade Pose. She photographed Kim from every angle with her wonderful old Nikon with its huge motor drive, better than the clichéd Hasselblad most photographers flashed like Rolexes. They'd smoked almost a carton of Winstons before they got it right. Not *smoked,* actually, Kim pointed out, as they collapsed in laughter and Kim finally threw on a robe. They just *puffed.*

While Kim rested from the photo shoot, Jeanette and Marcus finished the food. She wrapped slices of bacon around fresh, briny-smelling prawns, and then made fondue in a large pot, a votive illuminating its tarnished silver finish.

"You know this little rendezvous of ours will be in the gossip columns tomorrow," Jeanette said.

"One can always hope." Marcus returned to trimming the tree full of tulle bows and bubble lights. With his Vandyke beard, his velvet jacket and his dark hair parted in the middle, he looked as if he belonged in a Renaissance painting. "If anyone can keep the press off my ass, it's your lovely self on my arm."

"Why, thank you, sir." She nodded at the Edwardian jacket. "Right now, you look like anything but a television doctor."

"I'll cut the hair, maybe rearrange the beard a bit when we start shooting. What do you think?"

"You're preaching to the choir, Marcus. I think you're the sexiest actor in Hollywood, with or without the Vandyke."

Standing at the primitive counter across from

him, Jeanette added the flour-dusted shreds of Swiss cheese into the chafing dish, nudging the mixture with a wooden spoon until it began to separate and thicken.

"Mistress Eve," she said, just to test the sound of it in this large room, determined to hide the stab of pain with humor. "But I'm the only legitimate mistress. Kim's getting a divorce. Eddie's doing what he refers to as *freelancing* after that embarrassing breakup with Miss Fluffball. And in spite of what you say, you haven't been dumped, my dear drama queen. This is just the latest of yours and Hal's many tiffs."

"Tiff, is it?" Marcus raised a bushy brow. "I'm gay, so it's a tiff. But Kim splits with her husband, you get stood up by the prez, and it's the end of the world."

"At least you don't have to picture the man you love celebrating with the first frigging family while you're alone. No matter how free they say they are or how much of an understanding they say they have, married men always head home for Christmas. Even the president of the United States."

"I know you're hurting, honey, but pain's pain. And alone's alone," he said. He stood up from the tree, still only partially decorated by his standards but splendid by anyone else's. It conjured a multitude of memories and wishes of every Christmas she'd celebrated since childhood, this tree that managed to balance both nostalgia and style. "And I think it's time we had some champagne."

He opened the refrigerator, pulled out a bottle and placed it on the other side of the block. Jeanette leaned across and touched his cheek. He could always make her smile, even when he was chastising her. "Why do you have to be so damned smart?" she said. "You're absolutely right, of course. These days, I can't seem to see past my own soap opera."

"It's not a soap opera." Marcus rocked the cork gently out of the napkin-wrapped bottle. "To your misfortune, I fear it's the real thing."

"It is," she admitted. For years, she wouldn't have cared, would have danced away like the bubbles in their champagne if a man of hers, president or not, had stood her up. But she'd made the major mistake of indulging in what she believed would be only a one-night stand. "The prez, as you call him, isn't as bad as you think," she said, as much to assure herself as him.

"Of course not." The scowl only enhanced his smoky features. "When you're in love, sometimes you have no choice but to be alone," he said. "Sometimes, the love has to be enough."

"I wish it were that easy." Jeanette took the flute he handed her, watched it fill with bubbles. She wouldn't let herself give in to sadness or wonder what President Michael Theodore Remington was doing right now. She refused to let pain and memories spoil this moment. "I don't know what I'd do without you, Marcus."

"Nor I without you." He finished filling his own

flute, and soft mousse formed at the top of the glass. "No matter how screwed up our personal lives are, we have each other."

"Sounds like a toast to me." She lifted her flute, tipped it toward him. "To Mistress Eve."

He touched his flute to hers, clinked. "To Mistress Eve. Long may we wave."

The champagne tasted happy, carefree, the way she should feel tonight. "I'm sorry I downplayed your problems with Hal," she said.

Marcus grinned and took another sip. "A mere tiff," he said. "He'll be begging to come back before New Year's."

Palm Springs
1976

The doorbell rang. Jeanette moved slowly toward it, remembering the year before in Cabo—the toasts, the champagne, the laughter, Mistress Eve. She could still see the four of them—Eddie, Kim, Marcus and her, at the piano, could still hear her own broken voice, far too late in the evening, trying to sing "Santa Baby" the way Eartha Kitt did.

Mistress Eve. Only one year ago, and everything had changed.

Four

Reebie

Thanks to the doorman's insistence that we were the only ones he'd allowed in the building in two hours, the police officers decided to question Daphne and me separately. The older, soft-spoken African-American one introduced himself as Officer Morgan and took Daph somewhere upstairs. I got stuck on an unoccupied patio with a smart-ass, short as the doorman without his lifts, with white-blond hair buzzed to his skull.

"And you came here because—?"

"Because I got a call from a woman who said she was Jeanette Sheldon," I said.

"You get many calls like that?"

"Never."

"So why was she calling you?" He had the watery lie-detector eyes that assured me he had heard every story in the book. Something about him made me feel guilty before I as much as answered him. I could almost feel the mechanism in his mind trying to decide yea or nay. He still wasn't sure if I was the source of the bullet in Jeanette Sheldon's head.

"She said she'd been President Remington's mistress back in the sixties."

He raised a colorless eyebrow, wrote in his book. "Did anyone hear you talking to her?"

"My friend, Daphne Teng. She's a photographer for the newspaper," I said. "I'm a temp for the catering service."

"She heard the conversation?"

I felt trapped on the too-small patio with the cold eating into my skin. I hadn't done anything, but he was going at this with the gusto of someone who'd cornered a killer.

"She went to the bar when I made the call," I said.

Just then, the other officer joined us with a look I couldn't read.

I moved closer to him, shivering from the icy air, trying to distance myself from his partner. "Where's Daphne?"

"Ms. Teng's downstairs." He cocked his head, with a friendly checking-me-out kind of expression. "She said you were acquainted with the victim. Is that correct?"

No point in lying. I'd done nothing to lie about. Tell them what I knew and maybe I could get out of here. "I've seen her before, at my other job. I work as a makeup artist, too. She came in a couple of days ago."

He urged me on with a nod, the other cop fading into the evening. "Could you be more specific?"

"Tuesday, I think. Yes, Tuesday." I hadn't recognized her from the old photos on the Internet, but just one glimpse of her dead—that splendid hair with the unusual golden taffy color—and I was convinced it was the same woman. "She came in for a makeover," I said, "but we ended up just talking. She bought a lot of product."

A slight frown, borderline distasteful. Bushy eyebrows pinched together. "Product?" he asked.

"Cosmetics," I said. "Moisturizer, I believe. Night cream, foundation." It had been my largest commission of the day. That's why I remembered it. Rent money, I'd thought at the time.

The smart-ass pulled his chair from the table with a loud scrape. "Want me to check on the other one?" he asked Morgan, who was clearly his superior.

A short nod. Eye contact. "Why not go on down there?" he said. "Ms. Mahoney and I can finish up here and join you." As if it were a party and not an interrogation. As if I were here by will. This was good-cop/bad-cop all the way. One had frightened me. This one was going to help me. Only one flaw in that theory—I hadn't done anything, nor did I know anything.

"So," I said to Morgan, after his partner departed. "What's next?"

He gestured toward the chairs. "Why don't we sit down? You smoke?"

"No." I stared at the chair he pulled out for me.

"Mind if I do?"

"If I have a choice, I wish you wouldn't."

His chuckle sounded genuine, a sign of a good interviewer. "My wife says the same thing." He settled into the opposite chair, and I perched on the one he'd designated for me.

"Am I a suspect?" I asked. "You surely can't believe that doorman. Someone else had to be in the building. He just doesn't want to admit that whoever it was got past him."

"Think he's trying to cover up for being away from his station?" His tone implied more colleague than suspect, more insider than outsider. I couldn't help answering the same way.

"No doubt. He probably went out for a cigarette, nothing personal, and now he's trying to save his own behind." I pressed my palms into the cold glass of the table. He leaned forward, as if we were sharing drinks in a bar.

"You say you talked to this woman. Can you remember what you talked about?"

It came back to me with a start. I still wanted to get out of here, still wanted no involvement in the story connected with this murder. Until my moment of escape, maybe I could help this guy, this decent cop. If I could, I would.

"The cosmetics," I said. "She had a lot of questions about how they worked. And my job. She asked me about that." Crisscrossing my arms, I tried to rub away the sudden chills that sprang from within and not from the fog-chilled air. Her interest had seemed a little strange at the time, especially in that narcissistic world of cosmetics when customers want to talk about *their* skin, *their* flaws, real or imagined. Now, knowing who she was, our conversation seemed stranger still.

"What about your job? Can you remember?"

"If I liked it. How long I'd been there."

He nodded. "And what did you say?"

"I just answered her questions."

The fog thickened as darkness descended onto this tiny roost. He tapped his pen against the notebook in front of him. "Odd," he said.

"How's that?"

His grin broke through the fog. "Hey, sorry. I was thinking aloud. "How'd she pay for her purchases? Did she write you a check, use a credit card, maybe?"

Again that memory returned. "Cash," I said. "Twenties." Crisp and brittle bills, sticking together, as if she just removed them from an ATM.

He nodded. "So, that means she didn't have to show ID. She didn't give you her name, did she?"

"Not until we talked on the phone." Even if they were good-cop/bad-copping me, I liked this tall, rangy guy who couldn't hide his smile when he spoke of his wife and who wouldn't smoke if someone preferred it that way.

"You're aware the apartment is in a different name?"

"Yes. I'm not even sure that woman is the real Jeanette Sheldon."

"Why not?"

"Because as we spoke in the pub, I did a computer search for her on my laptop. The only Jeanette Sheldon I could find was supposed to have died in nineteen seventy-six."

"So who's the woman who was killed?" he asked, as if I should know. Although his voice was serene as the moist breeze that glided over us, I knew from his tense shoulders, his frozen smile that he was going for something, something that I couldn't even begin to guess.

I rubbed my arms again, trying to warm them. "I don't know," I said.

His eyes looked like hollow shadows in the darkness. "And other than that one time, Tuesday, at the department store, you've never seen the victim before?"

"Absolutely."

He leaned just a little farther across the table, close enough that I could smell the subtle scent of his cologne, a scent that would be understated, maybe even sexy, if it weren't for the tone of accusation that accompanied it.

"Why, then, Ms. Mahoney," he asked, riveting his gaze to mine, "does she have a photograph of you in her apartment?"

Five

The Mistress

Palm Springs
1976

The scent of bayberry followed Marcus and Jeanette down the shag-carpeted hall, toward her bedroom. Kim had sent three glittery, carved candles, "for new beginnings," she'd promised. They'd both been surprised when Kim's candlemaking business became more than a hobby.

In November, the flavor of the month had been gardenia, which Kim had assured would encourage commitment. Better request a barrelful of those for the new year.

They reached Jeanette's bedroom. She met his eyes at the door. "I can't believe it's been a year since Cabo," she said. "And now—" She fought tears. Why did love have to be so difficult, or did some people just need to make it that way?

"It's going to be okay." Marcus threw back the double doors of her closet, looking first inside, then at her. He. He'd need to change soon, and so would she. That was the tough part. How could she go through with Mistress Eve tonight? How could she pretend everything was the same?

"I remember when I had only one black skirt." She flipped on the one dim bulb and stared into the closet full of black—dresses, sweaters and, yes, skirts—mini, micromini, leather, jersey, angora, silk, even one made of paper and resembling the Yellow Pages in the phone book.

Marcus followed. "What did Sophie Tucker say? 'I've been rich and I've been poor. Rich is better.'"

"One black skirt, Marcus, and a couple of sweaters. One jacket." Remembering it brought back the empty, shut-down feeling of being without anyone, anything, even hope, back in those Las Vegas days before Eddie Palacios changed her life and her luck. And now, it was all going to change again. How would Eddie feel about that? This one might be even too big for his solid shoulders.

"That was then." Marcus began sorting through the garments hanging on the opposite side—holding out, discarding, holding out, discarding. And when he realized she was watching him, he asked, "May I?"

"Of course. You're the expert. In all honesty, I don't really care tonight."

"You've got to care." He frowned at her over his shoulder. "You need to be with people who love you tonight."

"Rem loves me." It came out unbidden and angrier than she'd intended.

"I'm not debating that point. But the prez is spending the night elsewhere."

"He can't help it. You know that. The whole damned nation wants to snoop on the White House during the holidays." The closet seemed to close around her. "I know you'll never believe it, Marcus, but he is in love with me."

"Oddly enough, I do believe it." He reached across the tiny space between them and squeezed her arm. "Listen, honey. We'll make it a grand Mistress Eve. Better than last year, even."

She moved closer to him, so close that she could smell his exquisite scent that reminded her of old castles, tapestries. "I notice you haven't shaved for a while. Guess that means you and Hal broke up again."

He returned to shuffling through the clothes, his back to her. In a muffled voice, he asked, "Hal who?"

One thing the early days in Las Vegas had taught her was when to speak and when to smile. She smiled.

He turned. "I mean it, Jeanette."

She smiled again.

"Say something, damn it."

"I said something last year and got in trouble."

"Ah, yes." Spoken in the actor voice. "The *tiff* word. I forgave you then. I forgive you now. And, by God, I'll shave tonight, right after I find you something to wear."

"I told you I don't care."

"And I told you this is the most important time to care." He reached into the darkness and pulled out a memory she'd forgotten, a slinky dress, more pimento than red. "Oh, this is fabulous. Remember that day?"

How long now? Three years? Marcus had spotted the flawless empire gown that he insisted carried, "all the energy of red without shouting." Ed Palacios had paid for it, of course, shrugging off the price by saying that true fashion was eternal.

As she reached out to touch its silken surface, Jeanette realized this gown was a link to something good, something lasting.

"I remember," she said. "But tell me, fashion maven. Is the empire look still in?"

Marcus gave her one of his snobbish sighs. "You tell me how many years it takes fashion to travel from Paris to the States. May we all live that long."

She touched the gown again. "It's really lovely. More than that, the memories are lovely."

"So, put it on." Marcus shoved it into her hands. "I'll step outside. You get dressed. Then, we'll go meet Kim and the others, and you will, as always, movie stars or not, be the most desirable woman in the room."

She didn't feel desirable. The gown was far too clingy for her mood. "I can't do it," she said.

Before he could answer, the phone rang. "Want me to get it?" he asked.

"Please." She took the hanger from him, left the closet and, standing before the narrow mirror at the foot of her bed, molded the dress to the curves of her body. Its bright optimism underscored her own, far more complicated, conflicting emotions. How could she go through with this? How could she possibly?

Pacing the room, phone to his ear, its long, beige cord snaking behind him, Marcus appeared to have forgotten her.

"No way. No way in hell, and why now?"

"What?" she asked. He waved her away, squinting as he absorbed whatever the caller was telling him, as if the words hurt his eyes as well as his ears.

"I see your point, man." He sank down on the padded bench at the foot of her bed and shoved the phone out to her.

She shook her head and whispered, "I don't want to talk to anybody."

"Not even Ed Palacios?"

"Eddie? He's on the phone? Why didn't you tell me?" She nearly tripped over the bench getting to him. "Of course, I'll talk to him."

Marcus handed her the receiver. "All yours."

Still holding the dress in one hand, she settled beside Marcus and pressed the phone to her ear. "Merry Christmas, Mr. Palacios," she said. "Aren't you supposed to be on some TV special tonight?"

"It was prerecorded." His voice was ragged and raw, as if the nightlife might be catching up with him.

"We're going to meet Kim, but wherever we are, you can be sure I'll be watching you singing about that merry little Christmas. It still brings tears to my eyes."

"Jeanette, honey." His voice. Something was wrong with his voice.

"What, baby?" she asked.

"You trust me, don't you?"

Her skin went clammy. Why would Eddie, of all people, have to ask? "I trust you with my life. But you know that," she said. "What's wrong?"

"I trust you, too, and I love you." He hadn't answered her question.

"What's *wrong?*" she repeated, her voice more strident than she intended.

"We've got a little problem," he said. "It could be a big problem, and unfortunately, this is the only night we might be able to fix it. Jeanette, from now on, I want you to do exactly what you're told to do, even if it doesn't make sense."

"Do what I'm told?" she asked. "I'm going to a Christmas party, Eddie. What are you talking about?"

"There's no more time. Just remember what I said, and remember I love you."

Before she could respond, the phone went dead.

"How odd." Still seated, holding the phone in one hand, the dress in the other, she looked up at Marcus, only to find his expression as unreadable as Eddie's voice had been. "Did he sound weird to you or what?" she asked.

"No." He reached out, took the phone from her and hung it up, the way he always attended to the details of her life.

"He sounded weird to me. Is it because of what's happened? You didn't tell him, Marcus, did you?"

"That's not important now." His stubbled jaw clenched and unclenched. He stood and reached for the dress. Without thinking, she handed it to him. He slammed it down on the bed and put out his hand, as if expecting her to take it.

This wasn't the Marcus she knew. Something had happened, something he'd kept from her. She tried to joke, to bring him back with the easy banter that might help hide her uneasiness.

"You're right about the dress. It's perfect, and I can pull it off, I really can. But I need to change right now. We can't be late for Mistress Eve, now can we?"

He didn't appear to hear her, cocking his head, as if listening to voices farther away than she could hear. "No."

"No what? No dress? No Mistress Eve?"

"Nothing." He moved closer, so close that she could see his flat, glazed eyes.

"But why?" she asked, as she felt herself shrink back from him.

"We're going to have to leave now."

"We can't. I need to change my clothes. We are going to Mistress Eve. We're still doing that, aren't we, Marcus?"

His fingers locked around her bare arm, just short of uncomfortable.

"There's been a change of plans," he said.

Six

Reebie

The cop's question followed me home, hung around the apartment, rode in the truck to work with me the next morning. Why did Jeanette have a photograph of me?

The cop had refused to let me see it. When I asked if it was a recent photo, he seemed to let down his guard, as if my shock had helped me ace the truth test he'd set up for me. "Looked that way," he said. "It was taken at some kind of counter in a store."

Had Jeanette sneaked in a camera and photographed me without my knowledge? I hadn't realized how vulnerable I was in the store, with only a glass counter between me and anyone who wanted to approach.

I hesitated in the parking lot, wondering if I really wanted to go to work today. I didn't have a choice. At least, I'd have Sunny to talk to today. Being around my beautiful and upbeat co-worker always made me feel better.

I couldn't help thinking, as I walked across that cold, mostly empty parking lot, toward my non-job, that in a perfectly green, perfectly calm corner of Napa Valley, the sun would be shining over that little farmhouse winery that used to be mine.

When Sunny pulled into the parking lot, I remembered something my dad told me. "Never trust a person who doesn't have at least two close friends." For a while, after what happened with my marriage and the winery, I was becoming that person he warned me about, afraid to trust or let anyone close to me. If the camaraderie came and went with the job, why bother? But Irish logic, like Irish food, is based on survival. Thanks to Daph, who bought her cosmetics here, I met her friend Sunny, and now I had both a new friend and another job.

Sunny climbed out of a tiny silver car, one of those retro designs, all curves and angles. She was built the same way, so flawless in her smock and full-face makeup, as we called it, that it was difficult to understand how she had so many man problems. Her lips, glossed a vivid apricot color only she could wear, all but shouted, *Kiss me.*

When she was working on a client, especially another brunette, the eye shadows and lash enhancers almost flew off the shelves. I wondered how makeup could look so much like light and shadow, so much like perfect flesh. I would never learn to coordinate all of those brushes and powders we sold. And I could never glow in the dark, as I was sure Sunny Perry could. There was something off about her today, though. Instead of the usual hug, she turned from me and made a show of checking to see if the doors were locked.

"Where did you get that?" I asked, staring at her car and wondering what was wrong. "It's wonderful."

"Isn't it cool?" She turned back to smile at the car, as if it could see her. "I can't believe it's really mine."

"You deserve it," I said. "I wish I could afford new wheels, or old wheels, for that matter."

"You could, you know, if you'd spend any of your settlement."

"It's all I have. I don't dare." The very word made me angry. Some settlement.

"Sorry. I know how you feel about that." It was one of the things I liked best about her. In spite of her glitzy veneer, she cared about her friends and was quick to apologize if she thought she'd offended them. She looked back at the car one more time. "I'll be in debt for the rest of my life, but it's worth it. Besides—" she winked "—I had a little help with the down payment."

I wanted to tell her that what a man gives in the name of love he can take back in the name of the law.

No. That was a lesson she had to learn on her own, as I had.

Instead, I said, "I guess that means you and Parker worked it out." *Never trust a man whose name is trendier than yours.*

"Not exactly, and he'd best be careful how he treats me. As my grandma used to say, he's not the only pebble on the beach." Sunny squinted at the black face of her watch, as if she could see the invisible numerals the diamonds represented. "We'd better hurry. I'm glad you waited for me, though. Daph called me early this morning and told me about you guys finding that woman's body. What a bummer."

She shot me a glance, and I could almost see the uncertainty chasing around her brain.

"It was pretty awful," I said. "The woman was murdered."

"And you're a suspect?"

"Of course not. Where did you hear that? Certainly not from Daph?"

I felt her hesitation like a wedge between us. She bit her lip. Next to her pale, powdered skin and eyes more frightened than friendly, the apricot gloss now looked orange and garish.

"She was really blown away by what happened. I probably just didn't hear her right."

We punched in, Sunny first. Although she had her own smock, mine belonged to the store. I slipped into it and followed her inside, up the escalator. The multifragranced floor met us as we stepped off.

"We're going to have tons of stock to arrange," Sunny said, changing the subject. "Summer stuff is already coming in."

My dad always said, "All work is noble." To prove it, he'd insisted I help him on the farm in the summers, even when I was in college and landed a job as a sommelier at a restaurant.

Hey, Dad, what do you think about this? Unloading cartons of eye goo when you know where I should be?

All work is noble, darlin'.

Right, Dad, right.

Sunny moved with the stiffness of indecision. I knew this was the part of the job she liked the least, the reality that created the glamour, the setting for her stage. Still, I felt something other than this lackluster grunt work was bothering her. Surely she couldn't believe that I had anything to do with what happened to Jeanette.

"Remember I told you about that rich lady who'd made my day? The one who said she wanted to paint me?" I asked.

"*She* was the woman who was killed?" Sunny almost dropped a carton of eye goo on the glass counter. "The one you said was so nice, who asked about you instead of talking about herself?"

"She was Jeanette Sheldon. The next time I saw her was last night." I remembered that face of death again as clearly as if it were before me, as close as Sunny was, closer.

She set the carton on the counter. "Why you, Reebie?"

"I don't know."

"Do you think it has something to do with your settlement, your ex, the winery?"

"How could it? Jeanette didn't have anything to do with the winery." I didn't repeat her claim about being President Remington's mistress. That would come out soon enough. "Apparently, she had a photograph of me in her apartment."

"No!" Sunny looked up from the opened carton to me, and the fear I saw in her eyes almost made me feel sorrier for her than I did for myself.

"They wouldn't let me see it, but the cop said it was taken at what looked like a cosmetics counter. I wonder if she took it while she was here that day."

"Like she had the camera in her purse or something?" Sunny stopped the unpacking process altogether and grasped my wrist. "Tell me the truth. I'll help you any way I can. Parker will too, I swear."

"You don't believe me, do you?" I said. That's what was wrong, what had been wrong since I'd first seen her emerge from her new car. Sunny had already decided that I was involved in Jeanette's death. Decided—or been convinced. Parker was not only an attorney, but an opinionated man, and Sunny usually allowed him to control her beliefs.

Although she hated confrontation, she didn't back down from this one. Still holding my wrist, she lowered her voice to a whisper. "You don't have to take

the blame for something you didn't do. There are rumors about that woman. That she was the mistress
of a famous man."

I shook my arm free. "Where did you hear that?"

"Everyone's going to hear it soon," she said, ignoring my question. "I know you didn't kill her, but
why don't you tell me why she contacted you and
why she had that photograph of you in her apartment?"

So, I didn't have two friends in the world, after
all. Sorry, Dad.

I had one friend I could trust and another who,
well intentioned as she probably was, thought I was
crazy, immoral or both—enough so to lie about my
connection to a murder victim. This must be her
boyfriend's interpretation. Typical attorney.

"You're wrong." My voice was harsher than I intended. Maybe not, though. Maybe it was as angry
as I felt. "Let's get these boxes unpacked, okay?"

She bit her lip again, looked down at the packages
of eye goo before her. "I was only trying to help."

"I understand that," I said, "but I don't want to
discuss it anymore."

Silence, then, "Would you talk to Parker if I had
him call you?"

"Absolutely not. If I need advice from an attorney,
it won't be a divorce attorney." If I didn't need the
money so much, I would have marched right out of
there to the nearest escalator. But I did need the money.
I lifted up a carton and slammed it on the counter.

"Careful," she said, the agitation chewing up her voice, choking it off. "You'll ruin the glass."

I began pulling out boxes. "Don't worry," I said, still smarting from the loss of what I thought was a friendship. "I won't do anything to harm the precious counters."

She acted as if she didn't hear me, checking her watch, pursing her lips at the display mirror. *Vanity, thy name is Sunny.* When she caught me looking at her, she winked and said, "Don't be mad at me, Reebie."

"I'm not." *Just disappointed,* I wanted to say. Instead, I looked up at the first customers approaching us. "Let's get to work, okay?"

"Deal," she said, holding her hand in the air in an invitation to high-five her. I complied. "Hope you don't mind covering for me tonight." She winked again. "I need to leave a little early to meet Parker. You understand."

Seven

Sunny

Sunny told Ellie, their supervisor, that she had to leave early to meet Parker. She told Parker she'd be late because she was going out with Reebie.

"You understand, don't you?" she'd said. "Getting accused of killing that woman has really freaked Reebie out."

Parker told her to take her time. Told her not to get too wrapped up in Reebie's problems. Didn't say he loved her. Never had, not once in the five hot months they'd been together. *So, hey, whatever floats your boat, honey.*

Crazy, but she felt free, no longer locked in the cooped-up smells of the department store. Now she had options, and she was going to make the most of them. The car—her car—was the cutest in the lot.

The kind of car someone with her looks deserved. The watch, too. Guilt nagged her for a moment, then passed. *Five long months, Parker. You really think somebody else isn't going to notice me?*

The relationship with Phil might not be forever. Okay, admit it, some of the mascara she sold would probably last longer than her relationship would. But at least Phil wasn't a cheapskate.

Even in the dark, the car seemed to shine. Just a lousy down payment. It wasn't as if she were selling herself. She was doing the mystery man a favor, collecting information. He was probably getting way more than the couple of grand he was paying her for what she was telling him.

She pulled away from the blurred blaze of car lights on the freeway to the first service station she saw. After locking herself inside the station's cold little bathroom, she took off her smock and pulled on a bodysuit and matching black skirt, with just a touch of lace cut in above her right thigh.

In the smudged rectangular mirror she checked out her face, the only thing in this world she truly loved. Sculpted eyebrows, almost perfect skin, lips that could draw a man like a magnet. You know, maybe she did have a chance with Phil—if she could only get him to open up about himself.

She winked at herself in the mirror. Most women couldn't pull off a simple wink. They didn't know it had to do with how you smiled, how you barely flicked your lid. She had it down. Shallow as it would sound to someone sensible like Reebie, she hoped she died before she lost her looks. Instead, she'd better make the most of them while she could. She was hot. And with just a touch of lip gloss, she'd be ready for her mystery man.

Once she'd parked in the upstairs garage, she did just as he'd told her and went straight to the hotel, repeating the code to herself. Others on the elevator glanced at her. She was used to it. A handsome gray-haired guy in a suit gave her the once-over. She leaned back against the elevator wall and crossed her ankles. A white-haired woman gave her an uncertain smile and held on to her husband's arm. As if Sunny would look at that withered hunk of flesh.

Higher they went, one or two departing on each floor until only she and the gray-haired guy were left. Destination was the penthouse, at the top, where only a special code would get you in. She looked over at the older guy with the diamond cuff links.

"Guess it's just you and me," he said.

Oh, she loved this life, loved being beautiful enough to catch the eye of this classy man who looked like Tony Bennett in his prime. Sexy voice, too.

She stepped back again so that he could see how the fabric of her skirt fell around her, how that sneaky little piece of lace revealed her leg. She lowered her voice. "All the way to the top," she said.

"Only two penthouse rooms up there. Wouldn't it be fun if we had the same one?"

"Not tonight." She licked her glossed lips. "Maybe next time."

She expected him to ask for her phone number, her business card, but no. She just winked and punched in the combination to get them out. Too old, cute as he was.

He went left, and she went right. He was singing as he walked down the hall, and damned well, "It Had To Be You." For one moment, Sunny wanted to chase that song, that voice. Okay, admit it, that man.

How crazy would that be, Sunny baby? Go for it. No, she couldn't. Not tonight.

She could still hear his song as she knocked on the door of the other.

Phil opened it, whisked her inside, then stood before her, looking her up and down. He was stocky but pure muscle, his dark blond hair a little longer than was fashionable. Although she was supposed to be reporting information to him, she intended to learn something about her mystery man tonight.

"You're perfect," he said finally. "You know that." He thought he was in control here, that he was a match for her, but he hadn't seen anything.

She played dumb. "Perfect? Like a perfect steak, a perfect margarita?"

"A perfect woman." He pulled her into his arms, shoved the skirt up along her hips as they kissed. He tasted of brandy. So much for the skirt. She twisted out of it and pressed herself into the heat of him.

They did it right there on the sofa, not even making it to the bed.

Afterward he put on his underwear and shirt, almost as fast as he'd taken them off.

"What's the matter? You afraid someone's going to walk in on us?"

"I hope they do. They can see for themselves I'm with the most beautiful woman in the Bay Area."

She winked. "Maybe even the entire state."

He went to the bar, offered her a drink.

"Is there any wine in there?" she asked.

"Nothing good enough for you. Let me call room service."

Wearing only her watch, she got up and walked across the room, slowly, letting him take in the perfection of her. His wallet lay on the bar with his car keys, the edge of a hundred-dollar bill peeking out. He would shove a couple into her bag before she left, tell her to buy herself something sexy. She checked out the labels in the bar. "This is an excellent cab."

"You know wine?"

"I know this one." She ran her fingertip along the scar on his arm. He winced, although she was sure it could no longer hurt. "That looks nasty," she said.

"It was a long time ago."

"Is that why you always wear a jacket?"

"Part of the reason, I guess." He moved to the bar, opened the wine and poured it into a tumbler. "Sorry I can't offer you the right kind of glass, babe. They should stock these rooms better."

"This is fine." She sat on one of the two chairs overlooking the balcony, knowing how the light filtering in from the sheer curtain enhanced the shape of her body. "Do you spoil all of your women like this?"

His grin was lazy, satisfied. "You think I've got the energy for other women after what you do to me?"

"Just curious. You never ask me to your place, don't introduce me to your friends."

He pulled up a chair close to hers. "It's safer this way."

She turned, trying to see his eyes in the shadows. "Are you married, Phil?"

"God, no. What do you think I am?" He got up and slammed the heavy drapes over the sheers.

"I'm sorry." That was how you learned people's secrets. You made them lose their temper, spill their guts, then you backed off, apologized and went back for more. "There's just so much about you I don't know."

"I told you when we met, and I'll tell you again, I'm a private person." He stood in front of the closed drapes, his face tense, and she felt a flicker of doubt. Maybe she shouldn't have given him her phone number that day at the store. At the very least, maybe she shouldn't have rushed into such an intense relationship. It was Parker's fault, damn him.

"What were you doing in the store that day we met?" she asked.

He frowned. "Looking for a beautiful woman."

"No, really. You were trying to check out Reebie, weren't you?"

"Yeah, I was. It's my job. I didn't have any idea I'd meet you." The thought made him smile. "I'm sure glad I did."

"I have more information for you," she said.

"And I have a payment for you." He went to his briefcase and took out an envelope. She should feel bad about this, taking money for spying on Reebie, but she didn't feel any worse than she did about taking his gifts. She deserved nice things, and besides, nothing she told him would hurt Reebie. The envelope looked nice and fat. She'd better play this up for all it was worth.

"This wine?" She took a sip, then placed the tumbler on the table.

"It's okay?" He stood before her, still holding the envelope.

"Better than okay, but that's not the point. The point is Reebie made it."

"What the hell are you talking about?"

"Her married name was Desmond. She and her husband owned Desmond Vineyards in Napa Valley. When they split up her ex got it all because the winery belonged to his family."

"You're a very good girl."

He held out the envelope. When she rose to take it, he pulled her to him, kissed her, bit her lower lip. Her cheeks burned. He was sexy. Dangerous sexy, her favorite flavor.

"What else did you find out?"

"So why do you want to know so much about Reebie?" She brushed her tender lip across his cheek. "You're a detective, aren't you?" She knew that, of course, but it didn't hurt to pretend to be dumber than she was.

"Close enough," he said.

"Only, private detectives don't have your kind of money. They don't dress like you do."

"Some do." In one move, his hand slipped up her neck, twisting her hair.

Her head jerked to one side. The pain almost dropped her. "Phil, you're hurting me," she gasped.

He twisted tighter, brandy breath in her face. "No more games," he said. "Just tell me."

"That Jeanette woman, the one who was killed." She whispered the words, wanting only away, out of this sick game. "She had a photograph of Reebie in her apartment."

He released her suddenly. "Are you sure?"

"That's what Reebie said. The cops told her." She tried to rub the pain from her neck and moved slowly toward her clothes piled on the coffee table. She just wanted to get away, back to Parker, screwed up as he was. She wasn't as tough as she'd thought. She was scared. Phil didn't seem to notice. He finished dressing, too.

"So, why?" he asked, as if talking to himself. "Why would she have Reebie's photo?"

"I don't know. Neither does Reebie."

"She's lying. You can bet she knows, all right."

"Maybe." She didn't believe it, though. Reebie had looked too confused, too frightened. She was starting to feel the same way. She'd come here with such high hopes, but the reality had fallen short again.

She sat on the chair putting on her boots. He stood behind her, massaging her shoulders. "Sorry if I got a little rough, baby."

"Rough's okay," she said. Maybe that's all it was—playing rough, the way they did in bed. Maybe her imagination made it worse than it was. Still, she felt creepy, and for once, she'd be glad to sleep alone tonight.

"Forgive me, then?" He kept his hand on her left shoulder, kneading away the pain he'd caused. Maybe this would go her way, after all. She looked at the envelope lying on the carpet where it had fallen when he dropped it. Maybe he'd be even more generous than usual after what happened tonight.

"There's nothing to forgive." She looked up and winked at him, then reached down to zip the other boot. "I thought you probably knew about Reebie and the winery," she said.

"No. I thought she was just some loser."

Did that mean he thought people who worked at cosmetics counters were losers? Something else bothered her more. "I thought you were working for Reebie's ex," she said.

He laughed and began to stroke her shoulder again. "In his dreams."

"I know that now. This isn't some stupid divorce case you're working on. It's something big, isn't it?"

"Yeah. It's pretty big."

Wow, she was lucky, even when she thought she wasn't. She'd scored this time. "And you're trusting me with it," she said, as she smoothed the boot to the sloping curve of her leg.

"No." A click in her ear. Hair rose and prickled the back of her neck. "No, I can't trust you with it."

"Phil." She jerked to face him, saw the gun. *No.* A gun pointed at her head. He couldn't do this, not to her. "Phil, baby, please. I won't tell anybody anything."

"No, you won't." He grabbed her hair again, and even as her head blew apart in a flood of splintering spasms, she screamed. Screamed for her life.

Nicholas

Nicholas had set the vibrating alarm clock and put it under his pillow so that he could get up early and work in the garden that morning. He liked the dirt, and it liked him.

"It's best to grow them from seed." He shouldn't talk to himself out loud like this, but no one could hear him this early in the morning, except maybe God and his father. Just these baby tomato plants, ready to go into his garden now. "Stronger when you grow them from seed."

"What in the hell do you think you're doing?"

He was caught, caught on all fours like a dog beside the toolshed. It was too early for her to be up. He had to lie. "I couldn't sleep, honey," he said.

She came closer, and he felt himself draw back. She was a beautiful woman, a good woman, except when he made her mad. She looked pretty mad right now. "You sure you weren't meeting anyone out here?"

"Honey, who would I meet out here?" Darla, that's who. But he never would. He pinched himself every time he thought about Darla. "I'm a married man. Why don't you trust me?"

She just shook her head. "Come on. We need to get packed and to the airport," she said. "First Family, remember? Funeral, get it?"

Of course he remembered. His father's death wasn't the point. He looked down at his little tomato plants. Soon their roots would dig into this ground he'd prepared for them. Their leaves would bristle and smell of spice. Wanton, some people might say. He wanted to stay here with them and think about the other things later. The packing. Darla. "From seed," he said to her. "That's the best way to grow vegetables."

"You stupid bastard." She stomped across the soft rows of dirt and grabbed the hoe leaning against his toolshed. "Get off your ass right now, and let's get packed."

He scrambled to his feet. What would happen to the plants if she didn't let him get them in the ground today? He touched the hoe, his fingers sliding along the smooth wood. "Okay, honey. Whatever you say."

Eight

Reebie

I couldn't sleep that night. Daph had a date with a guy she'd met online, and I'd agreed to dog-sit Chico at my place. He was in a snit about something, maybe having to leave his digs, so I did what I do best, now that I can't do what I was born to do. I cooked. It's amazing how a little Thai beef salad, minus the lime, cilantro and chili paste, will improve a dog's disposition.

First, I had to take Chico home. Then, I had to turn in my paperwork at the newspaper so I could get paid, let alone explain to panties-in-a-wedge Alberta why I'd left the pub crawl early. After that, I'd go into the department store until nine. As Sunny would say, whatever floats your boat.

I'm sure Alberta didn't work every Saturday. I

hoped the meeting with me wasn't the reason she was coming in, and especially hoped she wasn't going to dock my pay. Although I could get by if she did, I could use the extra, maybe even buy a little more flank steak for Chico.

I signed in at the security station and went to the HR department a few minutes before eight. It was good to be early, Natalie, my temp rep, always told me, even when you're just turning in paperwork. Of course, there was no one there yet. I waited in the reception area and checked messages on my cell phone. Darned if I didn't have one and from Leo Kersikovski, at that.

"Yeah, Reebie. This is LK. Sorry I missed you. I know you're coming in this morning, and so am I. How about lunch?"

Lunch?

I don't know where you cross the line from okay good-looking to too good-looking, but Leo Kersikovski had been crossing it from the day he was born, I'd bet. He had barely looked my way at Daph's birthday party the month before. Now he was leaving messages inviting me to lunch. If he wanted to interview me about Jeanette, he could at least be up-front about it.

I didn't return the call. Instead, I double-checked the forms I'd had to fill out in order to get paid. The kind of work I could do in my sleep—but in my sleep, in my dreams, I did finer work—work I would never do again.

I'd been at it a couple of hours when Alberta came in. I looked up with a start. She wore a jean jacket over cuffed pants that hit just below her knee. I started to think she had good legs for her age and amended it to good legs, period. They didn't go with her bearing. I'd thought of her as old, but looking at her now, squinting down at me with anguished eyes, I realized she wasn't that old. Her pinched face wasn't about age. It was about attitude.

"We have a little bit of a problem," she said, wincing as if I'd caused about the same amount of discomfort as a splinter or a paper cut. I could tell from the set, stern look on her face that I'd had it. "Can you join me in the conference room?"

Did I have a choice?

She led the way. Her dark hair fell toward her face in a short bob so bottle-black you could see the blue highlights in it. From behind, I could tell that she shaved the back of her neck.

What could be worse than what I'd already dealt with? Was I going to be fired from the temp service for screwing up the pub crawl? No, not even Alberta had that power. We went across the hall and through an open door to a room with a large-screen television and a couple of conference tables. At one of them sat the two officers who had interrogated me at Jeanette's, both of them on the same side of the table with their backs to the TV.

"Oh," I said, as my breathing quickened.

Officer Morgan nodded and introduced his partner, Officer Stumph. In the bright light of the conference room, I could see that his eyes were an unusual green. His short-man partner drummed his fingers on the tabletop.

"These officers would like to talk to you," Alberta said. She nodded toward the end of the table as if telling me to sit, then walked around to what she probably thought of as the head.

I sat down and looked over at Morgan, the decent one, or so he had been Thursday night. "Shouldn't we go somewhere else? I'm only a temp here, and my job's over."

"We thought it was important to talk to you as soon as possible," he said. "We contacted Ms. Folger, and she was kind enough to let us meet you here."

Alberta heaved a long-suffering sigh, to underscore, I guess, what an imposition this was.

"Would you like to leave, ma'am?" the punk Officer Stumph asked Alberta.

"Of course not," she said. "Temp or not, Ms. Mahoney's still an employee of my department, and I have to sit in on this."

"What's wrong?" I directed the question to the decent one's green eyes. Officer Morgan. That was his name.

"You don't know, do you?"

"Know what?" His intensity made me dizzy. This was worse than I'd suspected, but what could be worse than what had already happened?

"I'll tell her," the other one put in.

"Not so fast."

I felt disoriented, the way I did the day that blank-faced divorce attorney told me Geoff was entitled to keep his family's winery. "Is it bad?" I asked.

Morgan nodded and leaned closer, so close that I could smell the cigarette he'd just smoked. "When was the last time you saw Adelle Perry?"

"I don't know anyone by that name." Finally, a reprieve. I felt myself exhale.

"She was known as Sunny Perry, as well."

Was known? I went numb, pushing what I was hearing away from me, trying not to feel. "Sunny and I work together at the cosmetics counter. I saw her just last night."

"What time?" Stumph asked, almost gleefully.

"She had to leave early." I glanced back over at his partner, as the reality began to seep in. "No."

"I'm sorry."

"No." I must have shouted it. I heard my voice, as if it came from someone else. "She was fine. She was going to meet her boyfriend."

"She was murdered." His face flushed an officious pink.

It was too much for me to handle. Not Sunny. Not murdered. "How?"

"Shot."

"Where?"

"That's being withheld."

I felt as if Morgan and I were in a verbal Ping-

Pong game. He just kept driving back the answers as fast as I could ask the questions.

"Shot?" My lip trembled. "Like Jeanette?"

"We're checking that out." He cleared his throat. I could almost see those hypnotic eyes narrowing their focus. "Boyfriend said she was with you last night."

"She was with him."

"He says she was with you."

"It's not true. He's lying." I had to choke back tears now. Sunny was dead, shot, and now Parker was trying to blame it on me.

"Mind if I join you?"

I turned toward the voice, seeing Leo Kersikovski, his hand lifted as if he'd knocked, but of course he hadn't.

"Come in, LK," Alberta said, patting the seat beside her. Although her voice remained professional, she couldn't hide the longing in her eyes. *Never trust a man who goes by his initials.*

Stumph bristled, his scalp beneath the white-blond hair a purple color that would make me want to call the paramedics if he mattered. I guessed that he lived his life this way. He didn't care that Sunny was dead. He just cared that a reporter was invited into our little visit. That didn't sit well with me, either, but I couldn't sort out my feelings. I was still thinking about Sunny, what had happened to her, and how it could possibly have anything to do with Jeanette, a woman she'd never met.

To the officers, Alberta said, "I asked LK to join us since he'll be covering the story. I'm trying to help. You can choose to continue or not." I would have cheered her on, if it hadn't been my behind on the line.

Stumph raised his white eyebrows. "We could take it downtown, Danny."

Without looking at his partner, Officer Morgan stood and stuck out his hand. "We're finished here. Ski, how've you been?"

No one called Leo Kersikovski "Ski," not even behind his back.

"Hanging in, Danny. Congrats on the new son. Hope he's not as ugly as you."

"Looks just like me, I'm afraid. It's good to see you, Ski. Have a seat."

Kersikovski sat across from him, to my left.

Alberta looked down at her hand that still rested in the empty seat she'd patted, as if she'd expected him to obey like a dog. "Welcome," she said, then fixed her smile and made eye contact with me, her look one of undistilled hatred.

She wanted him. That's the only reason he'd been able to join this little meeting, the only reason she was giving me the evil eye. Give me a break, lady. Sure the guy was a hunk, but he wasn't my hunk. I'd never gone for pretty, and he was about as close to it as a man could get. All that saved him were the crisscross scars that cut off his right eyebrow and a full lower lip that had too much pout in it to be pretty.

His eyes, though, were magnificent, variegated, the color and depth of chardonnay grapes in the sunshine. And his voice was a borderline mocking rumble.

"Sorry about lunch," he said to me, as if it was his fault, not mine, that I hadn't returned his call.

Alberta's head whipped around so fast that I could almost feel the wind in my face.

"As the officer said, I think we're about finished here." I tried to push back my chair. It scraped against the carpet, unwilling to budge. I tried to give Alberta a charming smile, to convey to her that I wasn't after this guy she so clearly desired.

She returned an expression of ice then looked over at him. "They're here about that girl's murder, LK. Someone Ms. Mahoney worked with at one of her other jobs."

"I have only *two* jobs," I said. "The temp agency and the department store, okay?"

"Danny?" Kersikovski said, and I could see that he respected the cop, trusted him. "You've checked out the victim? Lifestyle? Habits?"

"You think we're idiots?" Stumph said. "Victim's boyfriend said the victim was with *her*." He stabbed his pudgy little finger at me.

"How do you explain that one?" Although Kersikovski was probably trying to sound neutral, the arrogance in his voice pissed me off.

"Why should I have to be the one to explain? Sunny left early. I didn't. Haven't you talked to our supervisor, Ellie? Oh, God, does she even know what happened to Sunny?"

Morgan shot a questioning look to his partner, who avoided eye contact.

"Planned on talking to her tomorrow," he said.

"She doesn't even work tomorrow. Why are you coming after me when you haven't even talked to our employer yet? Is it because of Sunny's boyfriend, Parker? Because if it is, I can tell you their relationship wasn't all that smooth."

"Oh?" That got Kersikovski's attention, at least.

"No. He wouldn't commit. It drove Sunny crazy. She—" I couldn't go on. Sunny was dead, murdered. I wasn't going to gossip to a reporter about her now.

"What?" Kersikovski leaned closer, his face shoved so close to mine that I could smell his minty breath. Gum? I wondered. Mouthwash?

"She just wasn't all that happy with him. She told me she was meeting him that night. I can tell you what I did. I went home and took care of Daphne Teng's dog. Ask Parker what he did."

"Mr. Franklin was at a meeting with real, live humans," Danny Morgan's partner shot back. "He was there until after midnight. Ms. Perry called him once on his cell phone."

"What'd she say?" Kersikovski asked.

"Don't go there, Ski." Morgan stopped the conversation with a frown that meant business. "Ms. Mahoney, you're free to leave, for now. I have just

one more question. Was Adele Perry acquainted with
Jeanette Sheldon?"

"No." I could tell from his eyes that it wasn't
enough of an answer. "Sunny was off the day
Jeanette talked to me."

"She could have come back another time, when
you were off."

"Sunny would have mentioned it." Still, I shivered
at the possibility. Sunny would have told me,
wouldn't she?

"Why?" Danny Morgan nailed me across the
table with a gaze that couldn't have been more thor-
ough if I'd been naked. "Why would Ms. Perry mention to you that Jeanette Sheldon had visited the
cosmetic counter? You claim you didn't even know
Jeanette's identity."

I could tell by his voice, his eyes, that he thought
I was lying, and that made me even more nervous,
probably even more suspicious. I didn't know how to
answer. Someone had murdered Sunny, and even this
decent cop thought I had something to do with it.

For some crazy reason, I addressed my answer to
Kersikovski. "We always talked about our customers. I told Sunny about this beautiful older woman
who'd spent a ton of money and stuck around to talk
to me. If she'd had a customer like that, she would
have mentioned it."

Kersikovski nodded as if he, at least, believed
me. "Did Sunny talk to you about any of her other
customers?" he asked.

The punk officer grunted. "We're the ones asking the questions, sir."

"Ski…" Morgan began.

"No problem. You guys *are* asking the questions, but let me say this." Before they could do more than look at each other, he said, "This woman, Reebie Mahoney, has just found out that her close friend was murdered last night. Thursday night, she discovered the body of another murdered woman. From what I can see, she doesn't know jack about how or why these two events occurred, let alone if they're connected."

"You're probably right," Alberta agreed, the first words she'd spoken since she'd set Kersikovski loose on these guys.

"Of course he's right." I was on my feet, ready to kick over the chair, if it were the only way I could get away from here.

"Just one moment." Stumph leaned across the table at me with a full-of-himself smile, his voice a lazy drawl. "Perhaps you can share with us why the doorman at Jeanette Sheldon's penthouse swears that you and your friend were the last ones in the building before the murder, and that when he entered the penthouse, he found you standing over the body."

Kersikovski whipped around, and I could see the doubt in his eyes.

"It's not true!" I said.

"We need to talk to the doorman." Kersikovski rose, as well.

"*We'll* talk to him." The officer glared at me. "And we'll talk to Ms. Mahoney whenever we feel it's necessary. Two people have been murdered, you know."

"Oh, I know." Kersikovski stared him down.

Officer Morgan rose and slapped Kersikovski on the back.

"We'll talk later, man."

Kersikovski nodded. Then, as the cops filed out, he turned to Alberta and said, "I owe you. You didn't have to do this, especially not on a weekend."

"*I'm* not on the clock," she said, with a short, judgmental motion in my direction. "I knew you'd want to be here." She gave him a look full of as much artificial sadness as it was hunger. "So, what are you doing now? Have you eaten?"

How pathetic, I thought. I'd been that way over a man, but at least Geoff had wanted me, too. Once.

"No," he said, "and I won't until I run out of leads. And when I do, I'll buy *you* lunch."

"It's a deal." She slunk past him, looking damned fine in those little cutoff pants, and I realized as she switched her ass that letting the cops in here, calling in a reporter—it wasn't about my stupid temp job, and it wasn't about who killed Sunny. It was about impressing Leo Kersikovski. The fact that he must know it, too, made me like him less.

We were the only ones in the room now. I decided to leave without a goodbye, but by the time I reached the doorway, he was standing in it. I saw him for what he was then—a not-so-tall man whose attitude made him big, unlike the punk cop, whose attitude made him even less than his physical self. I walked right up to the door and looked him square in the eye.

"I'm leaving now."

"Me, too," he said. I could still smell his tooth-paste, mouthwash, whatever it was. He didn't move.

"What?" I asked.

"What will the doorman tell them?"

"I have no idea," I said. I touched his arm. It moved. I slid past him, without looking back. But I could feel him watching me with every step I took down that hall.

Nine

I left the office, wondering if I should have told Kersikovski about the man I'd caught Sunny flirting with in the store. Flirting, hell. That was an under-statement. Seeing the two of them meet had been like watching a match strike—hypnotic yet scary. I hadn't been able to look away from them, had tried to forget it ever since. I couldn't.

Now, with Sunny dead, I didn't want to say any-thing that would taint her memory, especially if what I had observed between her and the stranger was something they hadn't acted upon. I'd have to tell someone, of course, maybe Daph, maybe even Par-ker, if he got too pushy about what I'd been doing the night Sunny was killed. Not Kersikovski, though. Not now.

For some insane reason, I was a suspect in Sun-ny's murder, maybe Jeanette Sheldon's, as well. It was a far cry from where I'd been a year ago. For a moment, I remembered how it felt to walk out into the vines when the grapes were starting to ripen, trying to decide when to pick for optimum flavor. I always had to remind myself not to reach for the best-looking grapes, but to gather my sample from all of the vines.

I really missed it—those early mornings, the nights in the lab, the cellar rats, the way we'd drink a sparkler and toast to a good, safe harvest the night before we began picking.

As I left the building, I looked across the parking lot at my miserable truck, and I just knew I couldn't drive it where I had to go tonight. Instead, I took out my cell phone and dialed the magic number. I no longer had to look at Pargat's card.

We drove to what I still thought of as Jeanette's penthouse and parked discreetly, if a cab that gruesome green color can be discreet about anything it does. At least Pargat didn't pull up to the awning. He kind of loitered around the entrance like a dog looking for a hydrant.

He opened the door for me. Met my eyes. "You will call if you need anything." Not a question.

"Of course. Thank you, my friend."

"My friend," he repeated.

I stepped out of the taxi and followed the path up to the awning, the glass doors. The doorway was still taped off. I hesitated, then reasoned that the tenants had to be getting in some way. The lobby was smaller, darker than I remembered from my first visit. No doorman. A small brass bell sat on the wood podium. I started to ring it, then heard a noise in the adjoining office.

I moved closer, past the doorman's station, and lifted the heavy burgundy curtain covering the window. A man in dark pants and a denim jacket hunched over one of two desks that were separated by file cabinets. In the same way a normal person might take out a notebook, he pulled out a gun.

I gasped.

He jerked his head up, as if he'd heard me.

It was the doorman, all right, looking even shorter in his tennis shoes but every bit as threatening. Maybe he was supposed to have the gun. Maybe it was part of his job. As much as I wanted to rationalize what I was witnessing, I knew better. I started to run out the way I'd come, but he reached the door in seconds.

"Stop," he shouted, and I expected a bullet in my back.

Slowly, I turned, trying to reason with him. "There are people all over the place. You wouldn't be crazy enough—"

"You're right," he said, his eyes as desperate as his voice. "In there."

"No way. You lied about me to the police. For all I know, you killed Jeanette."

"You know I was down here when she was shot."

He grabbed my arm and shoved me into the room. The jolt was so hard that I barely kept from falling by grabbing on to one of the desks. "I'm small potatoes, honey. My job was to keep watch, that's all." He kicked the door shut.

"Then why'd you lie?"

"I didn't like your attitude," he said. "I still don't."

My mouth went dry. I looked around frantically. The room had one of those fake skylights, unlike the lobby that erased the sun and made everything pretty in a dim kind of way.

Now, in this light, I could see the ridges of his pockmarked cheeks, his watery brown eyes. I tried to ignore the queasy feel of dread slipping over me.

"Do you know who killed her?" I asked.

"I'm not paid to know." He gestured with the gun. "With cops crawling all over the place, I had to stash this. Figured I could get in and get out tonight without anyone knowing."

"You still can," I said, betrayed by my quaking voice. "I'm not going to say anything."

"Oh, you'll say plenty if you get the chance." He grabbed my arm. "Come on. You might just make me look like a hero to my people."

"What do you mean?"

He grinned to himself, almost as if I wasn't in the room. "Just shut up. I said, come on."

I scanned the room for a weapon, any weapon. File cabinets? Too heavy to lift. Scissors on desks?

Too awkward. Fire extinguisher? I wouldn't know On from Off. He was dragging me now. I knew what waited beyond those doors if he got me through them.

"Let me go," I screamed. "Help."

He slapped me across the face with such force that I dropped to the floor.

"Get up, bitch, and don't say another word. I mean it."

My head exploded in painful sparks, and I struggled to get back on my feet. In doing so, I spotted the one thing that might get me out of there. A plant stand only about two-feet tall, but with three pointed legs at its base. I couldn't see how sharp they were when I was standing, but I could now.

I pretended to fall down again and, in rising, lifted my hand as if trying to steady myself on the plant stand.

He poked the gun between my shoulders. "I didn't hit you that hard. Get the hell up."

I looked at him again and realized there was something out of whack with him. I had only one chance, and no time. "My leg," I said.

He stiffened his arm with the gun. "Make it fast."

I lifted myself up on my new best wrought-iron friend—slowly, ever so slowly. He had a gun. I had a plant stand. But I had the questionable advantage that he didn't want to kill me inside this room.

"Not sure I can walk," I said, holding fast to the stand.

"Oh, you can walk, all right." He pressed the gun against my temple. "Walk for me, baby. Right now. Walk right through that door."

I pretended to stumble again. "I'm trying. My legs just aren't working."

"Then you better make them work."

He stepped back, and I wondered if he was taking aim, deciding to go for another murder indoors, the way Jeanette had been murdered. Had he killed her? Was he going to kill me? I couldn't think about that. Not now. I grabbed the plant stand, flipped it and went straight toward him. The spikes connected. He howled, dropped the gun. I hit him one more time. His wail grew louder as I forced my broken body to run. Then, an explosion. I cringed, expecting the force of that noise to burst through me. But, no. No. I ran out the way I'd come, broke into the street, the fresh, cold air. I was okay.

The taxi's back door was open. I threw myself inside. "Hurry," I shouted to Pargat.

"Not again," he said, and sped away.

I didn't know where to direct him, was afraid to pick up my truck until I was sure no one was at my apartment. "Take me home. That man tried to kill me."

"What man?"

"That doorman back there. First, he lied about me to the police. Then, he pulled a gun on me."

"You can't go back to your place." The concern in Pargat's voice felt genuine. I knew he'd try to help me if he could.

"I don't have anywhere else, not anymore," I said.

"Your friend? The camera lady?"

Daph. I didn't dare on a Saturday. She saved that day for the best of her Internet date matches. But she hadn't asked me to watch Chico when I'd brought him back this morning, and she'd been devastated when I'd told her about Sunny. Maybe she would be home after all.

"Let me call her," I said, glimpsing escape, anonymity, in the darkening sky. "But first, I need to make another call."

As much as I didn't want to, I took out the card Officer Morgan had given me and dialed the number on it. We were approaching the Bay Bridge now. Soon I'd have to decide where to direct Pargat. I hoped to get Morgan's voice mail, do my duty as a citizen and keep running. That hope didn't last through the first ring. He answered with his last name, and I responded with both of mine.

"Tell me what happened." Cop voice. No time for pleasantries.

"I went to see the doorman at Jeanette Sheldon's building." I couldn't decipher the noise on the other end—agreement or disgust. "He pulled a gun on me."

"What then?"

"He tried to get me out in the back. I fought him off with a plant stand."

"Where are you now?"

I looked around at the car-lined landscape. "The bridge, in a taxi. I'm going to try to stay with a friend tonight."

"Not yet," he said. "Just turn that taxi around and get back here."

"Back where?" The night no longer felt like a friendly place to disappear inside. "Why?"

"To the apartment building. The doorman is dead."

"He can't be. I didn't—"

"Murdered." He finished the sentence for me. "Now, get back here as fast as you can. We need to talk to you."

Because the sound of my own voice made me feel less alone, I explained what I thought I had just heard to Pargat as we drove.

"You could be killed," he said. "Like all of those cabdrivers in Richmond. Why would someone want to kill a cabdriver?"

With three cabbies shot down in a month, no wonder he was worried. And here I was, assuming he was just my carefree, turbaned protector.

"I read about the cabdriver murders," I said. "Please don't drive after dark until they find the person who's responsible."

He drove in silence, his hands stiff on the wheel. Finally he said, "It's after dark now."

"Then, don't pick up anyone else, not another fare tonight. Promise me."

He turned to flash me a sad smile that failed to hide the fear his eyes. "Promise. Now, you must tell the police the truth."

"Why would I lie?" I asked, but he'd already turned up the music, a whispery Norah Jones singing about love.

The music didn't fit. Pargat didn't fit. I sure as hell didn't fit. The rest was a nightmare ride full of garish images—the doorman grabbing his stomach. The blood. Had there been more blood than I'd seen? Had I gone into some self-preservation mode and done something awful? No, I couldn't believe it. Terrified as I was, I just shoved the spikes of the plant stand at him, tried to push him away from me. I didn't kill him. I couldn't have.

Ten

They were taking away the body as we pulled up to the curb. Without waiting for Pargat to get out, Officer Morgan opened the door for me.

"Don't give me that look," I said. "It was self-defense, I swear."

"So, why'd you leave the scene, Ms. Mahoney?"

"I didn't know it was a scene, okay? He was alive when I left. Besides, he was going to kill me."

Just when I said it, the wind picked up, and I shivered inside my blood-splattered pink sweater. Morgan didn't seem to notice. Nor did he appear to notice the officers like ants on a hill invading the posh establishment where the doorman had once held court. "Tell me what happened," he said.

"I already did, on the phone."

"Tell me again," he said, harsher now, all but snapping his fingers in my face. I tried to hurry up.

"I wanted to know why he lied about me. That's why I came back."

"And he was alive when you got here?"

"Of course. I told you what he tried to do. He got me in the back office and took out a gun."

"What kind of gun?"

"I don't know. Some kind of pistol. He shoved it against my head." I touched my temple again and began to tremble. The feeling came back, that horrible cold spot pressing against my skull, readying itself. To my shock and embarrassment, my eyes filled with tears. "He wanted me to go out the side door," I said. "He hit me. Here." I could feel the burn, the swollen flesh, relived every nightmarish moment.

"And?"

He didn't care. This was just another case for him. "I fell, okay? I thought I was going to pass out, but then, I saw the plant stand."

Soft rain began to fall. It made me realize how hot my tears were. "Here," Morgan said, guiding me under the burgundy awning. I went reluctantly, making sure I was still within bolting distance of the taxi.

He looked at me, professionally but also almost apologetically. "Tell me about the plant stand," he said.

No way could I hold back the tears, not now, not remembering how frightened I'd been. Not just remembering the fear but connecting with it. He waited with a patient expression, but there was nothing patient about his tightly coiled body, his fixed straight lips. "I charged him with the stupid plant stand," I said. "He fired the gun. He came after me with it." Now, I couldn't control the sobs, the reality of what had happened. "I didn't mean to kill him, I swear. I was just so scared."

"You didn't shoot him?" Morgan's eyes scanned mine, reading, searching.

"Of course not. He was the one with the gun."

"We found a revolver at the scene. Looks as if it might have been the murder weapon."

My thoughts scrambled in a mishmash of possibilities, no longer caring about the officers around us, the crime-scene tape, not even the videos in my brain. No, all I cared about was what Officer Morgan had just told me.

"A *gun* was the murder weapon?" I had to say it, had to hear it, had to hear him confirm it. Oh, please, Morgan, confirm it. "You mean the plant stand didn't kill him?"

"Hardly." Something broke through in his eyes, something I could see, in the dark, tears or not. He believed me, or at least he wanted to. "The victim appears to have died from a gunshot wound," he said.

I sobbed in earnest now. I was scared, but I wasn't a suspect. I could go home, wherever home was.

I hadn't killed the doorman.

I hadn't killed the doorman.

Standing there, under the starched, smart awning, I looked at his still-too-solemn face. "Then, I'm not a suspect?"

"I didn't say that. You were the last person to see the man alive."

"Except for the killer." I felt suddenly cold, and tried to hug the warmth back into my bones. "I don't even know how to use a gun."

"Witnesses heard two gunshots close together," Morgan said.

"The first was when he shot at me."

"The second was right after that." He frowned. "Within minutes."

I rubbed my arms, trying to get the feeling back. "So," I said, "whoever killed him was in that room when I was."

He didn't say anything, just stared at me and let the feeling sink in.

"Well, isn't that right?"

"Looks that way," he said, "but it's too soon to know."

But not too soon for me to know. Not too soon for me to go home or to Daph's fearing for my life. I shared a silent, ironic laugh with myself. *Fearing for my life.* Every time my life goes to hell, my thoughts get so Irish that I can almost hear the brogue. This was one of those times.

An old VW bus pulled up behind Pargat's cab.

"Ski," Danny uttered in a toneless voice.

This vehicle made the taxi look as if it belonged at the Concours d'Elegance. But, sure enough, Kersikovski got out. I would have figured him for a red Vette man or something equally predictable.

He wore a navy windbreaker over a gray T-shirt, and even in my frantic state, his polish-black hair was so silky that my first impulse was to stroke it. That's what beauty does to us. Our first thought is that of the child. *Touch it. Make it mine.* But the child grows up and learns what happens when you reach for those bright balloons bursting with color.

He marched up to me, confusion, maybe anger in his set expression. His jeans were tight enough to attract my attention, but only momentarily.

"What are you doing here? What happened to your face?"

Officer Morgan answered for me. "She was the last to see the victim alive."

"The doorman," I said. "He tried to kill me. I hit him with a plant stand. Now…" I was too cold, too scared, too wasted to say more. I wasn't even sure I could continue standing.

"I heard the news at work and recognized the address." Kersikovski took off his jacket and handed it to me. When I continued holding it, unmoving, he said, "Put that on. Are you finished here, Danny?"

"Not quite." He watched me slip into the jacket. "Ms. Mahoney can go, though."

"I have a taxi waiting," I said, half-expecting some ridiculous fantasy moment when Kersikovski would offer me a ride.

"Good," Kersikovski said. "I'm going to give you my cell-phone number. Don't take any chances. Call

me, and don't worry if it's too late. Call me if anything happens that seems the least unusual."

"Don't you think she should consider calling us
first?" Stumph leaned against what had once been a
spot-free glass door, running his hands through the
sparse grizzled fuzz on his pink scalp.

Kersikovski met the challenge, crossing between
Officer Morgan and me to confront him head-on.
"Maybe she'll hear a noise. She's not going to call
you over a noise. I want her to call me, okay? Do you
have a problem with that?"

"I have a problem with you," Stumph spit back.
"I have a problem with a junkyard journalist thinking he's the frigging *Enquirer.*"

"Damn it, Stumph." Morgan turned to his partner
and threw up his hands.

"A reporter, Danny," he said. "He's a reporter."

"Is that what bothers you?" Kersikovski's voice
got scratchy, as if he were biting off the words. "Get
used to it, because I'm not going away. And why the
hell don't you think about trusting me?"

Stumph's pale finger pointed straight at Reebie.
"Because of her."

"Stumph!" Danny Morgan motioned as he spoke,
and Stumph shut up.

After a moment, the other officer said, "I was just
trying—"

"I know what you're just trying." Morgan moved
closer, forcing Stumph to make eye contact with him.

"Listen, friend." Even in his T-shirt, Kersikovski

seemed a match and then some for the uniformed punk. "I have a job, too. If I find out something important, you folks are the first to hear it. Danny knows that."

"Right after you print the story," Stumph said. "And in the meantime someone gets away. Leads go stale. Somebody else dies." He made a noise that sounded as if he were going to spit and said to Morgan, "I'll be inside."

Kersikovski muttered something under his breath that sounded distinctly like, "Asshole."

"You've got to understand Stumph," Morgan said as the angry little man scrambled inside the building.

"The hell I do."

"He's a damned sharp officer. I wouldn't bullshit you on that, Ski. And if you'd been through what he has, you'd hate the press, too."

"So, enlighten me, Deepak Chopra Daniel Ray Morgan. Unveil the secrets of this asshole you're proud to call your partner."

Morgan's gaze flitted to me so fast that I wasn't supposed to see it, I guess, then back to Kersikovski. "We'll talk later," he said.

They exchanged looks I couldn't decipher, and whatever match in which they'd been engaged must have ended in a draw. "I'll call you if I find out anything," Kersikovski said, moving away from the building toward me.

Morgan frowned at the door to the place, its ornate etched-glass grotesque now that I knew what lay beyond it. "I better get to it, my man. We'll be talking, I know. Ms. Mahoney, we'll be talking to you, too." He crossed the yellow tape, and I shivered again, remembering—no, experiencing those moments with the doorman.

Kersikovski shrugged as he watched Morgan disappear inside. Made a noise like a sigh. Turned back from the building toward me, as if debating with himself.

"Let's go," he said.

"Go where?" I hugged myself in the oversize jacket.

"Out of here. I'm taking you home, to Daph's, wherever you want to go."

My teeth began to chatter. "I have a taxi waiting."

"Get rid of it."

I had a swollen, probably tearstained face, a blood-spattered sweater and a shivering body that felt as if it would never again feel warm. I should take the safe way home, with Pargat. Or I could ride with this guy. "Give me a minute," I said.

Pargat gunned up the cab as if expecting another quick getaway. I shook my head as I approached his door. He turned off the engine and got out.

"I have a way home," I told him as he reached for the passenger door. I didn't have much cash, but I wouldn't be able to sleep if I didn't do something to let him know how much I appreciated being able to depend on him. I reached into my wallet, found the two fives sandwiching a couple of ones and handed them to him.

"Can't take." He frowned and shoved them back at me.

"Must take." I shoved them back into his palms and closed his hands around them. "Not for the ride. For the friendship."

Before he could argue, I turned and returned to Kersikovski.

Only Kersikovski wasn't where I'd left him. His junker of a van was empty. He'd disappeared from beneath the awning, manned by only one cop now. As Pargat's cab pulled away, I felt stranded, lost. Then, I saw him, leaning into the driver's window of a white Mercedes. Before I could join them, a man in one of those black, down-filled jackets that make even skinny people look like fullbacks got out of the car. Old fullback shot past Kersikovski and started raising hell with the officer at the door to the penthouse.

"I manage this place. I have to get inside, crime scene or no crime scene."

I reached him about the same time Kersikovski did, in time to hear the officer promise to return with someone in authority. It wasn't good enough for this hefty loud-talker in the sunglasses.

He jerked toward us, immediately dismissed me, then asked Kersikovski, "You have any clout around here?"

"Not enough to disturb a crime scene."

"Crime scene, my ass." He looked over at me as if trying to decide whether to apologize for his language. "The doctor who owns this place is going to be pissed. Sixteen years, and we've never had anything worse than a bounced check before that Sheldon woman died."

"You have worse than that now," Kersikovski said. "Why not just let the officers do their jobs?"

"Because my job is protecting the owner's property." The big man patted his jacket. "The tenant who called me said he saw a woman running away. Our guy was killed by a woman, right?" He jerked his head, and although I couldn't see his eyes, I knew his attention had slid over to me.

"Your guy attacked me." I stepped forward, looking up into the glare of his glasses. "And I didn't kill him. Someone shot him after I escaped."

"You don't have to tell him anything." Kersikovski grabbed my arm. "If you don't know who killed your doorman, you're not going to be of any help here," he told the guy. "Why don't you try doing something useful, like notifying the victim's family?"

"You're lying." Ignoring Kersikovski, he took off his glasses and peered down at me with small, dark pupils like the hooded eyes of a snake. "There's no way he would attack you." And to Kersikovski. "If she'll lie about being attacked, what else will she lie about?"

I felt Kersikovski's grip loosen, his attention return to my face. For that one second, I wished I could make a run for it, escaping this insanity as I'd escaped the last, only with more to lose this time.

Kersikovski spoke, make that exploded. "Bullshit."

"Don't get tough with me," the man said, "just because you're trying to protect your girlfriend."

Color flushed into Kersikovski's face as if he'd been slapped. I felt it in my own, a wondrous palette, no doubt, with the bruises I'd received from the doorman. "Maybe you don't think the little punk would attack me," I said, "but he did. He also tried to kill me." My voice grated. I liked the sound. Bone-cold scared as I was, I almost liked this opportunity to finally rage.

"Henry Wong would never attack anyone," the man shouted.

"He attacked her," Kersikovski said.

"No." My voice was a peep. I tried to sort it out, the shuddering fear returning again. "The doorman." I looked at Kersikovski, trying to pretend the creep wasn't there, leaning against the wrought-iron column as if he owned it. Kersikovski nodded, urging me on.

"What about the doorman?"

"His name couldn't be Henry Wong," I said. "He was no more Asian than I am."

Eleven

The Widow

June could see them from inside her mind, probably as well as, if not better than, anyone watching them trudge this path could—the delicate but not fragile widow, her sightless eyes round and blue—startling some said, her best feature. And he, the former chief of staff, the forever friend. She could tell by the heavy texture of David's jacket that he'd overinsulated himself against the weather, but that's how he was.

She'd dressed herself, checking with her housekeeper to be sure she'd picked the right dress, not black, but the deep blue Rem loved her to wear. Although she couldn't tell all colors by touch, she could almost always feel the blue tones, especially the ones he'd loved.

She started singing, "'Jimmy crack corn and I don't care. The master's gone away.'"

"That's racist, sweetheart," David said.

Ever the gentleman. Out of respect for him, she stopped singing, but she continued to hum. The hill they'd been climbing seemed to reach a plateau. His breaths were more gasps now. "Rem wouldn't think it racist," she said. "He'd love being the master, still being in control of us."

"You're right." He chuckled, and his breathing evened out. Fast recovery, even now. "Yes, I guess he would. Just a few more steps now."

A blast of sea air caught her by surprise, sudden and sharp, like ether.

"The girl," she began.

"We're still checking. For now, it looks as if Jeanette picked her at random."

"But, why?"

"Because she wanted to come out about—you know."

She realized she'd squeezed her eyes shut. How many gestures in her life were futile now? "I always knew about her. I just didn't know her name."

"It didn't last that long." He brushed her arm. "Don't think about it now."

"So, you knew?"

"I'm sorry."

"Oh, David."

"I said I'm sorry. If it's worth anything, I never approved."

"And now someone's killed her. It's going to reflect on Rem's memory. We can't have that."

"No."

"What can we do about this girl she contacted?"

"You're in charge now."

The reality of his words stopped her. Yes, she was, and how odd it felt to be the one left to protect their legacy. "I want to know everything you can find out about her," she said.

"There's not much. I'll fill you in later. She's divorced, no children. The ex-husband owns a winery in Napa Valley."

"Do you really think Jeanette picked her at random?" she asked.

"There's no evidence that they knew each other before. The girl told the police that Jeanette called her when she heard that Rem had passed away."

"The bitch." She shuddered, saw a blaze of color and realized she was squeezing her eyes again. "She waits until he's gone, didn't have the guts to deal with him when he was alive. Can you imagine what he would have done to her if she'd come forward while he was here?" No answer. Only the breeze, cold now and wet, against her face. "David?"

"I'm here."

"Did he love her?" And before he could answer, "Don't tell me what I want to hear. Tell me the truth."

He made a noise in his throat, a mumble.

"Tell me, David."

"It was too long ago, sweetheart. We all thought a lot of things we don't think now. Rem never loved any woman the way he loved you. You don't need me to tell you that."

Odd that her cheeks could still prickle, that she could feel pride in such meager praise. In her lack of sight, she could still always see Rem's silence, feel his longing for something, someone other than her. She could never allow herself to think about it, didn't want to think about it now, but she had no choice.

All at once, her legs went weak. Vertigo struck, and for a moment, she faltered. David pulled her to him, steadied her.

"You were a good friend to him," she said.

"And he to me." He squeezed her arm, urging her to take the next final steps. "This is the real funeral, you know."

"Yes." Her sadness was overcome by something better, truer. "Is there a way," she asked, "that you can get rid of that shop girl?"

"You don't mean—?"

"Of course not. I'd be willing to give her money to send her away from here."

"But why?" he asked. "If Jeanette didn't tell her anything?"

"We won't know what Jeanette told her, or didn't, until she writes a book or shows up on a television show. Let's just get rid of her, pay her off. I don't want to spend my brave last days, as the tabloids will no doubt call them, being reminded of my husband's mistress and what she might or might not have told that shop girl."

"How much?"

Dear David, always looking at the bottom line.

"I'll discuss that with her," she said.

Now he was the one to stumble. "You want to negotiate with her face-to-face?" he asked.

"Absolutely." Yes, it was the only way. She must.

"I'll do my best." He cleared his throat. "And now—"

"Yes." She reached across him, tapped her fingers on the cold urn, too small to contain such a large man, such a large presence. "We're close to the edge, aren't we?"

"Very close, sweetheart."

"Should you do the honors, or should I?"

"He asked for you to do it, sweetheart. I'm supposed to read the poem, remember?"

"That's right," she said. He handed her the brick-like container, and as the cold wind seemed to blow through her, he began to recite *The Emperor of Ice Cream*. It was Rem's favorite poem. Besides, this was how he wanted it. As David read, nearing the end, she pitched the urn high in the air, and moments later, heard it splash in the sea. In that moment of impact, she saw colors—blue, green, gray—the colors of the ocean. Saw or imagined. It was really all the same.

They didn't speak again until they were in the car with secret service men in front of and behind them, winding back along this road to reality.

"Are you okay?" he whispered.

She nodded, then asked, "What differentiates a

bona fide mistress from a one-night stand, anyway? Do you pay for them, their homes, I mean, their groceries?" Her voice escalated against her will. She couldn't pull it back.

David's sigh was heavy, full of the ocean and this day of dirty duty. "It was a long time ago, sweetheart." An explanation. Not an answer at all.

"You will find that girl? You'll bring her to me?" She hated the strident urgency in her voice. She would have never talked to Rem this way.

David squeezed her arm, and for a moment, she could see his face, the way it had always looked, handsome but understated, strong but loyal. "I told you before," he said. "You're in charge now."

Reebie

A message from my temp rep, Natalie, was waiting for me on Saturday when Kersikovski dropped me off at home. I wasn't surprised to hear that Alberta had called the catering company to complain and that the catering people requested I not be assigned to future jobs. When I called her back I could hear the concern in Natalie's usually upbeat tone and realized that her compassion wasn't faked. No wonder she was so good at matching misfits like me to temporary positions. She promised that she wouldn't give up on me, reminded me that I had strong qualifications. She said not to be depressed. I told her I wasn't. I thanked her for her help. I didn't say I'd suffered greater losses.

I decided against my walk that morning. After Kersikovski had driven me home, I'd gotten on my computer and dug up everything I could find online about Jeanette Sheldon. Her romance with Marcus Olson, the TV star, in the sixties. Her rumored relationship with President Remington. Her affair with Ed Palacios, the mob-connected singer-turned-philanthropist. The lady had gotten around. Yet, she'd lived the last half of her life in obscurity. Hiding? Where did I come into this? Why did she want me to be the one to hear the Remington story?

I continued my Web searching Sunday, keeping the television on without sound. CNN showed the mourners moving past Remington's casket, which was lying in state in the Capitol Rotunda. I couldn't help being drawn to it. He'd been president around the time I was born, and still he commanded more respect than any of today's leaders. The sadness of it struck me. He had a wife, a blind wife at that, a son and a grandchild on the way. Was his personal life anyone's business?

If I'd been paid for the number of hours I spent squinting at that screen, I'd have earned more than my weekly take for selling skin firmers, under-eye serums and aromatherapy purification masks. I got so absorbed in thinking about the past and trying to assimilate the slew of gossip and facts about Jeanette that it was afternoon before I could take my walk, the only constant in my pathetic excuse for a life and the only thing that allowed me to vent some of the pent-up pain and, okay, fear that had hold of me most of my waking moments.

My doorbell rang just as I was about to leave.

I squinted through the peephole. Leo Kersikovski's gorgeous self stood on the other side. Here I was wearing gray sweats, a matching T-shirt without a bra, and no doubt reeking of my last romp with Chico. Kersikovski, although in equally casual attire, looked as if the word *sweat* didn't exist in his vocabulary.

I inched open the door. "You can't look at me," I said.

"Of course I can." He strode into the room, took in the place and headed straight to my Art Deco chaise, one of the few pieces of furniture I managed to hang on to when the marriage crumbled around me. "I've been checking out Jeanette Sheldon," he said.

"Me, too. Can you believe Ed Palacios?"

"And what about Marcus Olson?"

Still standing, I looked at the shabby landscape of my life—the decent glass coffee table, the umbrella stand and its contents of my former life, the former dining-room chairs trying to be part of the living room because my only dining area was no larger than the bistro table that occupied it. I glanced over at the counter, the pot of Peet's coffee, a gift from Daphne. The warmer light had gone off hours ago, and I'd happily drunk my last cup, down to room temperature.

"Can I get you some tea? Decaf?"

"No." He rose from the chaise with a half smile.

"First, I'm taking you to lunch, and then we're going to talk to Parker Cobb."

"Parker?" I asked. I'd called his office because I wanted to talk to him about Sunny's memorial service. He hadn't returned the call. "Why him?"

"Because he's been telling lies about you," he said. "I think it might be interesting for us to confront him face-to-face."

Kersikovski's van, The Green Tambourine as he called it, was the color of canned peas. The only good thing about it was the heater, which thawed me on contact today as it had last night. Even the smell of it was warm.

For a moment, back in my apartment, I'd panicked, thinking we were going somewhere fancy. So I'd pulled on my Uggs and the short pink skirt with the carwash pleats, a hand-me-over from Daph, who tired of her clothes about as fast as she tired of her men. Add a baggy turtleneck, and I was prime date material, if you ignored the bruises that even my expensive cosmetics left mottled, and the fact that I was, if not a suspect, at least a consideration in two murders, three if you counted Sunny's.

Sunny. Her death was the strangest of all. The memorial service was scheduled for Monday. I didn't know how I was going to get through it.

"Is this an antique car?" I asked. "One of those classics?"

"In a way." He reached for the shift, an amber knob of resin containing a replica of a daisylike flower. His hand brushed my knee, not his whole hand—his knuckle, just his knuckle. I could feel it that intensely. We both pretended not to notice the physical connection. He returned his hand to the steering wheel. "My dad," he said, "drove this bus when he was in the navy. Named it after some Dylan song."

He'd obviously never spent any time listening to Daph's oldies collection. "The Dylan song was 'Mr. Tambourine Man.' 'Green Tambourine' was the Lemon Pipers," I said. "You never bought a newer car?"

"I didn't feel the need, especially after he died."

"Oh?" So, I was riding in a monument.

"I had the seat belts installed later, and the CD player. It's as safe as a new car, I promise."

"That wasn't what I meant," I said. He gave me a look that was part question, part evaluation. I looked away from it, out the window. I hadn't figured him as sentimental, but I wasn't about to say so. We drove the rest of the way in silence.

Our destination was a hot-dog place across from a small park with wooden picnic tables and a set of old-fashioned swings with only chains and sagging seats. After my first bite, it was all I could do to keep from shoving the chili dog into my face.

Without touching his food, he studied me from the other side of the picnic table. "You're a foodie. How do you rate that?"

"Superlative."

"I thought you'd say that." He smiled as if I'd just given him something lovely.

"What have they done to it? The tiny, tiny little pieces of onion, maybe. Red onions, right? And don't you taste a little sugar, and what?"

He nodded, the sun lighting him from behind, like a silhouette etched in gold.

Suddenly, I stopped. "What makes you think I'm a foodie?"

"Listen to yourself."

"But you called me that before I rattled on." I spoke slowly as suspicion crept in.

"True." He bit into his paper-wrapped frank, then putting it back down into its flimsy white cardboard container, wiped the brick-red smear from his lips in a gesture that would make me shudder if I thought about it. "A foodie. But not a food snob. I like that."

"But how'd you know?" The splintery wood of the bench felt itchy on my leg. I didn't like being figured out, like a tidy little puzzle someone had decided to outsmart.

"Daph's party," he said. "That dip you brought."

"Hummus," I said, hoping it didn't sound like a correction.

"And the round pasta things on skewers."

"Tortellini."

"With that garlicky green sauce."

"Pesto." I couldn't help it. "Only I make mine with pistachios and sun-dried tomatoes instead of pine nuts."

He leaned across the table, so close that I could see the smudge of chili above his lips. "Tell me, food lady. What's your story? Your real story?"

I was a possible murder suspect, a possible target. And he was a reporter. "You're looking at it," I said, and stared him full in the face, until he was the one to look away.

Nicholas

The day they returned from Washington, he'd made sure she was gone, that she hadn't just circled back to catch him at something. Then, he sneaked fast out behind the house, past the lavender plants clumped all over the back, grown from seed. The hoe still leaned against the shed, but he couldn't see his little baby plants. What could have happened to them? She wouldn't have hurt them, would she? They'd been together almost every minute since they'd gotten on the plane.

He stopped walking. Maybe he should just go back inside and never come back here again. But if the plants were still alive, what would happen to them without him? She wouldn't care. No one would. He walked all stiff-legged toward the garden, then stopped again. There they were, all of his tomato plants, higher, fuller, sturdier than when he'd left them.

"How?" He rushed to the first row, knelt down and touched the wet circle around a plant. Someone had not only planted his seedlings but watered them, as well.

The sound of footsteps through the pines startled him. He jumped to his feet. It could be her, coming back again.

"Hi, handsome." Darla stepped from behind a pine tree and brushed her black hair behind the scrunched-up headband she wore when it rained, as it was bound to do any minute now.

"Hi." He squinted against the sudden glare of the sun he hadn't even noticed before. Then he got one of his crazy ideas. "You didn't do all of this, did you?"

"Plant your garden, you mean?"

He could see her clearly now, lit from the back and magnified by the sun. Her delicate face, those eyes, were full of life. "Yes," he said. "You didn't do it, did you?"

"Sure did." She seemed ready to laugh, but not a teasing laugh. A happy laugh. Then, she put out her arms. "Welcome home."

Twelve

The Mistress

Palm Springs
1976

Eddie had told her to trust whatever happened, but she couldn't. Marcus had acted too crazy. He'd almost broken her wrist as he dragged her from the house. It didn't make any sense, no sense at all.

"You think you're driving me somewhere?" she shouted. "Just let me tell you right now, that I'm not going until I hear frigging where and why."

"Come on, Jeanette. Get in the car."

Oh, yes, the big, black Mercedes. She'd get in all right, but he couldn't control her if he was driving. She'd get her answers.

He opened the door of the back seat and pushed

her inside. Great. Back seat was better. If he didn't tell her what this was all about, she'd be all over him, pulling his hair.

"Crazy bastard," she whispered, just to make herself feel better.

"He's not."

Jeanette whipped around. She couldn't believe it. Kim sat beside her in the seat. It was the first time she'd seen Kim's strawberry-blond hair pulled back from her face. It made her look gaunt, hungry almost.

"What the hell are you doing here? Marcus has gone bonkers. Please don't say you have, too."

"It's for your own good, Jeanette." Kim made a noise, and Jeanette realized she was crying. "It's going to save your life, honey."

Reebie

The attractive yet nondescript blonde who opened the door to Parker Cobb's condominium told us he was working at his office. I wondered if the lady was a relative. Surely he couldn't have replaced Sunny this soon?

Kersikovski drove us downtown to a three-story building that appeared to be occupied primarily by attorneys, psychologists and a teachers' credit union.

We took the elevator to the top floor and followed the carpeted hall to a frosted glass door labeled Cobb & Cobb. It was unlocked, but the reception area was empty. Kersikovski headed toward the back. I followed.

Parker came out of the conference room, wearing a shirt and slacks. Overdressed for any occasion. I'd forgotten that about him. I'd also forgotten how tall he was, how muscular. He spent a fair share of his considerable earnings staying in shape. I wondered briefly how much the suntan and short, too-blond-to-be-natural hair had cost.

"You looking for someone?" he demanded of Kersikovski, then he saw me. I caught him wincing as he surveyed the damage to my face. "What the hell are you doing here?"

Before I could answer, Kersikovski said, "We want to know why you're lying about Ms. Mahoney."

"I'm not lying, and you'd better reconsider those accusations." His face flushed beneath the tan and he strode past Kersikovski until he was only a few feet away from me. "The question is, why did *you* lie? I talked to Sunny right before she left the store Friday night. She said she was going out with you."

"And she told me she was going out with you," I said. "I know she wasn't with me."

"And I can prove she wasn't with me. Can you prove likewise?"

"You bet. I was dog-sitting for Daphne Teng."

"The dog's your alibi, I take it?"

He was an arrogant bastard. His confrontational manner reminded me of the nightmare I'd escaped, the attorneys, the judges. "Daph's my alibi," I said.

"This guy?" He jerked his head back at Kersikovski.

"I'm a reporter." Parker's double take earned him a grim smile.

"You're covering Sunny's murder?"

"Among other things." Kersikovski stood beside me. "The point is Reebie's telling the truth. I believe her."

His words made me feel vindicated, free, almost fluttery. I looked into Parker's doubting blue eyes. "Sunny was my friend," I said. "I don't want to be disrespectful, but I'm not lying, and I don't think you are, either. If she wasn't with you, and she wasn't with me, she was with someone else."

"Where the hell else would she be on a Friday night?" The courtroom voice had lost some of its punch. "Where?"

"It's just a guess—" I didn't want to say it. I looked up at Kersikovski, begging him with my eyes to fill the silence.

"Go on," he said.

"Yeah," Parker said. "Where the hell would she be?"

"Maybe with the person who helped her buy her car?"

The moment I spoke the words, I regretted doing so. Parker winced as if I'd struck him and sank against the reception desk. Kersikovski's face was a handsome mask, but his eyes were alive, taking it all in, recording it, maybe even relishing it.

"What person?" Parker asked.

So, I'd been right. My gut had told me Parker didn't buy her that car. "How do you think she bought it? You didn't give her the money, did you?"

He shook his head. "No."

"And the watch, the bracelet? You really think we can afford trinkets like those on what we earn at the makeup counter?"

"If she'd needed anything—" His look was pleading. "I guess I was too wrapped up in my career to understand."

"Maybe you were," I said. "Do you at least believe me now, that I wasn't with Sunny that night she was killed?"

"You made your point and made it well." The sadness in his eyes overpowered the assertiveness in his lawyer voice. "Maybe I wasn't the best partner in the world, but I cared about her, I loved her. I really loved her, and I never told her, not once. No wonder she—"

We said our goodbyes and got the hell out of that law office before Parker Cobb had to verbalize what Sunny had done.

I hurt for Sunny more in that moment than I had since I'd learned of her murder. She'd loved Parker. I knew that. He'd loved her, but he'd never told her. Why? He said he was too busy. And because he didn't give her what she needed, she'd found someone else—Mr. Money. Mr. Car Payment. Mr. Bracelet. Mr. Watch. And this man was probably the last person to see her alive.

"Why didn't you tell me Sunny had another boyfriend?" Kersikovski asked the moment the elevator door slid shut.

"I wasn't sure. I mean, I'd guessed, based on what she said about Parker. Basically, I was faking it."

"You fake well."

"Thanks, I think. I feel bad about it, though."

"He didn't feel bad about calling you a liar."

"Guess he didn't."

"So? I mean, I know a lot of women like that look of his."

It took a moment to unscramble the meaning of his words. "You can't possibly believe—" I was rescued by the elevator door. Walked through it, straight into the foyer, trying to bite back the obscenity that pressed against my lips like a wad of gum I had to fight against spitting out. We walked without speaking through the glass doors. Once in the car, certain that I was calmed down enough, I said, "I don't find that sleazeball in the least appealing. Still, I didn't want to destroy his memories of Sunny, okay?"

"Okay." He pulled his van out of the parking lot. "On that happy note, could we have dinner?"

Good God in heaven. The d-word. Less than three hours after lunch, and Leo Kersikovski had just invited me to dinner. His whole little tirade about Parker suddenly looked like jealousy. He'd invited me to dinner. He really had. And I couldn't go.

"I promised Daph I'd watch Chico," I said, feeling as hopeless as the lime-green plaid interior of the Green Tambourine. "She was devastated by Sunny's murder and she needs to get out."

"Damn. One-upped by a dog."

"But a very cool dog, you must admit. Way cooler than that attorney back there."

I almost asked if he'd like to join Chico and me and the flank steak, but it was too soon. And maybe it would always be too soon, and if so, that was okay, too. Instead of saying anything, I just studied that amazing profile, shocked that I could feel a ripple of hope in my life again, and grateful—yes, that, too— grateful to be walking around in the same world with the likes of Leo Kersikovski.

For the first time since I'd entered it, I wondered if there might be an end to this tunnel of darkness.

Daph brought Chico over about six. He gave me that flank-steak look, and I was glad I'd gone to the store.

"Which one tonight?" I asked.

"The architect." She checked her hair and rearranged the blue streak in the Pier One pewter-framed mirror beside my front door. "He's taking me to a place to paint pottery."

"Why?"

"Because it's a date. Because it's better to observe each other in activities than to just get drunk and jump in bed, then wake up with a stranger." She sighed. "I almost cancelled, but I don't want to be alone with my own thoughts right now."

I watched her watch herself, wondering if I could ever care about my appearance in such a focused way again. "Dating," I said. "I wouldn't know how to start."

"I'm not so sure about that. Where'd you spend the day?" She turned from the mirror in time to see what felt very much like guilt heating my cheeks.

"It was business."

"Still, Mr. Workaholic's been asking a few too many questions about you. Oh, he's good at sounding casual about it, but I can tell. Do you like him?"

I turned away. "Never trust a man who's prettier than you are."

"He's not." She marched around to face me. "But you do like him, don't you?"

Chico rubbed my leg, squeaking the beige furry toy we called his "baby."

"I could like him." I reached down and tugged on Chico's curly spaniel ears. He looked back at me with devotion no doubt motivated by memories of flank steak. "But I can't like anyone. You know that." I turned away, back toward the front door, so that she couldn't see the sudden tears in my eyes. Picked up Chico's baby and flung it into the kitchen. He skittered after it, retrieved it, circled the two rooms, the baby dangling from his mouth.

Daph moved behind me. In her best American accent, she said, "Divorce is a bitch, ain't it?"

"Especially when you're divorcing someone you thought you'd be with for the rest of your life. That's the worst part, Daph, realizing that the love is dead. You don't really watch it die. You just wake up one day and it's fucking gone."

We pretended to ignore my tears, and Chico didn't seem to notice. Daph left for her date and I took Chico for a walk, down to the end of the street and back, stopping just before the darkness.

I took a deep breath and was reminded of what I'd left behind. I'd become so used to exhaust fumes and city smells that I'd forgotten damp grass at dusk, pungent gardenias and jasmine, not to mention this musty little animal who tugged at his leash then bolted back and heaved a fetid burst of canine breath in my face.

I'd never had a dog. Now, I understood why women loved them. We'd never find this kind of obedience in any other area of our lives.

Sit, Chico. Good dog. Off, Chico. Pee-pee, Chico. No, Chico. Sit, Chico. Good dog, Chico. Very good dog. No way to find that any place else.

We returned home, Chico leading me through the fading light. He was no doubt thinking of the flank steak I'd already decided to give him, and I was thinking of many things in this fresh, cool air. About Kersikovski, of course. But most of all, about Jeanette. Why had this woman singled me out from all of the other people she could confess to? What was her link to me? A link that had involved me in three murders?

I might never know the answer to that one. I'd searched every link I could find to Jeanette Sheldon, knew every bit of gossip and fact. But her life had ended in 1976. Chico stopped to decorate a tree, and I realized what I'd overlooked. Jeanette Sheldon disappeared in 1976, probably the year she had decided to change her name. What had she done between then and now? I hadn't seen the obvious, hadn't even come close.

"Come on, boy," I urged Chico. No, it wasn't Jeanette I should have been researching. It was the woman she'd pretended to be. Nora McFarland.

Thirteen

The Mobster

It goes, Jeanette. Youth goes. It just seeps away, so slow you don't even notice. And me, hell, I'm the last to see my own flaws. Full of myself, you used to say. So vain I packed a hand mirror right next to my gun. A little less full these days.

The giving a shit. That goes, too. There's not much I care about anymore, and tell you the truth, I wish I didn't care about this little trip, but I do, and that's that.

I still pack the mirror though, and the gun. Got them in my briefcase.

If you'd have told me back than that I'd outlive Rem, I would have said it was wishful thinking. If you'd told me I'd be flying to D.C. to pay my respects to his fucking remains, I'd have said you lost your mind. The changes were so slow that I can't even remember when I quit hating that bastard.

It's been years since I did business in the backs of limos, but it's like riding a bike, all of it, like sex, you used to say.

It's about four o'clock when I land at Reagan International. No luggage. Just this mourner's suit, the pointy-toed shoes you teased me about a week ago. God, a week ago. And the cuff links, Venetian blue glass, we bought on that last trip to Siena. I've got to cut those thoughts right out of my head and just think about what I'm going to say.

The limo's waiting. I don't know the driver, Peter, but I know he's safe, checked out by people I trust. As instructed, he's already picked up David Ritchey.

"Rich," I say as I climb into the seat facing him, my back to the driver. Ritchey, too, is in a dark suit, but then he would be. He looks older than his photos, all jowls and nasty creases cutting up the heavy flesh of his face. He smiles as if telling me he knows what I'm thinking, but this is just the way it is.

"It's been too long, Eddie." He reaches out for my handshake. "How's the restaurant business?"

"It's been good to me."

"I should say so." He settles back in his seat, taking me in with that way he has, never missing a detail. I make sure he catches the cuff links, the shoes, the jacket and what it might or might not be hiding. "How do you do it?" he finally asks.

"Clean living."

He laughs harder than he needs to, but he was always good at laughing, good at backslapping, good at being the first on his feet to applaud. Rem's built-in audience when he needed more than June, which was most of the time. "I wasn't surprised to hear from you," he says. "Not after—I mean, there's no way that woman who was killed could be our Jeanette, is there?"

"That's not why I'm here." I finger the stone of my cuff links. My voice feels that cold to me. Oh, yes, Jeanette, the old ways come back in a hurry. "I want to make a donation to the nonprofit Rem established for the visually impaired." I take the silver-gray leather envelope out of my briefcase, open it and hand the check to him.

He glances down, as if embarrassed to be caught counting the zeroes. "That's very generous." He holds it like a hot potato, shifting it from hand to hand, until he finally smoothes it across the broad plane of his right leg. "Very generous. June will be so pleased. She's still one of your greatest fans. She keeps hoping you'll do one of those Tony Bennett comebacks."

"How's she holding up?" I ask. It's only right to ask.

"Taking it pretty hard." For the first time, I see a glint of sincerity in his weary, watery eyes. "He was her world."

"Give her my best," I say. "I'll be visiting the Rotunda later today to pay my respects."

"You're a class act, Eddie." Then, as if realizing he's let too much emotion slip out, he gets all solemn on me. "I'll convey that information to June. I know it will be a comfort to her."

The limo stops before my hotel, and I can almost feel his sigh of relief. What he doesn't know is that my man, Peter, has instructions to keep the doors and windows locked until I tell him otherwise. Ritchey doesn't have a clue. He thinks he's out of here, scot-free with a check and maybe an iffy friendship with me.

"It's been good talking to you," he says, wiping his hand across his shiny, fleshy forehead. "With Rem's passing, and that situation in San Francisco, I didn't know what to expect today."

"But you still met with me."

He nods. "Of course. It's my job."

"And exactly what is that? Your job, I mean." I'm nice, but I'm tightening the noose. I still know how to tighten the noose.

"Well." He runs his finger around his collar, as if he can feel what I'm doing to him right there. He's not the first one. "I might be officially retired, and I pretty much manage my investments since I sold the law firm. I've worked for Rem one way or the other since I was in my twenties, though."

"And now?" I ask. "You work for June?"

"Not for a salary, of course."

"Of course not."

His hand creeps toward the door lever. He thinks

I don't see him try it, that I don't see it not budging an inch. He's no longer David Ritchey, Rem's one-time chief of staff. Today, he's just another fat man, sweating, maybe even scared. It's that easy to erase him, to see only what I need to see, a man who's starting to figure out that he's in the wrong place with the wrong person.

"Now." I lower my voice, keep it scratchy, the way it was when I was still a smoker and a lot of other things I'm not today.

"What do you want?" Good, he's getting it.

"To give you a donation, in Rem's memory."

"What else?"

Now. Time to strike. "There is something else," I say.

"What?" He can barely get it out. I make it clear, bring it home.

"Junior."

"What do you mean?"

"Rem's son."

"Nicholas?" His face is a dangerous purple color, but I've got to scare the crap out of him—I have to, if this is going to work. "What about Nicholas?"

I might not be as young as the stud boy singer I used to be, but I haven't forgotten how to give The Look. There's still enough power in me that I could smash this worm here and now, and he knows it. God, does he know it.

"He could die," I say.

"Good God, man. What are you talking about? Why would anyone want to hurt Nicholas?"

"Not anyone, David. Me. My people."

"But—" He reaches for the door again. I take the liberty of shoving him back in his seat.

"With all due respect," I say. "If anything happens to that little girl in California, Reebie Mahoney—"

"I've never even heard of anyone by that name," he whines.

"Shut up." This time I don't need anything but my voice to shove him back into his seat. "If anything happens to that girl—"

"You rotten bastard."

"Which one of us is the rotten bastard, Davy?"

He draws back from my voice. "Why don't we leave that one up to God?"

"Works for me." I switch on the speaker and say, "Okay, Peter." The click is instantaneous. "I'm going to my hotel now," I say. "You can stay here, and Peter will take you wherever you like." I give him The Look again. "Just remember what I said. The son is only as safe as that little girl in California."

"Got it." The hatred in his puffy eyes is more intense than I'd expected, only because I hadn't figured the asshole to have this much passion in him.

I open the door, and when I do, he scrambles over my feet, like an animal freed from a cage. Peter scurries to the side of the door, waiting for his tip. I slip a big bill into his hand, a bill large enough to make him remember, the way all of my drivers used to, that Eddie P is good guy to work for.

Now, I'm tired, Jeanette. Walking past Rem's casket today made me go head-to-head with the stuff I've been putting off for later, the stuff that never happens in the here and now. Like my casket.

How many people will mourn me? And you, baby girl? What are we going to do about that? How do we bury you? What name do we use, and why the hell didn't we ever talk about it?

Fourteen

Reebie

Jeanette Sheldon was Nora McFarland. Or maybe Nora McFarland was Jeanette Sheldon. The moment I decided to focus on Nora, I began to uncover Web sites with images similar to the paintings in the murdered woman's home. And on one of those numerous sites, I discovered the location of Nora McFarland's studio. And I learned that it would be open Tuesday night.

None of the sites had photos of Nora, only of her eerie paintings. From what I could learn from the short bios of her, she began her career just a couple of years after Jeanette Sheldon's death. Now, Jeanette was dead, for real this time, not killed in that supposed auto accident back in the seventies. I knew I had to see Nora McFarland's studio. When I called

Kersikovski—I had to call Kersikovski—he agreed with me and said he'd pick me up and take me to the Hop, as it was called by the hip East Bayers who attended it.

The concept wasn't new. A handful of art galleries stay open one night a week, plying browsers with wine, cheese and an opportunity to mingle. This mingling was limited to the downtown area, a series of studios that were housed in the former bus barn, only one other like it in the country, the brochure boasted.

Each of the four parking stalls had been converted to studio space, with industrial rails balancing overhead lighting and white L-shaped dividers breaking up the enormous space. Stepping into it was like stepping into my past. The women wearing monochromatic tones and jewelry that looked as if it had been hammered out by hand. The men with shaved heads, coarse, clinched ponytails, or both.

We approached a table of goat cheeses, and I guessed that Kersikovski could sense my apprehension. In my valley, my town, we'd display the cheese with labels that addressed the field in which each herd had grazed. No one here cared.

"Wine?" he asked.

"Sure." I turned toward the long, black-paper-covered table, saw my bottle and almost toppled. My sandals managed to contain me. Before Kersikovski noticed, I forced myself to go through the motions and take the plastic glass the smiling server handed to me.

"Desmond Vineyards," she said. "This cab is awesome, believe me."

"I believe you." I looked over at Kersikovski.

"Make it two," he said.

I had to do this. I couldn't think about similar gatherings of food and wine. I couldn't think about Desmond Vineyards. I started to lift my glass and stopped, on the dime, as my dad would say. Then, I realized if I sipped one drop of this wine, I'd break down and bawl like the disenfranchised misfit that I was.

"Which part of this was Jeanette's studio, do you suppose?" Kersikovski tasted the wine, then smiled the same way I've seen countless others do. Took another taste. Smiled again, a big, broad grin, a man in love. If he only knew.

"Let's find out," I said.

We blended into the crowd, as much as a man who looks like Kersikovski can blend, at any rate. The apron-clad wine server trailed after us, offering us refills.

A handsome, horsy type with thick, streaked heiress hair galloped right up to introduce herself.

"Gaylene," she said, in a seductive drawl. "This is my studio."

"Amazing." Amazing. The all-encompassing adjective.

It was the word Daph used to describe anything she liked, from a film to coffee to sex.

Gaylene hadn't shifted her focus from Kersikovski's face.

I looked around us at the pottery displayed on white pedestals. She did nice work, something I wouldn't have guessed, judging from the overabundance of lilac glitter adorning her eyelids. Her pots and vases were clunky, colorful, almost mocking in their intensity. If I wasn't so broke I would have bought a crooked iris-colored vase etched with circular symbols.

I looked down at my clenched fists. Yes, I was angry that I couldn't buy that vase, that I didn't dare drink this wonderful cab—my cab—I held. I turned away and stalked toward the open area in the back, Kersikovski beside me. Gaylene caught up with us, watching him, as all women did, the way you'd be compelled to stare at a flower or a mountain when God got it just right.

"Doesn't Nora McFarland have a studio here?" he asked.

Gaylene stopped in the tracks of her stiletto boots. "She's out of town. I'm managing the studio for her until she gets back."

"Where is it?" I asked.

"Right next door, through there." Although I'd asked the question, it was Kersikovski she answered. "Her work is amazing."

That word again.

She moved through the crowd, toward the back of the room, Kersikovski behind her, and I behind him.

"As I said, her stuff is just amazing. I posed for

her a couple of times myself." Girlish giggle. "The Scheherazade Pose, you know. Like the Arabian Nights."

"You smoke?" I asked.

"Of course not." My unbidden question had thrown her off track—a track I'm sure she'd tried to direct straight to Kersikovski's bed. "There are other ways to get that effect. For my portraits, we burned sage." She turned and repeated it again into Kersikovski's face. "Sage." She exhaled the statement, like smoke. "She calls it the Scheherazade Pose because it's a metaphor."

Kersikovski's eyes met mine, and he almost smiled. "For what?" I asked.

"I don't know exactly. Scheherazade had to keep telling her husband those stories, or he was going to behead her, you know. The pose is about art born of desperation. At least that's how it was for me. Nora said it was one of her best pieces."

Spot lighting shone from the stall that must have been Jeanette's secret studio. No wine. No cheese. No patrons. To our left, as we entered, a white-painted wall displayed variations on the paintings I had glimpsed in Jeanette's apartment the night of her murder. Nude forms, more photograph than painting, all arms, legs, torsos emerging from filmy tangles of smoke, like two photographs in one frame. Faces without features, except the lips in a purple so vivid that not even our cosmetics counter could match it.

On the far wall, I recognized Gaylene at once and from his suddenly casual air, Kersikovski must have too. I could see why she wanted us to witness the painting. If her real breasts were anything close to the ones twisted in smoke swirls, all she needed beneath the painting was her phone number and the message: *For a good time, call Gaylene*. Scheherazade Pose, indeed.

As Kersikovski and I stood facing the painting, she wedged herself between us, turning first to him, then to me, as if to register our reactions.

"When did she paint that?" Kersikovski's voice hadn't changed. He might as well have been asking for extra onions on his chili dog.

"Oh, I'd say about last October. Pretty chilly weather, as I recall." That giggle again. "Nora brought along a little flask to warm me up, not to mention calm my nasty little jitters."

"How'd you meet her?" I asked.

"At an event like this one." She turned almost reluctantly and zigzagged around a large pedestal, heading into the open room and its smell of incense. "I came out here almost four years ago, you know. I was looking for some space, and I heard about a group of artists trying to buy the old bus barn. I had a little money from my divorce settlement." She shrugged and glanced at Kersikovski. "One thing about fried-chicken franchises in the South, honey— no one goes away hungry, not even the ex-wife."

In less than ten minutes, she'd been able to show

him an advertisement for her nude body and perform the verbal equivalent of handing him her bank statement. I had to admire her in a grudging, been-bested kind of way. "So." After that little display, I had to clear my throat. "You met Nora four years ago, then?"

"A little less than that. She bought in a month or two after I did. We hit it off right from the start, and that's not easy for me with another woman, especially not a beautiful one." Making a point of pretending to address me, she added, "I get along so much better with men."

"Have you ever been to her home?" Kersikovski asked.

"Why would I?" She crossed her arms, and I could see her composure change like that, from alluring to concerned and maybe more. "And why the hell would you ask that, anyway, if you're just here to buy a painting?"

He directed those eyes of his on her like headlights. "I'm a reporter. I'm sorry I didn't say that earlier."

"I should guess the hell so." Gaylene threw back her shoulders, and I got that vision of a horse again—all snort and size and stomping hooves. "And what does a reporter want with poor Nora, anyway? That lady's so sweet that she's damned near invisible."

She didn't know. She really didn't know who Nora was.

"Leo." It was the first time I'd used his first

name, but it got his attention. "We need to tell her,"
I said.

"Tell me what?" Gaylene was like a ball of yarn
someone had started to unwind. That toothy smile
became a grimace. Those flirtatious eyes narrowed,
no longer gleaming, just beady. She focused her
new, lovely self on me. "What the hell is going on?
What's happened to Nora?"

"I thought you said she was out of town."

"She told me to say that, okay? But she was supposed to call me, and she hasn't. What's going on?"
She turned on Kersikovski now, no longer trying to
intrigue him. "You'd better tell me, mister, and if you
don't, I'm going to the cops."

I looked at Kersikovski and said, "Well?"

She looked at Kersikovski and said nothing.

Kersikovski looked away from both of us, past the
paintings and the partitions and the pedestals, to that
wide-open doorway, wide enough to drive a bus into
this place.

At that moment, the space we watched was filled
by one man, only one man, but he filled it, not just
because of his size, but because of how he wore it.
I'd heard he was a looker in his day. I'd seen the old
photos, the handful of films he made before he gave
up singing and other less glamorous activities for the
restaurant business.

The gray of his suit was so dark that if it were a
car, they'd call it anthracite. His French cuffs were

so white that I blinked just looking at them. It was Ed Palacios, right down to his amethyst cuff links.

I heard Gaylene gasp, but Ed Palacios didn't notice her. He walked straight to me.

"You know this was her studio, don't you?"

Forget the hello—nice to meet yous.

I managed to move my head up and down in a semblance of a nod. His scent was as crisp and European as his shirt. "I know," I said.

"Her things are in there." He glared at me as if I had more power than I did. "The public can't just waltz in like this."

"I'm so sorry." Gaylene moved beside me. "It's my fault the studio's open tonight. I haven't heard from Nora, and I just thought—"

"With all due respect, I'd prefer you just shut up, okay?"

She gasped. "I only meant—" she began. But Eddie P was looking at me again in a way that made me nervous.

"What they're looking for—it's here," he said. "She told me, and she told you, too, didn't she? We've got to find it before the cops figure out who Nora really was."

"Won't happen, Eddie P." Kersikovski stepped up next to me, and Palacios moved back.

"What do you mean, and who the hell are you?"

"A reporter," Kersikovski said. "The cops know who Nora was, and they know about this studio."

"They do?" I asked. "Since when?"

"I called Danny Morgan right before I left home."

"Cops?" Palacios asked. Then, before waiting for an answer, he said to me, "We've got to tear this place apart."

"Someone's coming," Gaylene squealed. Sure enough, headlights filled the open door of the stall. The lights went out, doors slammed, and in came Officer Morgan and Officer Stumph.

"How y'all doing," Stumph asked, pausing inside the door.

"Just talking." I started to gesture toward Ed Palacios, but the big man with the French cuffs had disappeared. "Where'd he go?" I asked.

"Through there, through my studio." Gaylene hadn't moved since he'd arrived.

"Who?" Danny asked.

"Ed Palacios," she said.

Stumph whistled. "And what was the great Eddie P doing here?"

Although he directed the question to me, Gaylene gushed out the answer like a schoolgirl trying to impress the teacher.

"He said they needed to tear this studio apart before the police found out who Nora really is. Nora McFarland. These are her paintings."

Danny looked from me to the figures on the walls and dividers. He bit his lower lip, and I knew that he was making the same connection I had.

"What else did Mr. Palacios have to say?" he asked.

"He said that what they were looking for was in here. I don't know what exactly, but he said Nora told him. That she told her, too." She turned slowly and pointed a long orchid nail at me.

Fifteen

I woke up ahead of the alarm clock the next morning, and for a moment, I wasn't sure where I was. By the time I was fully awake, I was already remembering Ed Palacios's words, Gaylene's accusing finger pointing at me, the cops' questions after. Maybe I could miss my walk one day. No. I didn't need to lie here replaying my conversation with the police and Kersikovski.

A plus of early-morning walking is you don't remember much of pulling on the shorts and lacing up the shoes. I was on the street before I had a chance to decide, looking up into the moon's full face. The moon and the sun—sharing the same sky. I had to be crazy to get up this early.

I did it every morning, the same way I drank my juice and took my supplements, the way I had when Geoff and I were still together. I did it then because it was part of our routine. I did it now because I didn't know what else to do.

A woman in white shorts passed me, pumping her arms with so much energy that she might as well have been having sex with herself. She nodded a hello.

People who walk in the morning are polite, pleasant members of the same almost sanctimonious society. We step aside for each other, offering brief greetings through our sweat.

I tried to pump my arms like hers. Damned near knocked down a tree-trimmer, all buzz and short, spiked hair the color of ale. Soon, Pargat would arrive, to drive me to the gallery for a little snooping before I had to go into work. Then, I'd spend the rest of the day painting faces on the lookie Lous, the restless, the lonely.

And I'd be doing it without Sunny. I'd give anything if I didn't have to go in there today, but that was the problem. I'd already given everything. I had to go, to confront that space without her and to wonder, as I'd been wondering since this nightmare began, why?

The sun splintered light through a broken cover of clouds. I realized I was breathing the first air— before traffic, before all of the other people who would fill this empty street in a matter of hours, breathing in, breathing out the day. Instead of returning the way I'd come, I decided to go for the whole hour instead of my forty-minute minimum.

Turn left. Cross a narrow street, pass an elementary school.

An African-American man in shorts as well-worn as mine passed me and smiled a greeting.

"Good morning," I said, my words smothered by a guy trimming the trees across the street.

I continued to walk. Then, although my feet continued, my mind hesitated. *Nothing memorable about him,* part of my mind hummed. But beneath the static, a smaller part whispered. *Spiked hair. The color of ale.*

I took a short, shifty glance across the street. He'd moved along with me, buzzing his machine along someone else's tree. Probably a coincidence. It was morning. Bad things don't happen in the early moments of day.

I spotted a cul-de-sac two blocks down. I'd walk down there, just to convince myself. He'd move along to the next house on his path. I crossed the street, entered the cul-de-sac. Behind me, I heard the whir, faint but definitely coming my way. The sweat I'd worked up turned to ice. The bastard was following me.

I leaned down in front of a strange house, studied the grass as if it were my own. Time. I needed only time, only a moment. The offensive noise grew louder, like a plane, dipping down, then up again. Was it my imagination, or was he hovering, just waiting?

I should call the cops. And say what?

Kersikovski? I wouldn't know how to reach him. Besides, I'd left my cell phone at home. I pretended to tie my shoelaces and stood. Yes, it was the same man, walking briskly now, swinging the machine from side to side like a weapon.

I knew I couldn't make it to the end of the cul-de-sac. I couldn't run. Only one choice. Buy more time. I shot into the driveway of the next house, following the curve of its driveway up to the front door. The roar of the machine seemed to hesitate. I'd thrown him off. I pressed the bell and hoped someone was home. The house was in the good part of this northwest neighborhood, only a short walk from my end, where the homes were smaller, connected by driveways, and in my case, part of a thirty-unit apartment complex.

A woman wearing only a shower cap and the kind of bathrobe you get at ritzy hotels, opened it. She held a glass of what looked like orange juice but smelled more sinister. Just my luck.

"Please," I said, before she could speak. "Someone's following me. I need help."

"Don't we all?" she said, and started to close the door.

I hated Geoff all over again. He should be here, damn it. But he wasn't, and I had only one chance. I burst inside, nearly knocking her over, and slammed it shut behind me.

"What the hell?" Her breath was hot with attitude and the contents of the open gin bottle on her white-tiled counter.

Beside the bar, on an elaborate, phony pillar, rested a tiny gray-and-chrome object I recognized as a high-tech phone.

"I'm sorry," I said, "but someone's following me. I've got to get help."

"Honey, I've got problems of my own," she began.

By then, the phone was in my hand. I prayed she'd been sober enough to charge the batteries or whatever the hell the bored and wealthy did with toys like this.

Pargat answered on the first ring.

"Hurry," I said. "I'm five blocks down from my place, the block past the school, a two-story house, white with shiny black trim."

"I got here early," he began. "I am outside your place right now."

"You're here?" I couldn't believe it. Finally, something was going right.

"I told you I might be if I had no fares in the city."

"Someone, a man, is following me," I said. "Hurry." I looked at the woman, wide-eyed now, probably wondering if I were druggie or just plain whacked-out. "What's your address?" I demanded.

"None of your business," she said, pulling her robe around her.

I didn't have time for her, didn't have energy, didn't have patience. I gave her a look that I hoped conveyed all of that. "Don't make me go out there and look for it," I said.

She leaned against the counter and finished the rest of her doctored orange juice. "What the hell. It's sixty-three forty-three, okay? Now, get the hell out of my home."

"It's sixty-three forty-three, Pargat."

"I heard," he said, "and I am on my way."

The woman and I faced each other. I realized she was probably my dad's age, fifty something, but in worse shape. She yanked off her shower cap and put it next to the gin bottle. Her dark hair was cut as short as mine, only she hadn't bothered to unruffle it when she'd gotten up this morning.

Beneath her untrusting, bleary eyes were traces of eyeliner from the day before, maybe the day before that. I was in a stranger's home, leaning against a stranger's tiled bar, and the only thing more frightening than staying here was leaving.

"Please, believe me," I said slowly. "I'm afraid. There's a man out there, and I think he's following me."

The doorbell chimed. She turned toward it. Not Pargat, not this soon. Not even he drove that fast.

"No," I said.

"Don't worry. I have a peephole. Sure as hell should've used it when you rang." She pressed her forehead against the door. I could almost feel her squint. "It's okay. Only the gardener." She reached for the knob.

"Wait. Don't open it."

I covered the small space between the counter and

the door in a couple of breaths. I grabbed the knob, squeezing my fingers around her fingers, twisting the opposite direction, pushing forward with my knees. As she screamed, the door's grip loosened, and a heavy weight inched it open.

"This is my house," she shrieked.

A chuckle sounded from the other side, then we were both knocked back. Before us stood the gardener man, five-o'clock shadow, grimly handsome face, spiked hair the color of ale.

"Let's go," he said to me.

I backed off, looking for anything in the room I could use to fight him. In spite of the gardener attire, there was something familiar about him. "Who are you? What do you want?"

"I said, let's go." He closed the space between the two of us. "Right now. Come on."

"This is my house." The gin lady picked up her bottle. You get out of here right now, or I'll—" She swung it up, both hands around the neck of the bottle.

He turned, grabbed it from her, then hit her with such force that she collapsed on her tile floor with a moan.

"Help her," I said, unable to control my wavering voice. "She could be—"

He turned from her limp body to me, his eyes slanted like a lizard's. "Shut up, unless you want to join her. Now, come here."

I recognized him then, although I'd seen him only

once—at the department store. "Sunny—" I began, and he lunged for me.

I slipped around the other side of the bar, surveying the debris of the unconscious woman's life, desperate for a weapon. Bottle opener, pasta fork, serrated bread knife. I'd have to go with the bread knife, ridges and all. "Why me?" I asked.

"That's not any of my business." He stepped around the woman. She started to moan. Thank God she was alive, that she wasn't like the doorman and Jeanette. Like Sunny. I still couldn't think about Sunny.

"What *is* your business?"

"You'll find out soon enough." He swept past the woman toward my side of the bar.

I grabbed the bread knife by its mahogany-colored handle. "Stop right now."

He laughed. "You really think you can scare me with that? You think you can scare me at all?"

"I'm not trying to scare you," I said. "I just want you out of here."

"In your dreams. It's going to be a long drive to Seattle, so let's start out by making it clear who's in charge. Put the knife down, okay? Don't make me take it away from you." He looked me up and down, ran his tongue over his thin lips. "Although that might be fun, too."

I went for him, but he grabbed both wrists before I could connect. Drops of his sweat fell onto my face and sent a surge of nausea through me. His vise-lock on my wrists forced me to release the knife. I collapsed as the poor woman who owned this place had. Only I was still conscious. But I could pretend I wasn't. I tried to go limp, lifeless.

"Get up." A sharp boot toe connected with my side.

I yelped.

"Okay, you feel that, so you can get up. If you don't, the next one will be harder."

The bastard wasn't kidding.

I drew up my knees and reached for the edge of the counter. Slowly I pulled myself to my feet. "Why do you want to hurt me?" I asked. "I didn't know Jeanette at all. We'd talked one time. That was it. And that's why you're here, isn't it?"

"Shut up. Just shut up." He yanked me to him. "We're going to take a little drive to Washington."

I tried to pull away. "Washington, D.C.?"

"Relax, will you? Washington state. Seattle," he said. "The lady wants you to get there alive." He shot me a look that suggested how lucky I was that his employer didn't want me dead.

"Let her go."

Pargat stood in the doorway, his gun pointed at the gardener. I grabbed the knife from the floor, not sure what I would do with it, but feeling better just the same.

The owner of the house stirred again from where she'd fallen, then lifted her head and screamed.

Pargat steadied his aim. "Away from her," he said.

"Away from both of them. Over there, by the window."

I moved around the counter, took the woman's trembling arm and helped her to her feet. "Call nine-one-one," I told her. She nodded, her eyes large. Then, she looked at her home, at us.

"Oh, no," she said. "No. Help me. Please help me." Without as much as a glance at her high-tech phone on the faux pedestal, she ran out the open door, screaming.

"Quick, before the cops get here," the gardener told Pargat. "I have money. You need money, right?"

Pargat nodded. "I am not a rich man. Continue moving, please. In front of the window there."

"I'm moving, I'm moving." But he wasn't, not by much. The window was one of those floor-to-soaring-ceiling numbers, its top hidden by a fabric shade. Through it, I could see the dark-haired woman running away from us, across the street. "You need money," the gardener said. "I've got money, and I can get more. Can't we make a deal?"

"For what?" Pargat asked.

"Her. Let me take her."

Pargat hesitated, looking from the gardener to me. "How much money?"

Damn. Once again I'd trusted the wrong man. Still holding the knife, I looked at the door and the two men who blocked my way to it.

"How much do you want?"

"I want to know who paid you to kill this lady," he said.

"She doesn't want her killed. She just wants to talk to her." The gardener tried to edge away from the gun, but Pargat bore down on him.

"Who?" he demanded. "Who is this *she?*"

"You stupid bastard." The gardener's face hardened, and I knew he hadn't acquired those grim lines from working outdoors. "You just don't get it, do you? I could give you enough to take a month, hell, a whole year off that frigging cab."

"This deal sounds better and better. A month or a year, do you suppose?"

This time, I didn't cringe. I knew what Pargat was doing.

"You name your price," the man said. "I have about a grand on me. I can get you more, soon as we leave here."

Pargat nodded slowly, as if bowing to the money. "Forgive my ignorance, my friend. Who is the woman who wants to talk to this lady? And where is she? Perhaps I can drive you."

"You really think they give me their names and addresses, so I can look them up later, maybe, when I'm low on cash?" He swiped a hand across a nonexistent mustache. "Don't worry, though. No one's going to be hurt."

"You are right about that," Pargat said. "Because you're taking no one from this place."

"Don't be an idiot." The man jerked his head to-

ward me. "What's she to you? What's she to either
one of us?"

"That's not the point," I said, still gripping the
knife. "You said it yourself. That woman's going to
have every cop in town here in minutes. Why not tell
us who hired you to look for me?"

He turned to glance out the window, then returned
his attention to me. "I don't know what you've done
or what you know, little girl, but whatever it is, you
pissed off someone at the top, and you're not going
to get away with it."

"What do you mean? How? Is it connected to
Jeanette's murder?"

"You know it is." With that, he grabbed the pedestal and swung it into the window. Glass crashed, and
he swung it back, hurling it into Pargat.

The gun went off. Pargat fell. "Stupid bastard."
The gardener dove through the shards, shouting
words that registered only after he'd disappeared.
"I'm going to kill your ass."

Sixteen

I'm going to kill your ass.

I woke up with those words the next day, so close to my ear that I had to jump to be sure the man who spoke them wasn't lying there beside me.

No. The labored breathing came from Chico. After what happened yesterday, Daph had insisted that I spend the night at her place. She'd even broken one of her computer-man dates to stay home with me. I patted Chico's hefty hindquarters and whispered my *good boy* so that I wouldn't wake Daph in the next room.

I'm going to kill your ass.

I couldn't help it. For the first time since I lost my husband and my winery in one fell, legal swoop, I cared about something. I cared about Pargat. The man who'd followed me was no amateur. Even as he fled, he'd paused to take in every aspect of the room, especially Pargat. He'd be an easy target, too. Cab-drivers were being killed all over the East Bay. Not only did I have to find who the woman in Washington was, I also had to find a way to protect Pargat.

Daph drifted out for coffee about eight. Chico and I had walked around the backyard, but we hadn't left the premises. How she could drag herself from bed looking the way most women did after they'd showered, put on makeup and styled their hair always amazed me. Since Sunny's murder, though, there was a sadness about her, something more reflective than grief. It was as if she was mourning both Sunny and something else—something in herself.

She turned on the black-and-white television in the living room, an antique that probably cost her many times what it had sold for new. Scenes of President Remington's funeral filled the screen.

I turned away, knowing that the nightmare I was now living had started with his death. Why?

Daphne sat at the glass-topped table, patted Chico, reached for the full mug I placed before her and took a swallow.

"That's better than Starbucks. Thanks a bunch." Then she took another sip and asked, "How'd you sleep?"

"I slept, Daph. I really did. That's the unbelievable part. Thanks for canceling your date. I would have been under the bed at home."

"You should stay here tonight, too." She sipped

her coffee again and looked around for something more substantial.

"I put a couple of waffles in the toaster," I said.

"Works for me." Her chair, like all of the ones around the Formica table, was bright lipstick-red and chrome, like something out of a diner. She settled back in it. "Can you call-forward your phone to this one?"

"That would be great." My phone. I shouldn't be this far from it. I retrieved my cell from where I was recharging it on the countertop. "I'd better check for messages."

"Can't it wait until after you eat?"

"Probably. This just makes me think I'm in control."

A loud pop, and I smelled the yeasty, slightly burned smell of frozen waffles cooked in a fifties toaster. "Start without me, okay?"

She got up, almost said something, then sighed, tolerating my compulsiveness, I knew, only because she was worried about me. I punched in the code to retrieve my messages. The first was from Natalie at the temp service.

"I've found you something else," she said. "In a yoga studio. That should be fun. You have to call in by noon today, so get right back to me, okay?"

A yoga studio? Should I call her? I didn't know if I dared to accept a new job while the gardener man was loose. But I needed to work.

The second message came on. "Reebie, it's me. Are you there?" Geoff. I gripped the phone. Yes, it was his voice. "Damn it, Reebie. Pick up the phone if you're there. I need to talk to you. It's an emergency."

"What's the matter?" Daph stood beside me, her waffle forgotten on the table.

"Geoff." I felt myself tremble. I almost said *my husband.* Shows what I know—what I remember, what I retain. Like that Eddie Palacios song, "What Hurts So Much." It's not what you remember about love that hurts. It's what you forget. "I've got to call him. You go ahead, eat." I grabbed the cell phone and stepped outside into the yard where Chico and I had walked earlier.

My fingers picked out the number of his cell, and I pressed the connect button. I had sworn I'd never talk to him again, but *emergency* wasn't a word he threw around.

He answered in a voice both familiar and far-away. "Geoff," I began, uncertain where to go next.

"What in the hell have you gotten yourself into this time?" Anger wasn't a natural emotion for him, only at the end, when we'd screamed at each other daily. He sounded on the verge of that now.

"What happened?" I asked.

"No, Reebie. I'm the one who should be asking you that. Where are you?"

"At Daphne's. She's a photographer for the news-paper here."

"Tell me how to find the place. I'll be right there."

I couldn't make sense of his words. "You drove here?"

"That's what I said, and I spent the night outside your apartment, wondering what the hell had happened to you."

"Something did happen. I—"

"You can explain once I get there. Now, tell me where you are."

I gave him directions to Daph's, then regretted it once we hung up.

"It's okay," she said. "I have to go to work anyway. You stay here with Chico."

I decided to take her up on it. Not even nine o'clock yet, and already the smells of spring wafted through the vents of the security door. Geoff didn't have to glimpse spring through the white mesh of metal. He could throw his front door open wide, parade around naked if he wanted to, roll in the sun-warm grass, as we had once. Thinking about what he had and what I lacked had me warmed up by the time he came to the door.

The new black car, more Japanese art than auto, set me off. The Geoff I remembered wore jeans and silky brown hair to his shoulders. This Geoff had more tabs, loops and snaps than a carpenter.

I swung the door open, taking him in. I couldn't believe it. He'd buzzed his wonderful hair, all the better to show off the diamond stud piercing his earlobe. I glanced down at his empty ring finger. Of course it would be empty, and that diamond earring was about the right size. Only his clean-smelling cologne was the same, and I was sure it would be the next to go.

"You look different," I said.

"What kind of greeting is that after I drive all this way to see if you're okay?" He walked into the room of Daphne's Americana. Seeing it through his eyes—the Johnny Cash poster, the faux-cowhide bar stools shaped like saddles, the Felix The Cat wall clock with clicking pendulum tail—I realized it took some getting used to.

"It's not a greeting. I'm just remarking that you look different. You do."

"I made a few changes. But I didn't come here for your opinion. Just tell me what the hell you did to get the cops on your trail."

I began to tremble again. "I'm sorry. I had no idea they'd talk to you."

"Oh, they talked, all right. Make it he. The guy wanted to know everything about you."

I sank down onto a leather ottoman. "What'd you say?"

"He's a cop. I answered his questions." His voice rose. I could feel mine doing the same.

This was what had ripped our marriage to shreds. The addictive shouting and accusations were ultimately all we had left. That and his family's winery, the winery I had put on the map.

"I found a dead woman's body," I said. "It all started with that."

"Jeanette Sheldon," he retorted in a know-it-all voice. "She told you something about her affair with Remington, right?"

"Wrong."

"Don't lie to me. The cop let it slip. He thought maybe you'd said something to me. I told him we don't talk. We just yell."

"It's fine with me if I never talk to you again," I said. "I called because you said it was an emergency."

His suntanned face grew almost magenta. "Pardon the hell out of me. I was worried about you."

"If you were worried, you wouldn't have taken my winery."

"If you cared about it, you wouldn't have left."

"Anything was better than—"

"Than what?" He shouted into my face now, standing directly above me. "Better than living with me?"

"Yes, if you want the truth. Yes." Tears squeezed out of my eyes. I fought to hold them back.

Chico lumbered out of the kitchen and padded up to Geoff.

"A dog?" he asked, as if it were an accusation.

"Springer spaniel." I patted the side of the ottoman. Chico came over and thunked down beside me.

"All the times I wanted a Lab, and you said it was too much responsibility."

"He's not mine," I said. "Besides, I was working twelve- and fourteen-hour days back then."

"Because you loved it. You wanted it. You loved the work more than anything."

I patted Chico's side, in control again. "It paid off for you, didn't it? Helped finance that new chick-magnet car out there. You were the one who wanted to play. Now you can play all you want, on my dime."

"Your dime, my ass." He got the look that signaled a replay of the sad story of the boyhood that wasn't. Having to drive the tractor when he was too short to reach the brake pedal without jumping down on it. Not being able to be a kid.

I put up my hand. "Spare me. Since I last saw you, three people I've known have been killed. One of them was a friend. One was Jeanette, and one was Jeanette's doorman. I have been hounded by cops and attacked by one pretty dangerous looking guy who threatened to kill the one person who's been trying to help me. So, forgive me, Geoffrey, but I'm too tired and too scared to fight with you today."

"Ditto," he said.

"Why'd you come here, then?"

He puffed his chest up, melted his shoulders down in that confrontational pose I'd almost forgotten. "I want you to come home with me," he said, "until this investigation blows over."

"Home?" I tried to laugh but choked on it. "Whose frigging home?"

"Would you can it?" His voice rose again, as my heart beat faster. In a sick way, I almost enjoyed this. Ugly as it was, it was also familiar, and right now, I craved familiar like a drug.

"You want me to go back to the winery?"

"I've already figured out how to do it. I'll move into the stone building in back. You can have the house. The cop won't come back. He's already been there. You'll be safe, Reeb. Come on. For once, don't let your stupid pride get in the way."

"My pride is not stupid," I said. "But you are if you think I'd ever go back to that hellhole with you." I stood now, no longer concerned about Chico or the neighbors, who could hear, if they wanted to, everything we were saying. "I'm scared now, scared for my life. But I couldn't be scared enough to spend five minutes living the way we used to."

"Then you really are stupid." He headed for the door, his expression set. "And this is the most fucked-up house I've ever seen."

"It's not," I shouted at his back. "Just because you can't see beyond rattan and canvas doesn't mean everyone can't."

"I can't believe I wasted a trip trying to help you," he said, his expression incredulous.

"Trying to drag me back there," I shouted. "That's why you really came. And I wouldn't go back there, not for anything."

"I wouldn't have you back. Don't ever call me again." He slammed the door behind him. I stood there, rushing on adrenaline, tears hot in my eyes. The prick, the prick, the prick.

Then, I smelled it. His scent, the one part of him that connected me to the past.

Smell is a tricky bastard. As much as I hated Geoff Desmond at that moment—as much as I had almost relished screaming him out of Daphne's home—that whiff of the past that remained in the room reminded me of how passionately I had once loved him. I had believed we'd be together forever, known it. I'd trusted him. The left-behind scent brought it all back. Too drained to cry, I sank back down on the ottoman, staring at Daphne's Man In Black poster, and stroking Chico.

A noise at the door brought me to my feet. Oh no, I hadn't locked it.

"Just me." Geoff's voice was low-pitched, deceptively friendly.

"So?" I was almost grateful to feel my anger return.

"Met a friend of yours on the way out." He stepped into the room, his expression triumphant. Kersikovski followed behind.

"Hope I'm not interrupting," Kersikovski said. "Daph said you were here."

For just a moment, I felt as if I'd been caught cheating. My once laid-back, now-duded-up ex-husband glared at the hunky low-key reporter who was trying to make me his new big story. I took one look at Geoff and realized he was giving me far more credit than I deserved.

"Of course you're not interrupting," I said. "Leo Kersikovski, this is Geoff Desmond, my ex-husband."

"Not so fast." Geoff ignored Kersikovski's out-stretched hand and marched up to me so close that I could smell that haunting scent again. "You're coming back to the valley with me. Period. At least you'll be safe."

"I'm not going anywhere," I said. "Just get out of here."

"That's probably a good idea," Kersikovski said, his voice like gravel, those eyes of his waiting to photograph any response. "Why don't you just leave, man?"

"Why don't *I* leave?" Geoff's voice began to reach the pitch it did when he and I had those last horrible fights. "Why don't you get out of my wife's house?"

"Your ex-wife."

"Whatever you want to call it works for me. She's enough of a wife that I still care when a cop comes out to question me about her." Seeing Kersikovski's confusion, he delivered the next blow. "You've got to leave with me, Reebie," he said. "The cop won't come back. You'll be safe there."

"What cop?" Kersikovski demanded.

"He came to the winery," Geoff said. "I answered his questions. He'll leave us alone now."

Something akin to fear filled Kersikovski's eye, and I felt my skin prickle. "What was his name?" he asked.

Geoff looked sheepish. "I was so upset that I didn't write it down."

"He didn't give you a card or any kind of contact information?"

"No." I could see him trying to work himself up to another outburst again. "This cop comes to the winery, tells me my wife's in trouble, and I'm supposed to ask for a business card and a phone number?"

My wife, I thought. *My wife.* He just couldn't let go of it. I knew Kersikovski had caught it, too. "Can you describe this guy?" he asked Geoff.

"Hell, no, I can't describe him. He looked like a cop. Muscular. A little on the short side."

"Hair?" Kersikovski asked.

"Short. Brown. Cop hair. Not like yours and certainly not like mine."

"Certainly not," Kersikovski said, only just keeping the sarcasm from his voice, I guessed. "What did he ask about Reebie?"

"How we met, what I knew about her family, if we talked recently."

Kersikovski exhaled, shook his head as if trying to clear it. "Here's what I think," he said, "but it's only a guess. I don't think that guy was a cop. There are only two cops working on the case, and I know both of them. If they had talked to you, they would've gone together."

"Maybe, maybe not," Geoff said. "This was one guy, and he knew all about the case. He was convinced my wife had told me something she'd learned from Jeanette Sheldon."

"But she hadn't?"

"Of course not." He frowned, and I could feel the anger returning. "You might be right," he said. "The more I think about it, the less likely I am to think that guy was a cop. There was something odd about him, something hungry, but not in a good way. I'm serious, Reebie, you need protection."

As much as I wished I could accept his offer, I knew where that offer would lead. And I couldn't deal with another shouting match, never again. "We've had that conversation," I said. "And you were leaving, weren't you?"

Seventeen

Kersikovski watched Geoff storm out, then walked over and shut the door.

"So, what's the deal? Houses in Napa Valley don't have doors, maybe?"

"Don't." Pissed as I was, I wasn't going to snipe about Geoff behind his back.

"Why didn't you tell me you were a winemaker?"

"It didn't seem important. I'm not a winemaker now."

"Why not?"

"I got divorced. The winery belonged to his family, not community property, and even if it had been—" I couldn't finish the sentence, and he seemed to sense why.

"Were you good at it?"

"Yes."

"Then you ought to find another one. That's what I'd do if I lost my job. I wouldn't wait a day."

"You don't know what you'd do," I said in a voice angrier than I'd intended. "Speaking of your job, tell me why you're here."

"I wanted to fill you in on a couple of things," he began.

"And I've got a biggie for you," I said.

"Daph told me. I didn't say anything before because I didn't know how much your ex knew."

"He didn't bother to ask," I said. "It was terrible. That man threatened to kill the cabdriver. I think he'd do it, too."

His eyes changed. I guess they got clearer, or maybe he was just focusing on me. "You care about him, don't you?"

I nodded. "He was kind to me when he didn't have any reason to be. And now because of me, he's in danger."

Kersikovski frowned. "Do you think he'd talk to me?"

"I don't know. I'll give you his number."

"And?" He leaned against the door through which Geoff had stomped moments ago. "Are you considering your husband's offer to hide out in Napa for a while?"

"Ex-husband," I said, "and no way."

His smile made him look less intense. "On that happy note, how about lunch?"

I wondered if it would be a replay of the chili dogs, but Leo Kersikovski was full of surprises.

We bought it at a Trader Joe's and ate it on a park bench across the street.

"What do you think?" he asked.

"About the sushi?"

"Of course about the sushi."

Ginger and wasabi burned my nostrils, and the tears in my eyes felt clean, unlike the dammed-up ones I'd shed earlier for Geoff.

"I've never bought it here. I'm glad we came."

"I like it because it's fast," he said. "I come here all the time."

"You're always in a hurry, aren't you?"

He looked up from his California roll, meeting my eyes. "I love what I do."

I knew that feeling once, knew it on a soul level.

"You're a lucky man," I said.

"I got lucky today."

For one crazy moment, I thought he meant us, and I panicked. Geoff was probably still driving home, and here I was having lustful thoughts for a near-stranger. "How'd you get lucky?" I asked.

"On the killing at Jeanette's penthouse." His golden eyes grew even more intense. "That's what I wanted to tell you. The real doorman was indeed a Mr. Wong."

"Then, who—" I could still see the little man who had tried to drag me outside. Could still feel that horrible thud when the plant stand connected with him.

"A punk," Kersikovski said. "Strictly small-time."

"Are you sure?" I asked.

He nodded. "I could show you a list of his crimes, but believe me, you don't want to see it."

"So what happened to the real doorman?"

"Cops are still checking," Kersikovski said. "No one has seen Mr. Wong for at least two months."

"Not only do you love what you do, but you seem to be damned good at it," I said.

"I like to think so. I haven't told you everything yet."

I stood up. "I don't know if I can take any more."

"Jeanette's body."

He stood, too, and I followed him to the trash can and then across the lawn toward a small playground. I didn't want to think about the clinical details. I looked up at him.

"Do I really need to know about Jeanette's body?"

"You need to know who claimed it, and who's burying it," he said. "Don't you think you ought to know that?"

I nodded and leaned against the warm metal of a swing set. "Okay. Who claimed her body?" I asked.

Kersikovski moved behind me and lifted the swing, as if he expected me to sit there.

"Ed Palacios," he said.

The swing was the right therapy. Kersikovski still hadn't made it through my trust sensors. Too pretty, for starters.

Never trust a pretty man.

"So he must still have a thing for her."

"At least."

My feet sank into the sandy little gully created by kids trying to drag themselves to a stop.

"I can remember when I used to struggle to reach the ground," I said.

"Just push off. Pretty soon, it won't matter."

I tried it. Not a bad feeling, but I was too old for it. Memories came back, no more than that—sensations, smells. I realized that he and I shot up at exactly the same moment and swung down in a connection that to me, at least, was not without sexual connotations.

I felt I should say something. "You do this often?"

"Not as often as I should. As you pointed out, I'm always in a hurry."

"I used to be that way." It slipped out before I thought better of it.

"What happened?"

I could feel the breeze to my scalp. "I stopped caring."

"No one stops caring."

I stretched out my legs and let the swing slow. "I did."

"You care about the cabdriver."

His words brought back the helpless fear that hadn't been far from me since the scene with the gardener. "You're right."

"And you care about Daph and her dog."

"Right again."

"And your ex-husband."

"Don't go there," I said. "It's a long, bitter story."

"Breakups usually are."

He slowed as well, his legs dangling, and he no longer looked sexy, just kind of silly. I felt silly, too. Conversations like this didn't lead anywhere good. I needed to remember that he was a reporter and keep my association with him limited to that role.

"I wonder if Jeanette and Palacios really broke up," I said. "If he was telling the truth at her gallery, she confided in him about something before she died."

"It could be like Joe DiMaggio and Marilyn Monroe. He put roses on her grave until his own death. Maybe it's like that."

"Do you think so?" It was beyond my imagination that any love affair could survive a breakup, but I didn't tell him that. "He could be lying, too. Maybe Jeanette didn't want him to have whatever he claims is at the gallery."

He got out of his swing and leaned against the pole. "She didn't say anything to you to indicate what it was?" His eyes urged me to remember, as I was sure he'd done with hundreds of sources in the past. There was something else there, too. Was he still not one hundred percent convinced that I was telling the truth?

"I've been over it and over it," I said. "Have you talked to Ed Palacios?"

"He refused an interview. Said he's in poor health and needs to focus his energies on getting well."

My swing slowed. He reached out for the chain, stopped it.

"Palacios is the key to this. Every instinct I have tells me so," he said.

"Are you going to try again?" I asked. "Can't you reason with him? Surely if he loved her, he'd want whoever killed her punished?"

"Men like Palacios, even the respectable ones, have their own system of punishment, and it's outside the law."

He reached down to help me out of the seat, and, reluctantly, I took his hand. "What are you going to do? Try to convince him?"

He shook his head. "Wouldn't do any good. He won't talk to me." He released my hand and leaned closer to me, his expression serious. "He'll talk to you, though."

Daph kept an old hi-fi in the guest room, with real records and a built-in tape recorder. That night, afraid to damage her albums, I put on a greatest-hits tape by Ed Palacios, one of the many.

I give you me. I give up the me that I could be. Because now it's down to you and me. And we are forever.

I had once thought I could love like that, to give up the me for the we. But I hadn't. Had Palacios? I wondered. He sang as if he had. He thought I knew more about Jeanette than I did. Tomorrow, I would try to find out what he knew.

Eighteen

The Widow

June didn't have to see Friday to feel it. Even in her sightless world, the beginning of the end of the week was upbeat, often giddy. She felt anything but. How could David have been such an idiot?

They were supposed to be working out in her private gym, but the trainer had missed the ferry from Seattle, and it was just the two of them. Sitting on a parallel bench, facing the direction of the mirror, she finished her last bicep curl. She tried to keep the anger from her face, relaxing her muscles as she turned toward the blur that must be his face.

"Tell me again what went wrong?"

"Nothing went wrong, sweetheart." The blur moved closer. She could smell the woodsy scent that always made her feel safe. "The person I sent probably wasn't the right one. She refused to travel with him."

"Why?"

"She got carried away, scared, what can I say? She just freaked and called the police. Made a real scene."

June's legs went weak and watery. "What made her do that, David?" she asked.

She could feel him try to hedge, but he was decent and always owned up in the long run. "As I said, I picked the wrong person, someone Rem might have trusted, but not someone who was right for this assignment."

She put down the weights, one on each side of the bench. Her head felt ready to cave in. Rem would never trust the person David seemed to be describing.

"What could you have been thinking?" she said. "This was supposed to be a friendly meeting. I didn't ask you to kidnap her."

"You said do anything," he replied.

Yes, she'd said that. She'd said that, hadn't she?

"I didn't mean literally. I said I needed to talk to her."

"Confidentially, of course." His soft voice chided ever so slightly. "You didn't want me to just pick up the phone and invite her to dinner to talk about a friendly payoff."

No. What had she wanted? How did she picture this meeting taking place? "What exactly did this person do to her?"

"She wasn't hurt, if that's what you mean."

"Does she know that I'm involved?"

"Of course not. My guy simply told her that someone wanted to talk to her. Nothing was mentioned about a payoff or where the offer was coming from."

June felt weary, and not just from the weights. As much as she tried to stay strong, she could feel age eating its way in, taking over in increments.

"Don't look so sad," he said. "We can fix this. If you really want to talk to the girl, we can arrange it."

"That's what you said the first time."

"Maybe you don't need to talk to her," he said. "Maybe there's another way to get her out of the picture."

"I'm the one who should make the offer," she said. "Besides, I'm curious. I want to know why Jeanette picked her to confess to."

"You've got me there."

She could feel him move along the rack of weights, looking at himself in the mirror, she'd guess, patting his paunch. Odd how she could see him as if her vision were perfect.

"There's no reason she would just pick this kid off a cosmetic counter," he said.

"In a way, I feel sorry for her," she said. "Few would welcome that kind of intrusion. It was selfish of Jeanette, if it really was Jeanette."

"They're sure that it was," he said. "And, yes, it was selfish. She was a selfish woman."

June felt dirty even mentioning her name, and worse about encouraging, by her silence, David's defamation. She reached down for the barbell. This

was the only release she had. Other women her age
hid from their demons in a bottle, a handful of pills.
The discipline of her muscles burning from the challenge of the weights—this was her drug and her
demon chaser.

"You are still a very beautiful woman." He said it
as if he were inspecting a head of cabbage and finding it free of bugs. At least that's how he made it sound.

She turned from his voice, squeezing the cold
weight as if doing so could turn off her tears. "I always wondered—I wondered if I'd outlive him. Isn't
that terrible?"

"Everyone has those thoughts, sweetheart. You're
still dealing with too much grief." His voice rose.
"You were a loyal partner. That's all that matters, to
you, to God, to Rem's memory."

Leave it there, then. Don't say the rest of it, she
thought.

"This girl," she said.

"Why don't you let me talk to her? Give me a list
of questions, and I'll take care of it. She'll never need
to know it came from you. It would be terrible if she
went to the press, and she might, if she could get
someone to pay her for the story."

June went cold all over. That couldn't happen.
Rem's reputation was more important than her mor-
bid curiosity.

"That does it." She dropped the barbell, hearing
it clunk on the padded floor. "Jeanette wins again,

doesn't she? She talked about Rem to this girl, and now I can't risk trying to find out what she said or even paying the girl to keep silent about it."

"I told you I'd do it for you."

"No." Tears filled her eyes. When would they stop? She wished her mind could blend into the darkness of her vision. He didn't understand. He never would. "We've got to forget about the girl," she said. "She would do us more harm than good."

"Whatever you say." She could tell from his voice that he agreed with her and was relieved by her decision.

"I don't really feel like training today," she said.

"Let's go then. Frank will understand."

"You could take my hour."

He chuckled. "It's going to take more than an hour with Frank to reverse my sad decline."

"Don't be hard on yourself."

"Not hard, just honest. Most of us don't have the Peter Pan gene."

"As I recall, I'm a year older than you."

"And you look a decade younger. You'll get back to your routine, and maybe that will help. It's just too soon right now. Let's go back to the main house, then I need to leave. I'll check in on you tonight." He put her hand on his arm, and she took it, too tired to intuit her way home without guidance today.

"Sorry about the tears," she said. "They come when I least expect them."

"If you can't cry in front of me, who, then?" He patted her hand, and the gesture brought on a new wave. Was it grief for Rem that was torturing her like this? No, she felt that, of course, but this was something different.

"I wanted to outlive him," she said. "I wanted him to die first."

She waited for shocked silence, but instead he made a murmur of understanding. "What's so terrible about that? It's natural to fear your own mortality."

"That's not the reason, David. It's not because I feared death." She stopped, looked up into his eyes, that although she could not see them, she wanted desperately to witness the horror and self-loathing in her own. "I wanted him to die first, because I thought if I did, he'd find Jeanette and go back to her."

"That's insane. He'd never have gone back to her." His voice quavered, only slightly, but enough.

She clung to his arm as they walked through the woods, her woods, almost grateful for the lie. Almost.

"How's Nicholas holding up?" he asked as they neared the house.

"Better than I expected. He loved Rem, but—"

"I know." She felt the heaviness of his thoughts. "What is it, David?"

"Nita likes to travel, doesn't she? Maybe the two of them should get away for a while."

She stopped suddenly, feeling as if she were caught in a cold wind. "Tell me this instant what's going on."

"I just didn't want to alarm you," he said.

"I am alarmed. I am worse than alarmed. I just lost my husband. Tell me. Is my son in danger, too?"

"Perhaps," he said.

The Mobster

You'd want me to do this, Jeanette, I know you would. But it's tough.

"Nice cuff links, Mr. Palacios." Doesn't seem like the right kind of talk from a mortician. Forget the fancy counselor-consultant words. That's what he is. A mortician. "Violins," he adds. "You play?"

"Wanted to." The silver ones you gave me, Jeanette. I look down at them, remembering. "My mother wanted me to be a great violinist, but even she admitted I wasn't any good at it."

"So you found another profession?" His laugh is hearty and fake, and I realize the poor bastard thinks he's helping make this less painful. He's trying hard with that thousand-mile blue suit, the combed-back hair and the eyes a little too decent for someone in this line of work.

I lean back in the cracked leather chair and wonder how many of us, the ones left behind, it's held. "I want the best for her, the works." I don't like the way it sounds, as if I'm ordering at a restaurant, demanding the best, putting it on my tab. "I mean, I want her to have something dignified," I say. "The cost doesn't matter."

"I understand." I know he's trying to brace me for the walk though Coffin City. I went through that when I lost my mother.

"I have a few things in mind," I say. "White. It was her favorite color, that, and black."

He nods but doesn't get up to move toward wherever they've got the stuff stashed. His lips seem to tighten at the corners. "We can accommodate that."

"So, accommodate." The chair starts to creep me out—all of those grieving people who've sat here ahead of me. "Can we get on with this?"

"Of course." He's on his feet pretty fast for a big guy. "I'm sorry. There's just something I felt I should tell you before—" He swallows, and I notice an Adam's apple I didn't see before. "This is an unusual situation, because of her having two names."

"The police released the body, so what do you care?"

"I care about our reputation," he says. "I want to accommodate you, and I have the greatest respect for you."

I'm on my feet in a second. "And? I'm not good enough to bury the lady in your fancy mausoleum, maybe?"

"Nothing like that, Mr. Palacios." In spite of the respect in his voice, his eyes are darting, like a guy looking for the exit sign.

"What's the problem, then?"

"We've had reporters calling here."

"I can't control that."

"Neither can we. We're hoping that your involvement in Ms. McFarland's burial can be kept as low-key as possible."

"I feel the same." I want to correct him. Grab him by the back of his fleshy neck and yell, *Her name is Jeanette, you bastard.* I want to buy the frigging funeral home and fire him. I want to cry. Yeah, that's what I really want to do.

"Are you certain there won't be press at the services?"

"There won't be anyone at the services," I say. "Just me."

His forehead gleams, as if there's sweat trying to push through the oil. "That's very comforting," he says. "There's just one other matter I need to discuss with you."

"What's that? You need my credit report, maybe?" His expression embarrasses me. I'm being hard on a guy who doesn't deserve it because it's better than telling him my heart is ripped apart.

"A woman called here, asking us for contact information for you. Of course, our records are confidential."

"What woman?" I ask.

"Her name is Reebie Mahoney," he says in an apologetic voice. "I have her telephone number on my desk. I'll be happy to give it to you after—"

Reebie Mahoney. Son of a bitch. "No need to do that," I say. "I have her number."

He looks almost relieved. "Then, perhaps we should proceed?"

I nod.

Our little tour is worse than I imagined, Jeanette, as bad, maybe worse than with my mother, because what happened to you was so unexpected. Not to mention unfair. Not to mention all the stuff that would make me a crazy man if I started thinking about it.

Once I make all the choices, we return to his office.

"Should I let Ms. Mahoney know you'll be in contact with her?" he asks.

"Don't bother. I'll be calling her tonight." What I ought to do is just drive to her place. I might, too, if I don't settle down right away. I know you'd tell me not to, Jeanette. "You don't want to frighten her," you'd say.

The guy shifts from one foot to the other, hoping I'll leave, I know, hoping there won't be a crew of cameras at what he calls "the services." But it's only one service, Jeanette, and just me and just you, and Marcus, if he's up to it.

"Appreciate your help," I say. "See you Monday, then." I have only hundreds in my wallet. As I pull it out, I try to decide how many, like those healers on TV who press your arm up and down to decide how many supplements you need to take every day. My hand isn't pumping, but I feel two bills is about right for him.

"Thanks," I say, and slip them into his hand.

"My privilege, Mr. Palacios," he says, without glancing down at the bills. There's still more sadness in his look than gratitude.

We'll have a service. I'll talk to Reebie Mahoney. I might even record one more song before I die. It's all working, Jeanette, just the way I planned. But the world's a hell of a lot emptier without you.

Nineteen

Reebie

I woke up the next morning still freaked about seeing Geoff. It was easier to hate him from a distance, more difficult at close range. Not that I still felt a shred of love for him, just confusion and sadness. Anger was easier.

I wasn't surprised that Palacios returned my phone call. I could tell by the way he had reacted at the gallery that Kersikovski was right in guessing that he'd be willing to talk to me.

"So, he's a real gangster like Al Capone?" Daph was sitting at her table after work, going over the pages I'd printed from her computer while stroking on mascara a neon shade of green. "I wish I didn't have a date."

"For once I'm glad you do. I just hope you bring a can of pepper spray."

"No need. It's not one of the computer guys to-night. A friend from China and I are going out for American food. I wish I were going with you in-stead."

American food for Daph consisted of a T-bone steak at the International House of Pancakes. I'd never been able to figure out why, but it was proba-bly just as confusing to her to see what passed for Chinese food in this country.

"No way," I said. "This isn't show-and-tell."

"I know that." She blinked and turned away from me, and I was sure she was thinking about Sunny. "I've never seen a real gangster before," she said, her voice soft with apology. "And Ed Palacios is an icon. I love him."

"No," I said. "You love the idea of him. He's re-ally just a tired-looking, old, kind-of-scary man. Most of his time is spent donating money to causes." With that, I got up to return to the computer.

Daphne was my best post-divorce friend, and I'd always be grateful that we'd met. She'd been there for me as no one else had. But she hadn't had to stare into the face of the gardener man when he tried to take me with him. I could still feel his grip on my wrists, his sweat dripping onto my face. And now, Palacios. I'd give up everything except the winery I'd already lost if I never had to see him again.

"Reebie," she called as I started from the room. Finished with the green neon, she dusted a big blush brush over her cheekbones.

"What?"

She put down the mirror and, still holding the brush, looked at me the way she looked at something she was ready to photograph. "What's scary about him?" I could tell that she still didn't understand the reality of this, that she felt safe, as if watching a movie. "I mean if he's old and tired-looking, what could be scary about him?"

I thought a moment. "His eyes," I said. "They look—"

"Cold-blooded? Ruthless?"

"Haunted."

Palacios had been polite to me, but abrupt. I guessed that was the way he treated everyone. We agreed to meet at his restaurant, and I was relieved that at least there would be people around.

People was an understatement. A line wound around the deck leading to Eddie P's that Saturday night. San Francisco was a going-out-for-dinner town every night of the week, and with the addition of the tourists on the weekends, it was almost impossible to get into landmark places like Eddie P's.

A cold breeze had turned the air a ruthless cold that cut right through my black turtleneck and jacket to my bones. I'd worn my pink beret and was already grateful for the warmth. Pargat's brother accompanied us in the cab, and I wondered if the gardener's threats were the reason he wasn't traveling alone. They dropped me in front, and Pargat said he'd wait outside. I'd tried to talk to him about the encounter with the gardener, but he refused to discuss it, saying only, "You should not worry. I can take care of myself."

He had reported it to the police, which I knew would probably earn me another meeting with the officers investigating Jeanette's murder.

The people in front of me in the line talked to each other, stomped around in the cold, and a few blew into their hands. The feeling was one of merriment. The ones in the front craned to read the menu posted beside the door. Saturday night on the wharf always reminded me of how Christmas felt when you were a kid—giddy and surreal.

There had to be a better way to get in. I went to the front of the line where a woman in a black three-piece suit and tie was taking names and pointing the lucky ones inside. She avoided me politely, as I'm sure was her habit with anyone who tried to sneak in.

"I have an appointment with Mr. Palacios," I said.

"You do?" She looked down at her list, then up at me. "So, you won't be dining with us tonight?"

"I told you I have an appointment."

"Good, because it's at least a forty-minute wait for a table tonight."

"Is he in?" I asked, irritated.

"He was earlier." She went back to her list.

I moved closer. "I'd like to go inside."

She looked at me, evaluating, as if I were trying

a new tack to get past her. "If you have a meeting with Mr. Palacios, you ought to know where his office is."

"He just said to meet him at the restaurant." Now, I was getting pissed. Starting to think I didn't deserve to be treated like this. Starting to remember the last nine months of being jacked around, having everything but my life taken away from me. "Where the hell is he?" I liked the sound of my voice getting loud, liked the way she backed off, kind of sniffing with her pointed, no-longer-friendly face, as if hoping I were drunk, so that she'd have a reason to throw me out or call for a bouncer.

"His office is in the back, up the stairs, the only door up there." She kept her voice soft, wanting me out of her life with as little commotion as possible. "My apologies, but most of his friends park in the lot then take the stairs. I just assumed—"

I wanted to shout, wanted to tell her that I could help her boss as much as he could help me, but it wasn't her fault I was pissed off at the world. Instead, I did my best to smile and make eye contact. "Thank you," I said.

She stepped back as if I'd struck her. "You're welcome."

"Does the deck go all the way around to the back?"

She nodded. "We have it open when the weather's better, but it's closed tonight, and we keep pretty tight security." She straightened her already perfect tie and looked at me, as if for the first time. "You can go through, though."

I shot past her before she could change her mind. The wind had dropped several degrees, angry and cold as a knife. I silently thanked the suit lady for letting me take the forbidden short cut to the back. The patio area consisted of bistro tables and matching chairs, unlit pedestal heaters rising above them like science-fiction trees.

I wondered why I felt sad, then realized that I'd eaten here with Geoff before we were married, when we were so in love, so focused on pleasing each other, that a long wait in line and less-than-perfect weather couldn't begin to dampen our pleasure.

I didn't want to think about that right now. I couldn't. I needed to be tough when I faced Palacios, tougher even than I'd been that day I'd walked off of my own property, gotten into the black pickup and driven into that terrifying territory known as freedom. Still—I stopped and looked out at the ocean, chilled to the bone, overcome by memories, some of which I could visualize, some of which remained in the murky world of emotion.

Why? I wondered. And if anyone had asked me, "Why, what?" I wouldn't have known the answer.

A creaking noise froze me to the spot. Old wood, cruel ocean. Even the most modern buildings suffered from both in this city. It probably wasn't anything, but then again, I wasn't about to take chances.

I stood on the ocean side of the deck, out where

the tables were. To my left, a darker area, away from the overhead lights, hid pockets of shadow. I couldn't be far from the back. I inched my way along the outside, moving closer to the ocean and the light—what there was of it, at any rate.

The boards creaked once more. I might as well run for it. I'd tried to show off for Palacios by wearing boots, the worst choice I could have made. The soles slid along the deck as I picked up my pace.

"Stop." Just a voice. It came from the shadows. Someone was out there. Did he have a gun? I didn't dare chance it.

"Who are you?" I asked.

"Shut up." I recognized the fast-talking, slightly nasal voice of the gardener. And the realization hit me. He'd kill me this time, for sure. Any chance I took was worth it. "Come here," he said. "Walk slowly, this direction. I don't want to have to get rough."

"Okay." I turned back toward the sound of his voice, then suddenly bounded the other direction, screaming. "Help, help! Someone help!"

Gunshots exploded behind me.

I ran like hell, then bolted into a man so solid that I felt I'd hit a wall. I screamed, then tried to tear away from him. Another gunshot, so loud it felt as if it had blasted through me.

"Let me go."

"Shut up."

Through my sweat-streaked eyes, I looked up into the face of Ed Palacios. "Let go of me."

"Come on, will you? I'm trying to help."

I saw the gun in his hand and screamed again.

"Take it easy." Palacios released his grip on me. "Don't talk yet. Let's just get you inside."

He started toward the dark building. When he realized I wasn't following, he returned for me. "Come on. That bastard could be anywhere."

"The hostess said the entrance to your office is in the back." My teeth were chattering. He couldn't miss that.

"This is a short cut, okay? Get going, missy. You got to know that guy was no friend of yours."

I had a moment to decide whether or not to trust him. Although I didn't, he was my fastest way out. He led me to a side door, with a No Entry sign block-printed on it. "Through here." He took out something that looked like a credit card and passed it over the door. I heard a click, then he held it open. "Hurry."

I hesitated. I didn't want to go in, but I didn't dare stay out here. I knew what the gardener wanted, and Palacios could have shot me out there if he wanted to. He hadn't tried. The gardener had. I stepped inside, trying to slow my breathing.

"We can go up to my office from here." He stood before me in a dark suit. He wore no rings on his fingers, which struck me as odd for a man like this. His only jewelry was antique cuff links that looked as if they were made of mother-of-pearl. "You want something from the bar? You look like you could use it."

I couldn't answer. Instead, I looked at the tiny room into which we'd stepped, a dim room of racks holding what must be bottles of wine. Not just racks, whole walls. Except for one. To my right, on a stark white wall that provided the greatest illumination in the room, hung three paintings. Nudes, a figure superimposed upon itself, clouded by spirals of smoke, black, white, gray except for the vivid colors of their lips.

Stunned by the display, I must have made a sound or a sudden movement.

"Jeanette." Palacios stood beside me, blocking my exit, should I decide to take it. "She told you, didn't she?"

In this light, he looked terrifying, the still-thick hair and eyebrows almost cartoonish. I'd been off when I told Daph his eyes were haunted. They were more lifeless than that, empty. I had to meet them so that he could look into my eyes and know I wasn't lying. I had a feeling that in spite of his questionable relationship with the truth, this guy could recognize it in a heartbeat.

"She didn't tell me anything," I said, "except that she'd had a relationship with President Remington."

He cocked his head, evaluating me with far more sophisticated internal equipment than the cops had. I couldn't hide from those weary, wary eyes, although I wanted to. As we stood there, inches from each other, in front of Jeanette's paintings, I realized there was music, dim as the light, in this room. A young Ed Palacios sang, "They Can't Take That Away From Me," in that slow, jazzy style that made it clear he'd experienced the emotion behind the words.

He seemed to be listening, too, remembering. "Damn it to hell," he said.

I looked down at his hands, so smooth they could have belonged to a much younger man. "What did you think she told me?"

"Doesn't matter if you don't have proof." He looked from me to the paintings, and it was clear which held his attention.

"You paid for her funeral," I said.

He gave me a look that almost sent me back outside to the gardener. "Don't get cute with me, missy. I did what I thought was right. You got a problem with that?"

"I don't have a problem with anything. The woman called me, that's all. She was killed before I was able to see her again. I was hoping you could tell me why, or tell me anything, but I can see you're not going to. I didn't choose to be any part of this, and I don't intend to be." I edged around him toward the door. "Good night."

"Walk out that door, and you could die."

I swung around, expecting to see the gun reappear. Instead, he stood before the paintings, looking at me with enough anger that, for the first time, I realized the mobster rumors had to be true.

"Why's he after me?" I asked.

"Maybe he thinks Jeanette told you something."

"He's going to kill me for that?"

"If he wanted to kill you, he would have done that by now," he said. "He thinks you have something, or that you know where it is. I think so, too."

"But I don't." I felt trapped between the monster outside and this one next to me.

"She didn't give you anything?"

"Nothing. She bought cosmetics from me, that's all."

"She didn't mention anything to you? What did she talk about?"

"Nothing. Just small talk. She told me she was an artist, said I should pose for her sometime. I didn't take her seriously, of course."

"You need to disappear." He said it in a flat voice. "I can help you do that."

"Why would you help me?" I asked.

"Because it's the right thing to do." He glanced back up at the paintings. "Because Jeanette would want me to. I know a place. No one can find you there."

I looked down at his hands again, smooth and well tended.

Never trust a man with a manicure.

"Thanks for the offer, but I don't know what I'm going to do. I can't just disappear."

"You might not get a choice."

"I'd better get back," I said. "I wish I could tell you more, but I don't know anything."

"I'll walk with you, just in case. By now some-one's called the cops, but I don't want to take any chances."

I could tell by the way he said it that he was car-rying the gun.

"We're parked in front," I said.

"Good. Let's go on out through the restaurant. The guy's probably following you, so be careful. And be glad he thinks Jeanette gave you something. That's all that's keeping you alive."

"That's a comforting thought."

"Don't get smart, missy. This is serious, and so's my offer. Think about it."

We stepped into the restaurant, the milling crowds, the smell of shellfish, the soft, mournful voice of an Ed Palacios song. Some people turned to look at him, as if asking themselves if he was re-ally Palacios. A few men at the bar greeted them. We passed the hostess at the front door and her line of customers waiting for tables. She did a double take as we strolled past.

The wind had died down, but the air was still cold. I could see the cab at the front of the parking lot across from the entry.

"It's probably okay," I said, "but I'd feel better if you went with me."

"Me, too." As we walked, I wondered if he might not be just as dangerous, in his own way, as the gar-dener.

Then Pargat got out of the cab, and I felt safe

again. Palacios stood beside me as he opened the door. In the bright streetlights, I could see deep lines around his eyes, the kind that are carved not by age or lack of sleep, but by pain. I remembered that he'd said he was ill and wondered how much truth there was in that.

"Think about what I said," he told me. "I'm offering you a way out."

"I appreciate that," I said, and slid into the back seat. The sound of a siren grew closer. Police. Palacios's expression did not change.

"You need a place where no one can find you," he said. "I hope you figure that out before it's too late."

Twenty

The Widow

The requests for interviews had already begun. And one book offer already. June would deal with them in time, as she and Rem had discussed. As they had not discussed, she would deal with the questions about Rem and Jeanette by saying that rumors were only that, but her marriage was real. Not now, though.

Her first priority was protecting Rem's reputation—and protecting her son, Nicholas. She had to be careful how she broached the subject. Nita had her suspicious side, and they were all under pressure from the media scrutiny, even Nicholas, although he didn't show it.

She seldom missed her sight anymore, but she wished she could have seen her future grandchild, and she wished she could see Nicholas's new home. He'd described it to her numerous times so that she felt she could see the four-hundred-year-old windows from Italy, the stairs winding past the high beams. Two scents collided in the home, Nita's perfume, and something softer, a subtle potpourri scent, as if someone had tucked sachet bags in the drawers. She couldn't imagine Nita doing that.

They'd missed church, but she'd told them that they'd done enough praying this week. Besides, someone would surely sneak a photo of them, and then they'd have to deal with giving the tabloids a fresh reason for all of the same, stale stories they were running about Rem. She also didn't want Nicholas out and about. Although she had Secret Service protection, he did not, just one live-in housekeeper. She could buy him protection, though. The poor dear wouldn't know the difference.

When she argued about security, he said that was why they decided to make this and not their Los Angeles residence home, so that they could raise their child in a safe environment. If only it could work out that way. If only Jeanette hadn't robbed them of even that.

The house had been structured long and deep with a wall of glass bricks at the back. "A haze of green light," Nicholas had said when she'd asked him to describe it.

Nita sang at the piano. It was an old Ed Palacios song, but June declined to mention that. They'd planned to walk over to the complex of the architect who'd designed their home. She'd just completed a guest house, which she'd named The Tuscan Lady, and it was being written up in all of the magazines. Nicholas had insisted on "showing" it to her, and she'd agreed because it was the first time in a long time he seemed excited about anything.

She waited until Nita finished her song, then applauded along with Nicholas. "Before we leave," she said, "I want to make a suggestion."

"What's that?" Only her ears could catch the trace of a strain in Nita's voice.

"A trip. You two have been wonderful to me, but you need to get away from here, spend some time together." She leaned against the piano and turned in the direction she knew Nita sat. "I'm very grateful you came into our lives, my dear, but you need to think about yourself, and the baby."

"Oh, I don't know," Nicholas said from beside her. "Nita tires very easily now. Maybe after the baby's here."

"What kind of a trip?" Nita asked.

She was being tested, June knew. "You haven't been to Paris since your honeymoon."

"Too far," Nicholas said. "We shouldn't be that far away from you right now."

"It would be my present to you," she said, directing her voice to Nita. "Like after the wedding. All the shopping you can possibly do."

Nita made the little sighing sound that June had

come to learn indicated she was less than pleased. "I bought clothes the last time I shopped in Paris."

"You can't be showing that much yet. And there's always jewelry. And if you want to go on to Italy, there's furniture."

"True," she said.

"Nita, no."

"Stay out of this, Nicholas, dear," June said. "I know what you two need. You need to be spoiled a little."

"I don't think so." Nita made it sound like the final word.

June tried to make light of it, her throat dry. She had to get them out of here, and right away. "You don't think you need to be spoiled?"

"It's not that. We just built this house. Nicholas has just lost his father. There are those embarrassing stories in the tabloids."

"Honey, please," Nicholas said. "Show respect."

"That's what I mean." June spoke rapidly. "You've been under too much pressure. We all have. Spend some time in Paris. Indulge yourselves while you're still young and can enjoy it."

"While I'm still young." Nita hit the *I'm,* with just enough inflection to convey that she knew the power she wielded by being able to produce a Remington heir. June prayed her grandchild would be more like Rem than like dear Nicholas or, God forbid, like Nita.

"The time will fly," June said. "You'll never be as young and free as you are right now. Please, dear, let me give you this little gift." She paused. Could she say the rest? She had to. "If you go, it will ease this pain of mine more than anything anyone could do."

"Oh, Mom." Nicholas put his arm around her.

"I really don't—"

Before Nita finished her statement, the doorbell chimed. Nicholas rushed past her to answer it.

It was as if a rainstorm had just blown in to the solemn room. "It's the mountain coming to Mohammad." A woman, June thought, but with the voice of a girl. "Oh, gosh. I hope I'm not interrupting anything."

"You're not." Nicholas sounded as if he'd just come in from one of his bike rides. "You haven't met my mother."

"I'm so sorry for your loss." Cool, flexible fingers gripped her hands. "I'm Darla." Of course, the architect. It was all there in the fingers.

"Thank you. I feel as if I can see everything you've done to this wonderful house."

"You probably can. Wait until I get you inside The Tuscan Lady. Nicholas said he was bringing you and Nita, but it started to rain, and I thought I might have to come drag you over. It's a scaled-down version of this house. I hammered every nail myself, hand-painted my own tiles."

June caught her fragrance then, subtle, like a packet of sachet tucked into linens.

"And are you?" Nita moved beside her. Although June had never seen her, not even when Nita was a model and June still had her vision, she could imagine the look she was giving Darla.

"Am I what?" Darla asked, as if momentarily confused.

"A Tuscan lady?"

"I'd like to think so. Of course, a Tuscan lady may have little in common with a lady-lady. Come on, Nicholas. Can we go now?"

"Sure. You coming, Nita?"

"Of course, I'm coming."

For a moment, the two scents—Nita's exotic, designer one, and Darla's floral, nostalgic one—warred.

"Shall we walk," Nicholas asked, "or drive?"

"Drive, of course," Darla said. "Crazy man, you can't ask a newly pregnant woman to walk to my place. I brought my SUV."

"Sorry," Nicholas said. "I forgot." But he didn't sound sorry.

"June." Nita's voice pierced the air. She seldom called her by name.

Nicholas and Darla continued to chatter, their voices trailing as they hurried outside.

"Yes, dear?"

"I've been thinking about the trip," she said. "It's very kind of you to offer. Nicholas and I would love to go."

Thank you, thank you. She didn't dare let Nita see how relieved she was. Maybe now, Nicholas and her grandchild would be safe. June reached out for her arm, and they walked slowly out the door. "You've made me very happy, my dear. How soon could you leave?"

"How soon would you like us to?"

She paused so that Nita could hear the shared laughter ahead of them, guessing for once that sound was registering for Nita almost as quickly as it did for her. "Since the decision's been made, why dawdle? I think the sooner, the better. Just say the word, and I can have arrangements made as soon as tomorrow."

"I like the way you think," Nita said. And to Nicholas, "Hey, slow down, will you? Your mom's not a track star, you know."

"I'm all right," June called to him. She was all right now, and she'd be more so once her son was safely off this island.

For the first time since she'd met Nita, she was grateful for the simple, shameful fact that Nicholas couldn't stand up to this woman. That he couldn't stand up to his own wife.

The Mistress

Palm Springs
1976

How could her friends have done this? Jeanette sobbed in the back seat, her back to Kim, her fucking false friend. She'd held Kim's hand through her separation, but now, she and Marcus, and Eddie, too—they'd cooked up some plan to take charge of her life—and she could guess what it was. No way would she allow it. She was going to have this baby.

"Honey." Kim tapped her shoulder as the car slid around nauseating curves. "I'm on your side."

"Right. You have a kid. You ought to understand how I feel."

"I do understand, honey."

"You don't understand shit, and I'll tell you one thing. They can't do anything to me without my permission. So unless you have a tranquilizer hypodermic hidden in that macramé bag of yours, you're not going to stop me!"

Just then, the car jerked. Marcus shouted, "What the hell?"

"Marcus?"

He didn't answer.

"Marcus, please," Kim screamed.

No answer.

"Jeanette," Kim whimpered. "What's happening?"

The car careened off the road as if the wheels had been shot from beneath them. Jeanette turned, frantic. She and Kim hugged each other, holding on tightly as the car rolled over and over.

Twenty-One

Reebie

Within two days of each other, I'd been told by two different men—one a mere acquaintance and one my former husband—that I should hide until Jeanette's killer was found. I was afraid to return to my own apartment and knew I couldn't continue to impose on Daphne and Chico indefinitely. I grew more and more uncomfortable about going to the department store, parking as close to the entrance as possible and asking a security guard to walk me to my car at night.

That Monday, I had to force myself to dress for work and apply the full-face makeup required of those of us who painted the faces of the public. My hair had started to look shaggy. I trimmed it with my manicure scissors and used gel to hide the damage, a far cry from Daph's cuts in London.

Ellie, our supervisor, had been colder than ever to me since Sunny's death. In some irrational way, I knew she blamed me. The woman didn't have one good feature. Her narrow eyes, thin upper lip and overarched brows made her look mean and intimidating, which she was. But with her black hair slicked back from her face and her lips coated with our most daunting red, there was something undeniably attractive about her.

We were to press Shimmer for Spring, she instructed us that morning, and we were to shimmer, too, of course, and to sell, sell, sell. And don't forget the Rah-Rah Lashes. They were very trendy, and they could triple the thickness of your naturals.

I took a moment to stroke some of the rose-colored Glimmer Stick across my brows and cheekbones. Tarted up, my dad would call it, only half-kidding.

Aida, who had replaced Sunny, was a barely twenty-one-year-old part-time student who took a frisky-puppy approach to sales. She could talk the most conservative blue-hairs into purple eyeliner and Rah-Rah Lashes reaching all the way to their brow bones. I couldn't seem to get into the importance of Shimmer for Spring.

I was watching the clock, arranging product and waiting for my break when I spotted a tall blonde in an asymmetric black-and-white skirt making her way past the counters. At first, I just admired the way she carried herself. Then, I realized she looked familiar. It was Gaylene, the woman I'd met at Jeanette's studio.

"Oh, there you are," she said. "I wanted to apologize to you." She put her shiny red handbag on the counter. "I couldn't believe Nora wasn't who she said she was. I'm still in shock."

Aida glanced over at me from the woman she was making up. I tried to make it appear as if I were conversing with a potential customer.

"How'd you find me?"

"Leo told me you work here." Her cheeks went straight to shimmer mode without benefit of the Glimmer Stick.

"Work," I repeated, still stinging from her use of Kersikovski's first name and the fact that she'd talked to him since the night at the gallery. "Which means I can't be visiting. I appreciate your apology, but it isn't necessary."

"So pretend I'm a customer." She picked up a display-size compact of Sultry Shimmer. "If I wear this, will men find me irresistible?"

"It appears you're doing a pretty good job of that on your own." I watched her dust the product over her cheekbones. She had one of those rare faces that was made for cosmetics. The sparklies on her cheeks matched the glitter on her lids. Ellie strode by, giving me the lizard eye. *Sell. Sell. Sell.* "Amazing," I said, loud enough for her to hear.

"I'll take it. Do you suppose you could help me find a match for this nail polish?" She pointed an orchid-tipped finger at me, much as she'd done that night with the cops. "It's Shangri-la-la Lilac by OPI.

Discontinued, of course, and I refuse to wear anything else. So I bought up forty or so bottles of them
online."

This woman was not kidding. I couldn't help
wondering is this was what Kersikovski liked.
Southern gothic with orchid nails. "If it's discontinued…" I began.

"Sometimes, stores have an extra bottle or two
lying around."

I leaned across the counter into her scent. "You
didn't come here to buy nail polish," I said.

"I know that. I just didn't want to get you in trouble. That lady with the black hair who keeps looking over here's your boss, isn't she? Back home we
call that type a be-yatch."

"We have a similar term out here," I said.

"Here." She perched on the stool. "You sell me
stuff, and we'll talk about Nora."

Ellie made eye contact on her pass-by this time.
I had no choice but to drape Gaylene. "What do you
know about her?" I asked, as I removed her makeup.

"I never would have guessed she was someone
else." Her skin beneath the foundation was almost
as even as with it. And why shouldn't it be? Why
should I care? "I have stuff of hers, and I don't know
where it should go."

"Give it to the police," I said.

"That's what Leo suggested, but it doesn't seem
right. Her family should have her furniture, her
paintings and books, don't you think? I'm talking

personal items, nothing that could be used as evidence."

I touched the contour brush to her cheeks and jaw line. She didn't need much. "It's all evidence."

"Leo didn't think so."

My breath caught, but my hand continued doing what it had been trained to do. "You let him look at Jeanette's things?"

"Just the stuff I have at my place. I have this huge old garage, and I let her store some stuff there. Leo said it didn't look like anything important, but I should turn it over to the police all the same. It just breaks my heart to do that, if she has family out there somewhere."

I took the shadow and sponge to her eyelids. "Based on what I read about Jeanette, she had no living relatives."

"Nora McFarland didn't, either." She blinked, and a tear crept down her freshly sculpted cheek. "I cannot believe they were the same woman. Nora was just the sweetest thing, not like somebody who would, you know."

"Have an affair with a married man?"

"Well, yeah, and hang out with gangsters and all that. I would have trusted her with my life."

I could do nothing to improve on her eyebrows, which were already waxed to perfection. "What did she do?" I asked. What I meant was how did she spend all of those years between the time she was supposed to have died and the time she was murdered?

"She painted," Gaylene said. "And she kept to herself. She had friends she visited at holidays. And there was a man she kept company with. I never got a good look at him, but now that I've seen him in person, I think it might have been that Ed Palacios." She opened her eyes. They were clear blue-gray, something you wouldn't find in a compact or a tube. "I wonder if I should offer her things to him."

"I think you should let the police decide that. Have you told them what you told me?"

She nodded. "Leo insisted on it," she said. "It doesn't seem right. There has to be someone who cares about her, someone who'll remember."

"Leo Kersikovski knows what he's doing," I said, blending with my moist sponge. I was no artist, but this was, ironically enough, one of the best jobs I'd done. "I'd listen to him."

"Oh, I do. In fact, I'm seeing him tonight."

Interesting. Kersikovski had told me he had to work tonight. "Tell him I said hello."

"Gosh, I hope it was okay to say that." She put three Shangri-la-la Lilac nails over her lips.

I'd lost a winery that belonged to me. Kersikovski was only a man who didn't.

"Of course it's fine," I said. "I know this has to be awful for you."

"Oh, it is, and he's so great to talk to." Beneath the Sultry Shimmer, the Glimmer Stick and the aubergine eye crayon, she looked like anything but a be-yatch. Almost innocent.

"So," I felt downright magnanimous, all of a sudden. "You want to be really irresistible? You've got to try these Rah-Rah Lashes."

I gave her two coats on top of the primer. I painted her lips, powdered them through a tissue, then glossed and sealed them so that they'd look moist and inviting through all types of activities. I gave her several pods of Breakthrough skin texturizer, and what the hell? I tossed in samples of the new fragrance, called Shimmer, of course, that we weren't supposed to release until the weekend.

"No one else will have this scent until Monday," I told her.

"You're just a darling." She admired her face in the mirror and beamed at me. "Thanks for being so nice and all. I wouldn't have come if I didn't care about Nora. After that night, I was afraid you might be, you know."

"A be-yatch?" I asked.

She giggled, thanked me repeatedly and left all aglow with Shimmer for her date with Kersikovski. I remembered the feeling, waltzing off in scent, mousse and mascara, into an evening that couldn't start soon enough, with a man I believed would change my life.

I was glad I'd done my best makeover on her. Never let it be said that Reebie Mahoney was a be-yatch.

Thanks to Gaylene, my sales figures for the day would outshine even Aida's and make it look as if I'd sold, sold, sold.

"Good job, Miss Mahoney." Ellie approached as Gaylene departed. We were always *Miss* to her, as she preferred to be addressed. "Let's see some more activity like that today."

"Let's not," I said.

"What?" The crayoned brows rose higher.

I looked at the powders and paints before me. I looked at Ellie, her long-unkissed lips, and the kingdom of women over whom she presided. And before I thought through what I was doing, I took off my trendy smock, folded it into a trendy rectangle and placed it on the trendy, faceted glass of the counter. "I'm not going to do this anymore. You can send me my final check."

"You can't quit in the middle of your shift." She put her hands on her hips. Beneath the concealer around her thin, straight nose, I could see the red-ink spiral of broken capillaries.

"I just did." I glanced over at Aida, busily painting a face on a bored-looking teen with more body piercings than acne scars. "Tell Aida I said goodbye."

Ellie followed me toward the door, getting in front of me, her lizard eyes full of fire. "I was going to terminate you, anyway," she said.

"I beat you to the punch."

It reminded me of one of those oldies Daph played, made popular by one of the girl groups in the sixties and covered by Ed Palacios a few years later. I walked away humming.

Nicholas

Darla had planted his tomatoes. Darla had said, "Welcome home," and put out her arms to him. Darla had charmed his mother. His mother.

He'd been afraid to touch Darla, afraid of what he might do if he ever held such goodness that close to him.

It didn't matter, though. She came back the next day, early, with the sun. He knew she'd be there, and he made sure he was there, too.

"Aren't you supposed to be packing?"

She had that cute black thing scrunching down her hair, and that same laughter in her voice.

"I am packing," he said. "Just checking on the garden." Should he say the next part? Why not? "My mother really liked you."

He expected a smile but didn't get it. Darla moved closer.

"What happened?" she asked, placing a cool finger against the sore puff beneath his eye.

They sat on a bench he'd built around one of the trees. He was pretty good at building stuff. "Nothing."

"Something." She tapped it again, and that kind of made him mad. Maybe he was just mad at himself, though, because he couldn't remember. Maybe that's all it was. He just couldn't remember why, all of a sudden, in a place and with a person where he should have felt happy, he was miserable.

Twenty-Two

Reebie

For all of my bravado with Ellie, I'd walked out of my job without lining up another. I hadn't meant to quit, but my session with Gaylene and the whole shimmer number made me realize what I should have known since my first day there. I could never be Miss Mahoney.

I called Natalie, but of course, the yoga job was long gone. I can't say I was sorry. Something was happening to my attitude. After I lost the winery, I thought I'd just temp for a living, take whatever job that would have me and not care. "The whore works for money," my dad always said. "The slut enjoys it."

I'd been a whore. It hadn't worked, but maybe it would once I stopped worrying about whether or not I'd make it through the next day alive. If I had to dip into my settlement right now, I would do what I had to.

Daph couldn't hide her relief when I told her what I'd done. "Finally. You were like a sitting duck in that store."

She emerged from the computer room in a banana-colored crocheted top that showed just a trace of skin between it and the silky, low-slung khaki pants tied at the ankle. No way would she be wearing three-inch slides for an evening in front of the television with Chico and me.

"Another date?" I asked.

"You better believe it." She waved a chunk of papers toward me. "I printed some out for you, too. So? What do you think?"

I looked at them, the forced smiles, the nice- but not great-looking guys you see in the supermarket and the video store. All of the bios started out with something like, "I've done everything else and haven't found the right person, so thought I'd give this a try."

"Have you met anyone interesting, or do you just do it the same way you collect all of this Americana stuff?"

She sat down on one of the kitchen chairs and tossed a treat to Chico. "Maybe a little of both."

"You're one of the most attractive, intelligent women I ever met," I said. "It's none of my business, but you don't need to go looking for a man."

"Ah, but my biological clock might not agree

with that sage advice." She said it in her joke voice, but I wondered.

"Just don't make the mistake I made," I said. "Don't trust the wrong man, and don't mistake multiple orgasms for true love, 'cause it just ain't so."

"That could almost be a Johnny Cash song," she said.

"Not quite." Chico brought his treat to my chair and slid against it, butt first, thumping his tail on the tile. "I talked to a woman about Jeanette today," I said. "Her name's Gaylene. She's the one who shared gallery space with Jeanette."

"Scarlett O'Hara Gaylene? I met her. Don't you love that accent?"

"Where'd you meet her?" But I knew from the look on her face. "Kersikovski, you mean? She mentioned that."

"Oh, good. It's nothing. I mean, he just had lunch with her at the newspaper."

Right. Just had lunch at the newspaper, and dinner tonight. I wished Gaylene well. I was happy she had the Rah-Rah Lashes. If she were crazy enough, freshly divorced as she was, to trust a man, it might as well be Kersikovski.

"She said Jeanette went away on holidays."

I'd been thinking all about that, realizing that Gaylene was right. "Someone had to have cared about Jeanette," I said. "And she had to have cared for someone, too."

"Ed Palacios." Daph's face went dreamy. "You

know they had a thing back in her Vegas days? My old boyfriend and I stayed at the hotel he was supposed to have built for her."

Again she was ahead of me. "Palacios had a hotel built for Jeanette?"

"And he aged better than it did," Daph said. "The elevators smell like smoke. There are hypodermics and condoms in the planters outside. And those weirdo portraits she did make the rooms damned spooky. Must have been her early work. I had to sleep with the lights on."

"If it was that early, was she painting under her own name?"

"I didn't think to look. You could call and ask."

"I will."

"That other old lover of hers lives in Palm Springs," she said.

"You're the trivia queen. What other old lover, pray tell?"

She gave me the grin I'd seen too infrequently since Sunny's murder. "Remember the guy who did the doctor show back when doctor shows were big?"

"Marcus Olson?" I remembered him at once. Although I'd never seen the show, I could see him, bearded and elusive, the sexiest television doctor since Vince Edwards did Ben Casey and Richard Chamberlain's Dr. Kildare sang, "All I Want To Do Is Dream."

"That's the guy. They were supposed to be a couple. I have a bunch of old *Photoplay* mags I bought in a Venice Beach store. He sang a song called 'Dreamy Eyes,' and you better believe he had them. I could probably show you the photos of them."

"Where's the good doctor now?" I asked.

"I don't know. Let's check the mags."

We went into the back bedroom, which was really Chico's room, all blankets, beds and toys among the bookcases. Daph spread out her collection from the white shelves.

"Here," she said, placing a plastic-covered magazine into my hand. "Read the cover."

I did.

Tony Curtis and Janet Leigh celebrate Janet's Birthday. Judy Garland's Hollywood Opening, Hope Lange, Elvis Presley's Mother's Death, I Babysat for the Boones, Elizabeth Taylor Remembers Michael Todd, Gia Scala Tries to Take Her Own Life, Why John Saxon Doesn't Go for Sandra Dee, Dean Stockwell. Marcus Olson: Hot TV Doc Courts Las Vegas Beauty.

"Open it." I handed it back to her, not wanting to harm the pages of Daph's treasure.

She spread it out on a shelf, turning pages carefully until Jeanette's face appeared. Despite the poor-quality black-and-white reproduction that looked as if it had been printed on toilet paper, Jeanette stood out, even among these shots of the professionally beautiful. She wore a strapless lace dress, probably white, and held a champagne flute. Beside her, in a tux, stood Marcus Olson. I wondered

how it felt to be looked at the way Olson was looking at her.

"He was quite the hunk," Daph said. "I had a boss
who used to shoot this stuff back then. They posed
it all, and the giveaway is that they're wearing the
same clothes in every shot. For all you know, they
were just the couple of the month. They could have
hated each other."

I looked at their faces, their eyes, in the grainy
gray print. "You think so?"

She shook her head. "That's the thing about photos like this. They make you want to believe."

She was right about the clothes. Jeanette wore the
same lace dress in every photograph. The shoot
could have taken hours, yet there wasn't a sign of
exhaustion or impatience in her smile.

"She looks like a woman in love," I said, "not that
I'm an expert on those traits."

"And look." Daph touched the page, a party scene,
Jeanette clinging to Olson's arm with the same expression of Hollywood enchantment. On Olson's other
side stood a dark-haired man in a suit and, yes, cuff
links. His hair was a little too long and kinky, but those
smooth, well-tended hands hadn't changed that much.

I checked beneath the photo to be sure I was right.
*"Jeanette and Marcus chat with dreamboat singer
Ed Palacios. Could they be requesting a special love
song just for them?* Who wrote this stuff, Daph?"

"Oh, just the usual hacks. It hasn't changed that
much, just gotten more sophisticated."

I was no longer paying attention to what she said.
I was looking at Jeanette's face. It wasn't Olson who
made her glow like that. The magazine's readers
might have missed it, but it was clear to me.

"Forget Olson," I said. "The lady had the serious
hots for Palacios."

Daph scowled at the photo. "I told you that, but
I still think you need to check out Olson. If you
don't, someone else will."

Did she just want to get rid of me for a while, or
was she worried, as I was, that every day I stayed
around here, the gardener guy was probably getting
closer to making his next move?

"You're right." Looking through the old magazine
had made me feel as if I needed to sneeze, or cry
even. "I think I'll take a little trip to Palm Springs."

"Let Ski know," she said. "Maybe he—"

"I think," I said, "Mr. Ski has his hands full. I can
call on Marcus Olson with no help from anyone."

I could, too.

Secretly, I was glad to get away from here, from
putting myself and possibly Daph in danger.

"You want me to come?" she asked. "I could take
a couple of vacation days."

"No, you just check out those computer guys,"
I said. "Let me know when you find Mr. Wonderful, okay?"

She placed her magazine on the top of the book-
case. "Be careful," she said. "Chico and I would be
lonely if you went and got yourself killed." Then, she

turned away, back to the magazines, but not before I saw her bottom lip quiver.

Marcus Olson's voice was elegant with the slow, pronounced cadence of one who learned to speak by reading Shakespeare, maybe. I was somewhat but not entirely surprised that he agreed to see me and wondered if he'd talked to Eddie Palacios. It was almost too easy.

He lived in the Las Palmas area, right up against the mountain, where I heard many of the old Hollywood types went to retire. The sand-colored mid-century modern home surprised me, too. It didn't appear that different from any of the other houses, with its private entry and what looked like guest units peeking from behind palm trees.

I got there a little after three, and although it was warmer than what I'd left, a series of gray clouds darkened the sky. Marcus Olson was like any other older, amiable guy who happened to have been drop-dead gorgeous in his prime. He'd held on to his youth better than Palacios, and he didn't appear to have had any work done. The skin around his eyes crinkled with what looked like a lifetime of smiles, and the eyes themselves were the most hypnotic I'd seen on anyone, even Kersikovski. His arms, beneath the short-sleeved blue shirt were the smooth, moisturized tan that must be chemically induced. He met me at the gated courtyard in front of the guest unit.

"Let's walk out to the pool," he said. "It should clear up in a bit, and we might see some sun."

What the hell was I doing here? Walking behind some one-time TV star out to his covered patio, getting ready to ask him about an old love affair? I was the lady who didn't give a damn about anything, who was ready to spend my life moving from temp job to temp job. And now, here I was. The reason, of course, was fear. It hit me just like that, staring at the angles of the geometric swimming pool. As much as I hated my life without the winery, I didn't want it to be over. I was here because I knew if I didn't get to the bottom of what was going on, I was going to be very dead. And I didn't want to be.

I'd dressed in white cropped pants, shirt and visor, trying to fit in without overdoing it. I matched the patio furniture, so that was a good sign.

"Could I offer you something? Water?" He could have played a butler. His speech and manners were that precise.

"No, thanks." I settled on a white chair, and he pulled up one beside me. "It's kind of you to talk to me, Mr. Olson. I feel really strange about barging into your home like this."

"I wouldn't talk to most." He kept his gaze riveted to mine, unnerving for me, because of the power of his eyes. "I wouldn't talk to the press, of course, although I've had calls."

"I didn't want anything to do with it," I said in a

rush. "I only went to see her because she sounded desperate."

"That's why I agreed to talk to you. Jeanette was very dear to me at one time. When I heard what happened to you, that she'd tried to contact you, I knew she'd want me to see you, if only to tell you that there's nothing I can do to help."

He was saying two things. One, that he couldn't help me. Two, that he believed me. "You know I didn't do anything to harm her, then?"

He nodded. "I never believed that. Those investigating officers are idiots if they do."

"Do you think it had anything to do with President Remington?"

His lips tightened, and wrinkles I hadn't seen before appeared. "I wish I knew. I never believed in coincidence, though, and she did tell you that she wanted to talk about him."

"She said she'd been his mistress."

More stress wrinkles. He ran a hand through his short hair, more gray in front, more straw-blond on the sides. "Please understand that I can't discuss her personal life."

"Not even if it will help find her killer?"

He sat, motionless, devoid of expression, like an actor waiting for his lines. Finally, he turned those sad, fiery eyes on me. "You make a good point, my dear. If I talked about something that's better kept secret, would that really help anyone find out what happened?"

"It would if you think Remington's family had anything to do with it."

"Who, for Christ's sake? June? That son? The wimp of a chief of staff?" He got up and paced before the pool. I wondered if he were playing Mac-Beth or Henry the VIII, perhaps. "Rem may be dead, but let me tell you, he's still calling the shots, and he always will. He was the most controlling man I ever knew, and I was an actor. Controlling men were as common to me as cornflakes in my cereal bowl."

"What kind of man was he?" I asked. "And I don't mean the greatness, the war hero-ness, the strong-leader stuff."

"A dictator." He almost whispered it. "And, yes, a womanizer." He sat back down beside me and turned his head toward me. "He did love her, though."

"So he and Jeanette were—?"

He turned those headlight eyes on me again. "I'm not going to say they were, but I'm not going to deny it, either."

There it was, from someone who would have known. Jeanette hadn't been lying about her affair with Remington. And someone from Remington's camp must be responsible for her death. But which one?

Olson stood and looked toward the glass door to the house. Time for me to go. I wanted to, but something about his blustering made me feel just a little manipulated.

The sun had broken through the gray cloud layer, just as he'd predicted. I squinted as I looked up at him. Just say it. I'd just have to say it before he gave me what my dad would call the bum's rush and closed the gate behind me for good.

"I loved those photos of you and Jeanette in *Photoplay*."

His smile was a little quirky, probably trying to remember which photos, maybe even to reassess what I knew. "*Photoplay* was a couple of lifetimes ago. The photo shoots were set up by my PR people, of course."

"You two were a beautiful couple." I didn't ask, only stared at him, feeling like the most callow human on earth. A be-yatch, as Kersikovski's new lady friend would say.

His edgy expression softened into a smile. "That was a long time ago. I loved her dearly and respect her memory. One of my greatest regrets is losing touch with her."

That stopped me. "When *was* the last time you saw her?"

"When Rem was president. I'm not sure of the year. Then she went off to California. That's what I meant when I told you I couldn't be of much help. I haven't seen Jeanette since 1976. Indeed, I believed she was dead, just as everyone else did."

I had nothing but unspoken confirmation of Jeanette's affair with Remington, and I'd gotten that from Jeanette herself. I hadn't counted on this, that

she hadn't kept in touch with Olson. Chalk up another wasted trip.

"Thanks for your time," I said. "Can you think of
anyone else I should contact?"

He shook his head. "I'm sorry. It was just too long
ago. Let's go through the house. It will be faster."

We stepped through the sliding glass doors into
a kitchen of beech-wood cupboards, aluminum
appliances and floor-to-ceiling windows. I felt like
the world's biggest loser for intruding on this man's
pristine life.

We stepped down into the living room and its
stone floor. I looked around the room—at the ultra-
modern fireplace that stood from the wall like a
white screen in a movie theatre. At the photo of a
young woman, her features similar to Olson's. And
there, on either side of it, two paintings—nudes
superimposed upon each other, swathed in smoke.
Jeanette's paintings.

"Lovely room," I said, trying to subdue him with
the kind of language he might use. Before he could
respond, I went up to the closest nude abstract. The
smoke-colored signature against the white read: Mc-
Farland, 1993.

"What are you doing?" he demanded. "Would
you please leave my home?" All of a sudden, actor
man wasn't all that friendly.

"When did you say you last talked to Jeanette?"
I asked.

He moved from the door to where I stood, his

good manners washed away along with his tan, which now stood out on his pale skin like a cheap paint job. "I suggest you leave. Do you understand? Do you understand what will happen if you don't?"

I looked up into those glittery eyes and understood only one thing. I'd better get the hell out of there. And fast.

Twenty-Three

I'd checked into a nondescript hotel not far from Marcus Olson's house, a place so green and relaxed it made me wish I played golf. But one doesn't play golf when one is trying to stay alive. Marcus had lied to me about the last time he'd seen Jeanette. What else had he lied about?

This was supposed to be a safe town. I wanted it to be, but I wished I'd had Chico to ride behind me in the car, to growl at my door.

I arrived at the cheapo motel I'd booked online and hoped just to crash. I tossed off the visor. I took the plastic room key from the bored anorexic who looked as if she'd benefit from a nicotine patch, a hamburger and a stroke or two of Rah-Rah Lashes.

"Your other party's already arrived," she said.

"What other party?"

She pushed back her streaked blond hair, narrowing her eyes. "There's two of you traveling, isn't there?" she asked.

No one knew where I was, only Daph. Had the gardener man followed me here? "Is it a Ms. Teng?" I asked, trying to fight off the smothering dread.

"Isn't a miz anyone."

A man? "He must have registered. What name did he use?"

"What kind of game are you playing? Are you trying to say you don't even know your own husband?"

"The name?" I shouted it in her face. "Who did you register in my room?"

She jerked the computer monitor around and mashed her finger on the screen. "I'm not sure how to pronounce it. Maybe you can clue me in."

Leo Kersikovski.

My fear began to subside.

The blonde looked at me as if she needed a cigarette. "Mystery solved?"

"You don't understand," I said. "I've been involved in some very scary stuff. Is the man who registered about this tall with black hair and—"

"A hunk," she said. "Can't say the same for his wheels."

It was really Kersikovski. How many hunks with ugly vans could there be in Palm Springs? "Thank you," I said. "Sorry for the outburst."

"No problem." She reached into a drawer and

brought out a brown leather container the size of a pack of cigarettes. She looked down at it and, for the first time since I entered the office, smiled. "Anything else I can do for you before I go on my break?"

I shook my head, unable to speak. Why the hell had Kersikovski followed me to Palm Springs?

The moment I opened the door, I heard the sound of some kind of sporting event. There he was, sprawled on one of the two beds, pillows propped behind him, his shoes off.

"Hi," he said casually.

I didn't know where to start, but the lack of shoes upset me the most. "Why?" I demanded. "Why?"

He zapped the game into silence and got off the bed. "Because."

"Because why?"

"Because Daph was worried about you and called me."

We stood close to each other now. For some odd reason, I thought of my dad, how he'd always warn me to "simmer down." I felt as if I were doing that now, as if the air was slowly being released from this huge bubble of anger and fear.

"And?"

"That's it."

"In that case, thank you. Why did you tell the desk clerk you were my husband?"

"Easiest way to get into a room?" he said. "I should have called you first, though. It was stupid of me, considering what you've been through."

"It's okay." I couldn't move toward the bed, couldn't kick off my shoes or do any of the things I should have been able to do. I was both frozen and flushed. At least that's how it felt being inside my cold/hot skin looking out at Leo Kersikovski.

Those smoky eyes met mine, and I tried to think of a reason why I should never trust a man who smiles without opening his mouth.

"Cute outfit," he said, "but I like the way you usually dress better. I miss the beret."

Spell broken, thank you very much.

"I've been picking my own clothes since I was six," I said, "and I stopped trying to dress for someone else a long time ago."

"Me, too." He looked down at his well-worn jeans, then back up at me. "I meant what I said, Reebie. I came because Daph was worried about you. And because I was worried about you, too. You're more than just a source to me. You've got to know that."

I couldn't respond to what he was saying. I didn't know how to get away or even if I wanted to. "Why?" I asked.

"Because." He reached out for me, and in one tilted movement, I was in his arms, clinging to him, feeling the heat of his body through his thin, scratchy shirt.

The lips that remained closed when he smiled spread across mine, opened me up. His taste, his scent, mingled with my own, strange and familiar. I tried to pull away. He wouldn't let me. I wouldn't let me. I scrambled, and while still luxuriating in his touch, put my hands on his solid chest and pushed.

"I'm not sure I'm reading you right," he said.

"You are." I gasped the words. No wonder he wasn't reading me. "I don't want this, especially not with Miss Dallas on the scene."

He reached for me again. I pulled away. "You can't believe that. Gaylene's only a source."

"That's not what she thinks."

"What she thinks is her problem. Not yours, not mine. Not ours." He tilted his head to one side and gave me that tight-lipped, little-boy smile. "Gaylene's not the real reason, though, is it, Temp Lady?"

I forced myself to look back into his eyes. "Maybe not entirely."

He cupped his chin in his hand. "You've still got a thing for your ex."

"I hate him."

He nodded. "*I hate him.* That's symptom number one for still-got-a-thing-for-your-ex disease."

"Make it still-pissed-off-at-your-ex, and it's a bingo." I thought about everything Geoff had taken from me, about all of the dreams I'd lost because I'd chosen to love him. I hoped Kersikovski could read that in my eyes. Just because I didn't want a momentary thing with a man who probably had a dozen juicy Lucys on the side, did not mean I still wanted Geoff.

"You sure?"

He looked ready for another huddle, so I said, "I'm not sure of anything right now. I just met with Marcus Olson. He wasn't what I expected. None of it was what I expected."

I could almost hear a gear click. "What'd you learn?" Kersikovski asked.

"He let me know without saying it that Jeanette and President Remington were lovers, but he also lied to me."

"How?"

"He said his last contact with Jeanette was *before* she was supposed to have died in that auto accident. But guess what? He has two of Nora McFarland's nude abstracts in his living room."

"Mr. Olson has lied about more than that in his life."

I was more comfortable with this Kersikovski, the one who settled into a straight-backed chair with a frown. I wasn't comfortable with the other. I still couldn't believe what I'd allowed us to do. I'd have to sort that out later.

I pulled a straight chair next to his and sat. "What did Olson lie about?"

"For one thing, his orientation," he said. "He's gay."

"I don't think so. He has a family, an ex-wife, a kid away at college."

"His romance with Jeanette was studio-land," he said. His eyes gleamed with gold-gray lights, the way they had moments before he kissed me. "Can you believe this? I did a search on him and came up with one of his co-stars and roommates, guy named Hal Winston. His number was in the book, and Winston confirmed that they were lovers. He's never talked to the press about it."

"But he's going to talk to you?" I asked.

"To us, if you want to come along."

"Why would you want me to go with you?" I asked.

"Because." He rose from the chair, then lifted me from mine.

"No," I said. And then our lips connected again. And although I didn't dare speak it, my body screamed yes.

That cute little white Palm Springs outfit flew like feathers off me. Kersikovski's jeans didn't make it across the room.

"I want you," he whispered. "I wanted you from that first day."

He wanted me.

I wanted him.

Our bodies took care of the rest. I couldn't believe I'd never let a man this close to me again, let myself be lifted to his lips, throw my head back and just relish the joy of it. The pure joy.

"Leo." He'd never be Kersikovski to me again.

Leo. Leo. Leo.

I knew better, but I couldn't help it. For the first

time since I stood outside Jeanette's door and heard that gunshot, I felt safe.

The Mistress

Palm Springs
1976

It had been all lights and gunshots after the crash. She had somehow rolled down the hill and managed to grab hold of a bush. Sharp needles cut her flesh. Her baby, what was happening to her baby? And where were Kim and Marcus?

"Jeanette, don't answer. Just listen." Thank God. Marcus was alive, although his voice sounded weak. She wanted to call back, but held on to the bush instead. "Jeanette, honey, Kim and I weren't trying to hurt you," he said. "We were trying to get you out of here before the shit hit the fan. Be quiet. Don't come out, no matter what. Kim, you be quiet, too. Remember that—"

A screech of wheels drowned out his words. Jeanette heard the crack of something that sounded like a gun. She huddled under her inadequate cover, trying to protect the only thing in her life that deserved protection.

"You're here, aren't you, Olson?" The voice came only inches from her. "Where'd you hide her? Tell me that, and you just might live to see Christmas."

A boot kicked into Jeanette's side. She sucked in her breath, afraid to move.

A woman's scream broke the silence. "Leave us alone. We haven't done anything wrong." Kim, wonderful Kim, always thinking the world would get it right, if she could just explain it.

The boots left Jeanette, stomped toward Kim's voice. And then the shot. The scream. The voice of insane rage.

"I'll find you, bitch! You know I will!"

She could see his horrible boots, coated in mud. She flattened herself, praying that he couldn't see her hiding there, dark and hopeless as the dirt.

Twenty-Four

Reebie

Hal Winston owned an aged but classy-looking bungalow in the old part of town by the tennis club, which was where, he said with a shaky laugh, he really lived. He looked like a tennis player. Tanned muscular legs covered in sun-bleached hair, clear blue eyes and bristly silver hair buzzed short to the scalp.

Leo introduced us at the door to the bungalow, and the first words out of Winston's mouth to me were, "I like your hair."

"I like yours, too," I said.

"Takes guts to just cut it all off, doesn't it?"

"I don't know," I said. What it took was not giving a damn, just grabbing the scissors and hacking away. "Depends on how attached to it you were, I guess."

"I was attached, but now I'm detached." He laughed a little too hardily at his own cleverness, then, segueing into a strictly business voice, addressed Leo. "You were supposed to be here an hour ago."

"Sorry. I'm running late."

We looked away from each other, and I could swear I felt Winston's knowing gaze. Didn't matter. My face was already hot, and I felt as if the details of what had made us late were printed all over it.

"Maybe it's just as well. I don't feel right about talking about it just now, and I wouldn't if I didn't have to."

"Take your time," Leo said. "Do you mind if we come inside?"

"Let's not. It's just about martini time. I'm on my way to Melvyns. Want to walk with me?" He stepped out and closed the door behind him before either of us could answer. "I met a young man just last night who actually ordered a pesto martini. They make it with basil and vodka, of course. No gin drinker would tolerate such an aberration."

"Who's Melvyn?" Leo asked, as we picked up the rear.

"Melvyns, no apostrophe, in case you decide to write about it one day. A restaurant and bar you'll like, since you're into digging up dirt on old stars. Sinatra used to hang there. Two of the biggest sexpots in history were caught in flagrante delicto at the hotel there back in the early sixties. Female sexpots, by the by. I'll let you use your imagination."

The air had turned cold again. The back of Leo's hand brushed mine, and I shivered.

"Sounds like it must have been fun," Leo said, "but to set it straight, I'm not a gossip columnist."

Winston slowed his pace and waited for us to catch up with him. "Pity. I could tell you stories."

We turned onto West Ramon Road, and I caught sight of the structure toward which we were surely heading. I don't think I've ever seen such a heady display of bougainvillea. Even in the dimming light, fuchsia blossoms and green leaves glowed like neon along arched white entry walls.

"I'm interested only in Marcus Olson." Leo took my hand as we crossed the street. It was all I could do to keep from lifting his fingers to my lips. They felt that right.

The spell was broken the moment Hal Winston began speaking again.

"I don't want to harm Marcus. He was an important part of my life. But ultimately he betrayed me. That was what he had to do. This is what I have to do."

"How'd he betray you?" I gasped the question before I remembered that Leo was supposed to be conducting this interview. "Sorry."

"Don't be." Winston waved away my apology as if it were cigarette smoke some thoughtless person had blown his way. "I'm okay with what happened. The betrayal was the woman, of course. We'd had our ups and downs, but I fully expected to totter off into the sunset with him."

"Which woman?" Leo asked.

"I never knew. We'd had some problems. I was a lot less tolerant than I am today, far too jealous." He stopped, and I could almost feel him sorting through old memories, could see the pain in his pale eyes. "I don't believe that there's only one perfect person for you, and I've had good relationships since then."

"But?" Leo was good. He made the question so quick, so short, that Winston probably didn't notice it, probably thought he was asking it of himself.

"But he was the one for me, the closest one, at least."

"In spite of the problems."

"In spite of everything. I didn't count on her, that's all."

"Who?" Leo asked again, and I knew he was fighting himself, trying not to mention Jeanette.

"I told you I don't know. We were off. We were on. We were off. We were on. We were off, and I never heard from him again. When I tried to call him, he cut me off, said it was over, that he was sorry but he had a new life. And that was that."

But it wasn't that. I could see he hadn't gotten over it. "Did he give you any reason?" Leo asked.

"No, and I was too distraught to press him. I spent time in Europe working on a picture after our final breakup—after I heard he'd gotten married and all that. I came back here, just kind of hoping, but we've never as much as run into each other in the grocery store. We had the same agent, and I could get in touch with him if I wanted to." He gave us a don't-give-a-damn shrug that conveyed only how much of a damn he gave. "He's a private man now. The last thing I want to do is disturb his life."

"You knew Jeanette Sheldon?" Leo asked.

He threw back his head, laughing like a young man with more hope and more happiness than this congenial yet guarded man he was today, not mimicking the laughter of his youth as much as reliving it. "I loved Jeanette," he said. "And that whole thing about her and Marcus was for publicity only. If she'd been alive, she would have talked him into reconsidering the breakup and that whole drastic life change. And she would have warned me. Jeanette didn't know how to lie."

We'd reached Melvyns, where he would spend the evenings with old friends, old memories and gin versus vodka. And where would we go tonight, Leo and I?

His arm pressed into my back as if he'd sensed my thought. "I take it Jeanette was reported dead before you and Marcus split," he asked.

"Listen, my friend." Winston stood up to him. "I don't care what they're saying now. If Jeanette had been alive all of these years, she would've gotten in touch with me. It's that simple."

"Maybe she had a reason not to," I said.

"No reason could have kept her quiet." He looked at me and shook his head. "You would have had to know her to understand," he said. "She was the most honest person—the most honest *human*—I ever met.

She said once you told a lie, you'd keep telling them, and one day you wouldn't know the difference between what was true and what wasn't. You'd wake up saying the sky is green, just because lying was your way of life."

"You sound as if you were very close," Leo said.

"We were." He looked away from me, at his destination. "I had two major losses that year, my lover and my best woman friend."

"What year?" Leo asked.

I could see that Hal Winston still carried every day of it in his eyes.

"The year was 1976. I woke up the day after Christmas reading about Jeanette's death, horrified. I called Marcus, but—I'm sorry. I don't think I can continue."

"It's all right," Leo said. "You're saying that Marcus split for good right after Jeanette Sheldon was reported dead."

He nodded and wiped his eyes dry. "The two most important people in my life, and they were both taken away from me in one holiday."

"I'm sorry." I said it before I thought. I even took his cool hand in mine. "You must have loved them both very much."

"And they loved me." His gaze went to Leo. "That's why it's so difficult for me to do this. I never even told Marcus, although I would have, of course, if he hadn't decided to end it for good."

"To do what?" Leo asked.

He continued to walk, not speaking. The tension

in the air was so tight I felt as if a gun were pointed at my head. I looked over at Leo, begging him with my eyes to break the silence. He gave a quick jerk of his head, and I knew what he was trying to say. If I thought the strained silence was unbearable for me, imagine what Winston thought. By the time we reached the end of the block, it got too much for him.

Sweat gleamed on his brow. He stopped, grabbed Leo's wrinkled sleeve.

"I overheard something one night when Marcus and I were still together."

We waited again. Silent again. And again, he spoke.

"This is good stuff, stuff you wouldn't hear anywhere else. And it just might explain why Jeanette was murdered, not to mention who did it. I'm the only one who can tell you this. Marcus will take it to his grave, that is, if he's figured it out."

"Go on." Leo's voice was raw.

"I'm not greedy. I could have gone to the tabloids or done the talk-show circuits again, but I don't want the attention, and I want my name kept out of it."

"I told you I couldn't promise you that," Leo said.

"Well, try, will you? I wouldn't if there were an easier way. I'd die before I went to Marcus for money, though."

Leo's fingers went stiff in my hand. "You know I can't pay you for this information."

Winston's eyes took on a scared, desperate glow. "What do you mean you can't pay me? That was our arrangement."

"We don't have an arrangement," Leo said, confused. "You agreed to talk to me."

"No." He seemed to grow shorter, paler, before my eyes. "That's not what you told me last week."

I could feel Leo click into some silent, watchful mode. "I didn't call you last week," he said. "You know that."

"What are you trying to pull? We talked last week. I agreed to tell you what I know. You mentioned a fee."

"It didn't happen," Leo said. "I've never paid a source."

"But you promised. It's the only reason I'm talking to you. The only reason." He slumped onto a stone bench before an explosion of bougainvillea. "You called me and said you'd pay me to talk to you about Jeanette and Marcus. About what I've kept to myself about what happened before her death."

"I made no such call."

The man's sigh was enough to make me cry. He'd been confessing his history to us, expecting money, but I knew Leo hadn't promised him that, regardless of how much the story meant to him.

"If not you, I've been talking to the wrong person."

"You were talking to a liar," Leo said. "Or worse. Whatever you know, whatever it is, tell me. If you don't, just know it's cheaper for this new best friend of yours to kill you than to pay you off."

His expression, stark, seemed robbed of emotion, frightened. "I don't believe you. You promised me money, enough to take care of my problems. Do you know what it's like to be an out-of-work actor at my age? I took care of my brother until his death last year. That just about wiped me out."

"I'm sorry," Leo said, "but I never would have offered you money. I'm not allowed to. Did the other caller use my name?"

"I don't think so. I don't remember." He rose to his feet and straightened his shoulders. "You sound as if you're telling the truth, but that doesn't matter. All that matters is that I thought I had a solution, and now I don't. There's really nothing I can do, except go on in there and buy myself a real martini tonight."

"Buy more than one." Leo dug into his pocket. I don't know how many bills he counted out, but the wad looked decently thick. "This isn't for anything," he said. "Know that. Have a drink on us tonight, okay."

He dipped his head. "I shouldn't take this, but I don't have a choice. Thank you."

"No problem. And listen. Before you talk to any other reporters, be sure to check them out first."

His walk was almost jaunty as he headed through the entrance.

"That's called six-pack journalism," Leo said, as we watched him. "Like interviewing some old wino and buying him a bottle of Gallo as a reward. Very bad stuff."

"But that's not why you did it," I said.

"I hope not." He looked down at me, his eyes almost as sad as Hal Winston's had been.

I pressed my hand against his cheek. "It's not why you did it," I said again, tears in my eyes.

He wrapped his arms around me, and we stood there, in front of the famous site where Sinatra used to roam, where two female hotties had been caught doing who knows what back in the sixties, and we kissed each other with such eagerness that if I didn't know better, I'd believe it was the first time for both of us.

Hal

"You're leaving early," the valet parker called as he walked past.

"Getting old," Hal told him, "just getting old."

His little tap dance down memory lane had left him drained and sad, and the gin simply reminded him of better times. That was the only reason he or any of the others went to Melvyns anymore, not for anything that was happening right now. Only to remember.

He'd embarrassed himself with the reporter and his girlfriend, and he could see he'd embarrassed them, too. Money was such an indelicate subject, regardless of how you looked at it. He'd have to sell the house, that was all. Maybe it was a good thing. Even after all these years, he could feel Marcus in every room. Sometimes, even now, he'd catch a flicker of a shadow and think it was Marcus, coming in from the golf course, the study, the bath.

It had gotten dark early. Must be eight or so. Still time to call friends if he got too into the weird zone once he was back home. He had a feeling he'd be able to sleep tonight. He hadn't wanted to take money for the information. Maybe he should contact Marcus, tell him what he knew and just ask.

He'd kept the private phone number to himself yet never used it, like the partial pack of cigarettes he kept for years after he quit. Just in case. He'd never needed the cigarettes and finally threw the pack away. Not so the number.

Yes. It was time.

He stopped and took out his cell phone. If he didn't do it right here, right now, he'd lose his nerve.

As he started to dial, a sound drew his attention to the path he'd just taken. A man stood there, on the other side of the street, not moving. He looked familiar, but he was too far away for Hal to recognize him. Was someone following him? It had been a few years since that had happened.

Holding the phone, he waited for the man to cross the street, but he didn't.

"Suit yourself, asshole." Hal dialed the phone, amazed that his hand was so steady. When he looked up, the man had disappeared, and for the first time in thirty years, he was listening to Marcus Olson's voice.

"Marcus, it's me."

"No." He paused, moving out of a room, maybe. Hal couldn't tell. He was shaking now, but he had to do this. "Oh, my God."

"I'm not trying to cause you problems, Marcus, but there's something you need to know."

"I can't."

"You have to. It's about Jeanette. I think I know why she was killed."

Twenty-Five

Reebie

Leo spent the night in my room. During the course of the evening, while we ate pizza in bed and drank Corona from the bottle, he informed me that it wasn't my room at all.

"I upgraded for you, with Ms. Anorexic out front." He leaned against the pillows, pleased with himself in that way men are after sex, where every joke is funny, every insight profound.

The steamy cardboard pizza smell blended with the smell of us. Us. We were an us, for now, at least.

"This is an upgrade?"

He chuckled. "The honeymoon suite."

"No. With two double beds?"

"Yes."

"What in the world makes this a honeymoon

suite? The fact that there's a lock on the door, maybe?"

"And those candles over there on the dresser. The candlesticks are pink, you'll note. And the bathtub—" He whipped the sheet off me and patted my butt, the way I might pat Chico. "Yes, I think we could fit two people in there. Want to try?"

"Perhaps." No, I couldn't do this again. It couldn't go anywhere, be anything. I was afraid. He made me less afraid, but real life was just a few hours away.

"I think I spotted some bath foam, whatever the hell that is." He stroked the part of me he'd patted just a moment before. It had the same effect as a warm breath in my ear.

"Knowing this place, it's probably dishwasher detergent, traveling incognito."

"Maybe not." The stroking moved up along my side, nearing my breast, which was already on alert. "I'm game if you are."

I stretched out, blatantly carnal after having been shut down for so long, and hating myself for it. "Leo." I don't know what I was going to say. We both moved at the same time, and the pizza box slipped off the bed and hit the floor.

Leo ignored it and pulled my face to his. "What were you saying?"

I looked into those eyes and felt myself get dizzy at the thought that I was in bed with this man. "I'll race you to the tub," I said.

* * *

Later that night—how late?—I woke up feeling, even before I realized where I was, abandoned and alone. It was the way I'd felt after the divorce when Geoff had taken back the winery. I woke up with a gasp, reached out and realized I was alone in this strange bed.

He'd left. Leo had left me by myself in this room. No, Leo wouldn't do that to me. He was probably in the bathroom. The beer had left me with a dry mouth and an edgy, caffeinelike insomnia. I pushed the fear away and looked around the room until I found his shape in the darkness, sitting at the window, looking out into the night. At what? I wondered. At what?

Part of me wanted to go there, to put my arms around him and lay my head on his. But I couldn't. His demons were his demons, and my demons were my demons, and nothing that had happened in this bed could change that.

Maybe he was having second thoughts about this encounter, the same as I was. Maybe he, too, was doing the could've, should've, would've thing. I reached up and touched my hair, still damp from our clumsy frolic in the tub. "Leo?"

He turned, but I couldn't see his face. "Did I wake you?"

"I think the Coronas did."

"It can't be too bad. I drank most of the six-pack. Ate most of the pizza, too. You go back to sleep now, okay?"

"Okay." I rolled over on my side, so that I could look at him while I tried to ease myself back into sleep. It didn't work. "Leo," I asked. "What's going on with you?"

"Just thinking," he said. "You try to rest."

"Thinking about what?"

"That guy."

I shot up in bed. It wasn't the answer I expected. "What guy?"

"Old Hal Winston."

"Oh." He turned, but it was too dark in the room for me to see his eyes. I could tell from his voice that his thoughts and mine were worlds apart.

"I think he knows something," he said.

"Even if he does, he wants to sell the information."

"Not really. He's horrified by the thought of it. If I talked to him again, maybe, just maybe—"

"What?" I asked, reaching down and pulling the thin thermal blanket over me.

"I don't know." He moved, and for a moment, I thought he was coming back to bed with me. Then, I realized he'd turned his chair back, facing the window. "You just try to get some sleep. I promise to be more fun in the morning."

Hal

Marcus had argued, even when Hal told him he might be able to solve the mystery of Jeanette's death. He'd said there was too much to risk.

Something more important than finding Jeanette's killer? Finally, Hal did what he used to do, knowing how much Marcus hated it. He threatened.

"If you don't talk to me, I'm going to the police, the media, everyone."

"You wouldn't dare."

"I would. You know I would. I will."

It worked.

They met at his house. Marcus wasn't hot about that, but they counted off any number of places they couldn't meet, and Hal's came in first, with no seconds. Even now, Marcus was too well-known.

Maybe it would be different if they'd aged together. He probably wouldn't notice the changes. Now, though, looking at Marcus on the black sofa in his living room, he surveyed the sun damage, the wrinkles, the faux tan, too orange, way too orange. Only those magnificent eyes were the same.

"I like what you've done with the place." His smile was both warm and familiar.

Hal realized that they'd spent their most vital years in this room, this bungalow. What was that song they used to sing? "Our House." Something about two cats in the yard and everything being easy. They'd had that once. But now? "Thank you for coming," he said. "Can I get you a drink?"

Marcus stiffened on the sofa. "I won't be here long enough to finish it."

"Of course."

"Not of course. You always thought you had me figured out, but you didn't."

"You left me. That's all I know. You married a woman, had a kid and never talked to me again. How could you do that, Marcus? We were a couple."

"That's not why I came here and took the risk of somebody finding out. I came to ask you what you know about Jeanette."

"So you don't care about you-me stuff. You just want to know about Jeanette?"

Marcus's eyes filled. Yes, he could see the tears. "I loved you with my life," he said.

"And I loved you with my life," Hal said. "So what happened?"

"Everything. Everything happened. And if I had to go back and do it over, I wouldn't change anything."

"You like the straight life that much?" He couldn't help the bitterness he felt.

"That's not what I said. You told me on the phone that you think you know why Jeanette was killed."

"She was pregnant." There, finally he'd said it.

"That's absurd." Marcus sat unmoving, and as well as he still knew that face, Hal couldn't read his expression.

"She was pregnant with the president's child, and he either killed her or had her killed."

"How do you know that?"

"I overheard her talking to Ed Palacios on the phone. He knows it, too. I'm surprised he hasn't seen to it that the responsible parties were punished."

Marcus swallowed with difficulty, as if he needed a glass of water. He stood up meeting him eye to eye. "Stay out of it, Hal. It's not going to help anyone. That was all a long time ago."

"The older I get, the more it bothers me. You two were best friends. How can you not care?"

"I do care. There's just nothing I can do about it." He squeezed Hal's arm. "I care about you, too."

His eyes spoke the truth. Hal wanted to believe what he saw there. "I should have treated you better."

"We did the best we could for two crazy egomaniacs."

"*Au contraire.* I could have been better."

"I could have been better, too," Marcus said. "I didn't want to come here, but I'm glad I got to see you this last time."

He couldn't let him go, not now. "Why does it have to be a last time?" he asked. "Couldn't we get together now and then? Nothing else. Just talk once in a while?"

"I couldn't. I can't." Marcus shook his head and stepped away from him. "Let me help you, though. You can't have had an easy time of it."

Here he was offering him money, and not for any reason, just because he cared. "Ironic," Hal said.

"What's ironic?"

"Nothing. Just talking to myself. I don't feel right about keeping quiet, Marcus. If Jeanette was killed because she was carrying Remington's child, someone has to pay for it."

"Maybe someone has," he said. "Remington's last days certainly weren't very pretty. And June Remington's still alive. What would it do to her, to his son? I can't believe Jeanette would want that."

Hal wasn't so sure. He started for the door. "I had to tell you. I didn't know if you knew or not."

Marcus reached out for him, and in that moment, they were the way they'd been in the good days, perfectly matched, connected. He didn't know who made the first move. He knew only that their arms were locked around each other, their hammering hearts pressed close.

Marcus broke away, his eyes blazing. Like fire agates in the sun, Jeanette had said. She was right. There was anger in the eyes, passion, fear. But even as Marcus backed toward the door, Hal saw something else, too. Marcus still loved him. "Why?" he asked.

"I have to go." His voice was brusque, his smile gentle. "I'll have my attorney get in touch with you about the other matter. I want to help you out."

Hal watched him walk away. He hadn't answered his question and never would. Marcus still loved him. Marcus had left him. And he would never know why.

His dreams were formless, disturbing images, bright colors, fragments of conversation, like dialogue snipped from various films. Something—a sound, maybe, his own overworked heart—woke him, and he stretched out, feeling as if he'd just been beaten. He'd have to take something to sleep. He reached out and turned the alarm clock to face him, pressing down the top to illuminate the screen. Not even four-thirty yet. Missing Marcus was worse now because he knew their feelings were mutual. He had to take care of himself, had to get back to a life that was free of Marcus, free of wondering why.

He had started to get out of bed when he heard a noise. A tree brushing the glass patio doors. Still, it didn't sound exactly like that. He had nothing to fear, no reason for concern. Security in this place couldn't be better. He was just heartsick and off balance a bit because of the encounter with Marcus and, admit it, guilty that he'd considered selling information about him to that reporter.

He lay there for a moment, listening, and when the noise did not repeat itself, got up and sat on the edge of the bed.

Then, another noise. He turned. The shadow of a figure against the glass door. Someone was in the room with him.

"What the hell?" He jumped out of bed, but the man was on him, pushing him back down. Hal kicked him, heard a grunt. Good. He was fit for his age. He could turn this around. He grabbed the stranger around the neck, trying to squeeze the air out of him.

A hand shoved against his nose. Cool, painful flowers filled his nostrils. His hands turned to butter, melted off his attacker's neck. Hal tried to fight it, but his lungs ached, demanding air. He felt his head flop to the side of the pillow and tried to lift it. No, someone was holding his head like this at an odd angle. He began to drift, but he needed to stay here, to stay awake. Someone was coming to help him. Touching his chin, lifting it.

"Marcus."

"I'm here." Yes, it was Marcus, lifting his chin, touching his finger to his lips. No, not his finger, something cold.

He tried to call out again, but his words erupted into screams as his head exploded in blast after blast of fire.

Twenty-Six

Reebie

Leo had promised to be more fun in the morning. He kept his word, and I was more fun, too. Then, halfway into my bra, I asked him to drive me to the airport. He stood between the bedroom and the bathroom, wearing only his shorts. His black hair, still wet from the shower, lay plastered to his scalp, only underscoring his perfect features.

"Ride back with me. We can do obscene things on the road."

For one crazed moment, his invitation actually appealed to me. But I knew better. "My cabdriver friend's meeting me at the Oakland airport."

He tilted his head. "No way to phone a cabdriver from Palm Springs?"

I hooked the bra behind me. "I need to see him.

And maybe you should go talk to Hal again, considering he kept you up most of the night."

Leo didn't seem to get the dig. Instead, he nodded and said, "Well, if you're sure." Then, he turned those Kersikovski eyes on me. "Kinky sex on the road would be more fun, though. I'll think about you all the way home."

Leave it to Palm Springs to have lounge chairs and a putting green just a few feet from the terminal. The Tambourine was definitely out of its league among this upscale crowd.

"You don't need to wait with me," I said.

"I want to."

I felt a little guilty as we walked up to the resort-like terminal. I'd heard from other women about the Band-Aid man, the first lover after a divorce. I didn't want Leo to be that man.

"Are you feeling weird about what happened?" he asked.

"How'd you guess?"

"I could tell," he said, as we walked into the building.

"You, too?"

"No, but I haven't just been through a divorce, either."

"It's no fun."

"Neither's a broken engagement."

"Is that what happened to you?"

He nodded and walked with me to the ticket window. I was grateful that I'd decided to travel without baggage, which was the way I'd been traveling through my life since Geoff and I had split.

I got checked in, and Leo walked me to the gate.

"Sure you just don't want to climb in the Tambourine and forget about the flight?" His eyes glittered, but I could almost feel the clenched jaw of his smile.

"I need to get back," I said. "This isn't a good time for me."

He nodded. "That's an understatement. I've never been where you are, so I won't presume to say I understand."

"How long were you engaged?" I asked.

"Two years." He laughed. "That alone should tell you something. If it's not right after two years, it's never going to be."

I wasn't sure about that. I had known that I wanted to marry Geoff the first time I went out with him. "Which one of you broke it off?" I asked.

"I did. I should have done it sooner, but I kept thinking it would get better. She didn't understand my commitment to my job. It was as if she and the newspaper were in competition for me."

"So, she wasn't another reporter?"

"Oh, no," he said. "I met her while I was working on a story."

I went numb. "She was a source?"

He nodded. "It happens. It's not supposed to, but it does."

"Yes," I said. "It does."

His eyes darkened, and I could see him trying to

resist the urge to tell me to take a flying leap. That
would be fine with me, too—anything to break up
this feeling of dread in my chest. Instead, he said,
"She's a good woman. Even though it didn't work
out with us, I still care about her."

Big of him. *Never trust a man who stays friends
with his former lovers.* I nodded, unable to sort out
my jumbled emotions, just glad I'd be leaving.

"Are you going back to Hal Winston's?" I asked.

"I probably should." I felt him click into work
gear, and I was almost relieved. "I keep thinking
about that other reporter," he said.

"What about him?"

"No one reputable would offer money to a source.
I wonder…"

He didn't finish the statement, and I finally said,
"It's time for me to go now."

Our kiss was awkward and quick, and my smile
felt forced. I all but ran through the large glass doors.

Pargat met me, as we had arranged, in Oakland,
and from the moment I spotted him, I knew there
was trouble.

"Another cabdriver was killed in Richmond yesterday," he said.

"Oh, no."

"And last night, when I was taking a fare to the
city, somebody chased my cab, tried to run me off
the road. They fired a gun at me."

I stopped outside the cab. Here I'd been playing

house with Kersikovski in Palm Springs, and Pargat had almost been killed. "Why would somebody be doing this to cabdrivers?" I said.

"I do not know. And with me?" He shrugged. "I never know if it is this man who is murdering the other drivers, or if it's that man who tried to take you."

I looked into his eyes, a combination of pain and fear, and regretted climbing into his cab the night outside the pub. "I'm so sorry I got you into this."

He shook his head empathically. "It is not your fault. The other drivers who have been killed do not know you, and still they are dead."

"We've got to get you out of here."

"But how?" He held up his empty palms. "I have little money. The cab is the only way I can take care of my family."

Then, an idea hit me so solidly that I felt overwhelmed, dizzy, something that just might save Pargat and give him back the safety that had been robbed from him because of his friendship with me. It would take what my dad would call brass balls on my part, but it was the answer—for Pargat, and maybe for me. "Would you be willing to move?" I asked.

"How can I?"

"I have a friend who'll help us. He'll help you get a job where no one will think to look for you."

"This friend of yours. Is he someone you can trust?"

I winced all the way to my heart. No way could

I bear to answer that question. "He's already offered to help," I said. "I'm going to call him right now."

Geoff sounded surprised to hear my voice. "Are you okay?"

His demanding tone made me want to shout back, but I forced myself to stay calm as I stared at Pargat, still unsmiling, but different. I realized, that in the course of our short friendship, I'd never seen anything close to hope in his eyes. I saw that now.

"You made an offer," I said to Geoff. "I'd like to accept it, with one condition."

"I can't believe it. You finally figured out that I'm not a complete moron. When are you coming? Tonight, I hope. I'll have everything ready. Reeb, I am just so glad you're willing to let me help."

"There's more," I said.

"Not that reporter?"

"Of course not." How easily I could X out the weekend. How easily I could lie by omission to the man who had been my husband and trusted friend. But I had a reason to. I had Pargat.

"You have a lot of influence on the limo company that schedules the wine tours," I said.

"So what? You won't have to work once you're here."

The male platitude made me want to scream obscenities into the phone. "There's a cabdriver here. He's helped me, risked his life for me, and now a man who tried to kidnap me is after him. Apart from that, some serial killer is murdering cabdrivers."

"You want me to get him a job driving for the limo company?"

I clutched the phone, my hand slippery with sweat. "More than that. He and his family are going to need a place to live."

"The farmhouse? Is that what you're thinking?"

I nodded. He'd been decent before. Please let him be decent again. "Yes."

The pause was unbearable. Finally, he said, "I'll help your friend, get him a job and let his family live in the farmhouse."

"You will?" I felt light-headed. "You really will?"

"On one condition."

Oh, no. "One condition?" I repeated.

"That you come here, too. That you stay in this house and let me hide you here until the crazy stuff settles down."

I looked at Pargat, his hopeful eyes, his rigid demeanor, afraid to expect too much. He needed to get out of here. I needed to get out of here. And the last man on earth I would have trusted was the only one who could help us now. "It's a deal," I said.

"You mean it, Reeb? You're willing to come back here?"

His voice sounded the way it did back when I trusted him. "Yes," I said, "if you can help my friend."

"Tell him he has a job. Tell him he has a house. Tell him he's going to be safe here."

I hoped I could trust at least part of the message. "Call me the minute it's firm about his job," I said.

"Then don't move. I can make that happen in less than five minutes."

"I'll be waiting," I said, and switched off the phone. Pargat's eyes looked both hopeful and afraid. "Have you ever driven a limousine?" I asked.

He shook his head. "I could learn. Will you be there, I hope?"

Would I? I'd have to be. It was part of Geoff's bargain. "Yes," I said. "It used to be my winery, too. That's where we're going to live."

This was what I had to do now. I had to save Pargat from the violence in this city, from the people who were after me. And, okay, I had to save myself. Geoff called back while we were still on the way to Daph's.

"He has the job," he said, "starting Monday. Can you get here that fast?"

"Yes," I said. "Yes, I can." I leaned forward and touched Pargat's shoulder. "If you're ready to move, I have a place for you," I said.

"Thank you so much."

"You'll have a better life there," I told him, hoping that by saying it, I could make it happen.

I slept well that night, but woke up early Thursday thinking about Kersikovski. I couldn't worry about him right now. I had to worry about saving my life.

I'd told Daph about it the night before, explaining that I wouldn't be gone that long. She had insisted that I give up my apartment since I wasn't living there, anyway.

"Why keep throwing away rent money?" she said.

For a person who had a closet full of never-worn designer clothes with the price tags still hanging from them, Daph was practical when it came to everyone else's finances. I agreed, but told her I would do it only if she let me pay half the rent. She refused, as I knew she would, but I insisted. Finally, I would be rid of the apartment I hated. And, soon perhaps, I would be back here with Daph and Chico.

She had already gone to work that morning. Chico sprawled out on the bed beside me. I reached over and stroked his curly rag-doll ears, knowing he'd bide his time, letting me sleep in until I got up, and then it was treat time.

"I'll miss you," I told him.

He looked down that long spaniel nose at me as if he understood. Then, in a fit of barking, he bounced toward the front of the house. I threw on my robe and, following him, ran to the front window, my cell phone in my hand. No way was I opening the door unless it was someone I knew. The Tambourine was parked in the driveway. Not Kersikovski, not this soon. But if I didn't open it, he might think something had happened to me.

I gripped Chico's collar and opened the door. He had calmed down by the time Leo Kersikovski came inside and edged his way past him.

He was wearing the same shirt and jeans he'd had on the last time I'd seen him, when he'd given me that sad, short hug at the Palm Springs airport.

"Shouldn't you be at work?" I asked. Then I noticed his eyes. "What is it?"

"Hal Winston, the guy we talked to in Palm Springs. He's dead."

I stepped back, trying to process the information. "What do you mean dead? What happened?"

"This is all I know." He handed me a short computer printout headed, Former Actor Takes Own Life.

"You'll note it says he was despondent about financial worries and the death of his brother," Kersikovski said.

We had just talked to Hal Winston. Now he was dead. I couldn't sit, couldn't move, just stood there reading the obituary. "That poor guy. You were going to go back to his place last night."

"I didn't," he said. "Now I wish I had."

"Do you think he really committed suicide?"

"I've been asking myself that." He'd barely noticed me. He was living his job now, silently arguing with himself, sorting out facts. Even his voice had the same distracted tone as it had last night in the motel when I'd wakened to find him staring out the window.

"That second reporter? Maybe, as you suggested, that person wasn't a reporter at all."

"I've thought about that, too."

"Winston said he knew why Jeanette was killed. Of course, he didn't believe Nora McFarland was the real Jeanette."

"Didn't want to believe it," he said. "He couldn't believe that Jeanette could go all of this time letting him think she was dead."

"Poor man." I'd seen desperation in Hal Winston's eyes. Enough desperation, I wondered, to force him to take his own life? "It can't be a coincidence. So that means that Jeanette is the key to this."

"She is, regardless."

"And where the hell do I fit in?"

He looked at me and shook his head. "She didn't do you any favors when she called you that night. When we find that link, we'll understand it all."

"I have more bad news," I said. "Pargat, my cab-driver friend, was shot at. Someone tried to run his cab off the road."

"That might not be connected." He processed it like a computer, no emotion evident. "Cabdrivers are being killed."

"I think it's related." I forced myself to sit down across from him on the sofa. "From what I understand, the drivers who've been killed have been shot in their cabs. No one's been run off the road."

He nodded. "Okay. Good point. That man who tried to kidnap you threatened to come after him."

"At any rate, I'm getting him out of town."

He raised an eyebrow. "That's generous of you. How are you going to pull it off?"

"I'll tell you only if you promise to keep it to yourself." That bounced him right out of robot mode. "What the hell do you think I'm going to do, print it in the paper, along with your new address, maybe? Reebie, you should know me better than that."

"Cut me some slack," I said. "If you'd been through what I have, you'd be paranoid, too. I've gotten Pargat a job driving a wine-tour limousine."

His expressing was uncomprehending. Then, his lips tightened. "With your husband?"

"Ex-husband."

"And you'll be going, too?"

"I have to, at first. It's the safest place for me. But I won't be there long, only until this is over." I could feel my face heat as I stammered out my little speech.

"And you don't think the killer is going to find out where you are?"

"At least maybe I can buy some time," I said. "Will you keep me updated?"

At first he didn't answer. Then he said, "By any chance, was what happened with us…was it some little test to see if you still love your husband?"

"What do you think I am?" I said. "And he's my *ex*-husband, and I don't have to make love to someone else to know I don't love him. I hate him, I told you."

"Okay," he said. "You're doing what you think you need to for your safety, and I can't argue with that."

"You'll keep me posted on what's happening?"

"Of course." He gave me a lips-only smile and got up. "You have my cell-phone number. Call me if you need anything."

"You know I will." I followed him to the door, feeling only relief. It had been too soon. I didn't need a Band-Aid man.

"By the way," he said, his hand on the knob. "I like your bathrobe."

He'd been so preoccupied that it was probably the first time he'd noticed it. "Thanks," I said, and tightened the belt around my waist.

I watched the Tambourine back out of the driveway. No, it wasn't relief I was feeling. Fear had numbed me into a place where I could register little else. No, not relief, at all. I was feeling nothing.

Chico tried to distract with the mad gallop around the room that would end in a series of *good dog* and his morning treat.

"Okay," I said. "And then, you get to go for a ride. We are going to get me out of that apartment."

Twenty-Seven

Nicholas

Paris

From Dijon, they'd taken a high-speed train to Paris. Four nights on the Left Bank. Nita's attitude had brightened up the closer they got. He was glad he had her to translate for him. Phil, the Secret Service guy, couldn't speak French, and Nita knew it sideways. Besides, one smile from her and any man would fall all over himself trying to help them.

Phil knocked on the door and poked his head in the room. "You doing all right, pal?"

Nicholas had spread out cheese and fresh yogurt on the sofa. "Where's Nita?" he asked.

"She said she was doing some shopping. I'll be down the hall if you need anything."

He needed something, but for the life of him, he didn't know what. He was happy to travel where no one knew them, where rude reporters didn't hit him with questions about everything from why he had waited so long to marry to what he did for a living. Why was "I manage my investments" not good enough for them? Why didn't all of the time he spent on his mother's charities matter?

Face it. The press had never liked him. Buying the film studio hadn't helped, either. It was California. Why couldn't a president's son own a studio? Why couldn't a president's son marry a model, have a baby later in life?

Screw them.

That's what Darla had said when he'd told her how he felt.

Darla. Sure thing. That's what he needed, what he'd been missing. Here, he'd had Nice, Arles, Lyon and Paris, and all those Cezannes, cities and cemeteries he'd already forgotten. He'd had good sex with Nita, decent sex, considering her condition. But he didn't have Darla.

He looked down at the yogurt, creamy white with cherries, whole ones, hidden at the bottom, not blended in the way the health regulations required in America. He'd gotten it for Nita, but Nita wasn't here. What he really wanted was a big fat steak, something to hold him down and make him sleep, so the train dreams didn't grab him again tonight.

He picked up the phone and got a nice guy at the

front desk, a guy who could speak English and explain to him what he needed to do. In moments, he heard her sleepy voice.

"Darla?"

"Nicholas? Is that you? Do you know what time it is?"

He'd forgotten. "I'm sorry, Darla. I just missed you so much. I forgot what time it must be there."

"It's okay." Her voice got stronger. He could hear that laughter in it. "I miss you, too, but I'm taking care of everything. Wait until you see what I've done with your garden."

"I wish you were here." He looked at his purchases. "I thought I wanted a steak, but I have to tell you, I could eat this yogurt every day. The cheese, too. It melts when you touch it. I wish I could bring some home to you."

"Well, you try, hon. Is everything else okay?"

She always knew. Darla always knew. "I've been having them again."

"The same ones or a different one?"

"Different. Like this time it's happening on a train in France, not back home."

"That makes sense. Are you hearing the same voices?"

"Pretty much the same. Nita was in the last one, but I think that's just because she got upset with me the other night."

"What about?"

He didn't want to think about it, and he looked

back down at his plate. "Nothing important. I just wish you were here, Darla. You make me happy."

"I wish I could be there, but I'll see you soon."

Before he could answer, he looked up. Nita stood on those giant high heels, giving him a look that made him want to run out the door. "Nita's here," he said. "I better go." Then he slammed down the phone, hoping Nita hadn't heard, although from the look on her face, he could tell she had.

Her long, black dress draped over those wonderful hipbones, those small, perfect breasts. He wanted to touch her, the way he liked to touch pretty things, but he knew he was in trouble, that he wasn't going to get to touch anything tonight.

"What did I interrupt?" she asked.

"Nothing, honey."

"Nothing that you're telling a woman you wish she were here instead of me?"

"Not instead of you, honey. I just meant I wish she were here with us."

"You said she makes you happy. How does that old Darla crone make you happy, Nicholas?"

He didn't like to stand up to her, but this time he had to. "Darla might be older than you are," he said, "but she's not a crone. She's a nice lady, and she listens to me."

"Then she must be a moron." She clicked closer to him on those heels. Something was wrong with her. She could hardly walk. "You know why, Nicholas? Because you're a moron, that's why. Your parents bought you that law degree. Everyone knows it, too. The press is just too kind to come right out and say that President Remington's son is a frigging moron."

"I'm not a moron." It seemed like a pretty lame response. It made him feel slow and stupid.

"You're lucky to have me, me and this kid." She punched her still-flat belly, staggered across the room and slid down next to him, on the arm of the sofa. "Why would you devote one moment of your limited brain to that crone Darla, when you can have me?"

He caught a whiff of something sour. "You haven't been drinking again, have you?"

"Only a little champagne." She flopped against him. "Now, back to Darla. Maybe you don't see it, because you don't see much, but she's had laser or something on that skin of hers. No woman over forty can have skin like that."

"You shouldn't be drinking," he said, "not with the baby."

"Don't you ever tell me what to do." She slid off the sofa arm as easily as she had slid onto it. "Not ever, you bastard."

"I'm not a bastard," he said, "and don't you insult my parents that way."

The instant he finished, she drove her fist into his face. "Fuck your parents. Fuck you."

"Nita, please." He tried to duck. He tried to run, but her flailing fists hammered him every way he tried to turn. He lay on the floor, facedown, as she kept on shouting curse words at him. "Please stop," he said, cupping his hands over his ears. She would stop soon. She always did. He closed his eyes and tried to think about Darla.

Reebie

Chico and I took a little drive, and the moment I approached my old neighborhood, I got what my dad would call the heebie-jeebies. This was the place I'd landed when I wanted no job, no home, no anything. It was a place where I'd felt threatened, and from where I'd almost been snatched, supposedly at the request of some woman from Washington.

I left Chico in the truck and went to the manager, happily giving my thirty-day notice.

She nodded and said, "Been expecting it."

Daph had agreed to take most of my furniture. The rest I could give to charity. Again, I was amazed at how easy it was to let go of your past, how easy to let go of the things of our lives.

As I pulled out of the complex, I spotted a woman limping along the sidewalk. I slowed the truck. She tried to hurry ahead. I recognized her because of the short, black hair. Today she wore a pink jogging outfit instead of a bathrobe, but she wouldn't be jogging anytime soon. Yes, it was the woman whose house I'd invaded, and something was wrong with her.

I stopped, patted Chico. "Stay," I said. He wouldn't

hear of it. Those scratchy paws dug over my legs the moment I touched the door handle. "Okay, mister," I said. I leashed him, let him jump out first, then walked rapidly to catch up with my former neighbor.

"Could I talk to you for a moment?" I asked.

She turned her bruised face toward me. "What the hell are you doing coming back here?"

"That's not the point," I said. "The point is what's happening with you?" At least this time I didn't smell alcohol on her breath.

"I thought I had it bad before," she said, "but I didn't know bad. I don't know what kind of trouble you're in, little girl, but I pity you when that guy catches up with you." Her face looked like a healing wound, once-black bruises fading greenish. One eye was watery and red.

"When?" I asked. "When did this happen?"

"The day after you were here," she said. "Your buddy didn't waste any time. Now, leave me alone, I mean it. And tell your friend she better look out for this guy."

"What friend?" I asked, feeling that familiar tickle of dread.

"The one he thinks told you something." She ran her hand through the short feathers of hair. "He thought you and I were friends, thought you told me what she said—that Jeanette."

She resumed her slow movement down the sidewalk. Chico and I joined her.

"I thought he was going to kill me," I said. "That's the only reason I bothered you that day. I hope you called the police."

"He said I'd be a dead woman if I did."

"You have to."

"No, I don't, and don't you be giving me advice after the trouble you caused. I'll tell you what I did do, though. I joined the Neighborhood Watch group. I'm on the board already. And I got me some of this." She fumbled with her fanny pack and pulled out a short, black spray bottle.

"Be careful," I said. "That man is very dangerous."

"Don't I know it." She gave me a look that shimmered with determination. "He'd better not try threatening me again, though. I don't know any Jeanette, and I don't know anything about any photograph. Now, if you don't mind, I'd rather walk by myself. If someone drives by and decides to shoot you, I don't want to be in the way."

"Please," I said. "I'll leave, but tell me what he said about a photograph."

"Only said he knew you had it, and he wanted me to tell him what you did with it."

So, that's what this was over, some kind of photograph. I had to tell Kersikovski. Now. "I'm sorry about what happened to you," I said. "And I'm glad you're involved in the Watch program. You probably don't believe this, but I don't know any more about the photo and Jeanette than you do."

"Whatever." She seemed to soften for a moment and looked down at Chico. "Beautiful dog you've got there. I can tell he loves you a lot."

"Thanks," I said. No need to explain that one.

She looked over at me, and I could see the strength behind her marred skin. "My name's Betty, by the way."

"Hi, Betty. I'm Reebie. I just gave my notice today. I'm moving."

"Good," she said, then, still holding the small container, continued her slow walk down the street.

Twenty-Eight

Returning to the place where I had been happiest bought back not only the anger, but the joy of my marriage. Breathing in the musky air of the past, walking into the old stone wine cellar, no longer used but full of ghosts from the days before Prohibition shut it down, reminded me how it used to feel to be part of something eternal. I'd felt as permanent here as the gnarled vines on the hill, rich, true grapes that had outlasted those who thought they'd conquered them.

Now, I was—what was it Kersikovski had called me?—Temp Lady?

My only consolation was seeing Pargat in this environment. I had to thank Geoff for that as much as I hated him for what he had taken from me.

"You're a star, Par," he said, as we stood outside the old farmhouse where Pargat and his wife and two children now stayed. "The limo folks think you're cool. Can you believe they're thanking me for turning them on to you?"

"It is I who am grateful." He nodded at me, his eyes as shiny and alive as they had been subdued just days before. "The tips here…" his voice cracked before he could finish. "Most of all, I feel safe."

I wished I could say the same. The truth was, I couldn't imagine ever again feeling safe.

Geoff watched Pargat go into the house. "A week on the job," he said, "and he's charmed everyone from tourists to staff."

"He's a good man." *And so are you.* I didn't know where the words came from or how I could have possibly let them drift through my mind.

"What are you thinking, Reeb?"

I wasn't into his mind reading this evening, nor his nickname for me. "That I appreciate what you did for him. You've helped improve his life, maybe save it."

"I'm glad to do it. No, more than glad." In spite of the male-life-crisis hairdo and earring, I could see the decency in him, the part that had attracted me initially. I'd thought he was the least greedy human I'd ever met. "Want to take a walk?" It was one of our rituals, walking through the vineyards as the sun set. Part of me could fall easily into that routine, except the land we walked was not mine, had never really been.

"I need to visit my dad. He called yesterday."

"He's worried about you." His borderline smug

look reminded me of how he used to try to prioritize my life for me and how crazy that had made me.

"You didn't tell him anything, did you?"

"He's your father, Reeb. Don't you think he deserves to know what's going on?"

He was right, and that angered me as much as anything else. "I'm sure you convinced him that the only safe place for me was here with you."

"It's the truth." His jaw clenched as if he wanted to say more. I did, too, but I wasn't in the mood for one of our shouting wars.

"I'm not safe anywhere until this is over," I said. "You can't imagine how it feels."

"And you can't imagine how it feels to worry about you and not be able to do anything." We stood staring at each other, and I wondered if he was remembering, as I was, how it had been when it was good. "Reebie." He put out his arms.

"I can't." My voice shook. This was not my husband anymore, not my marriage, not my house. "I'm going to my dad's."

"Now?"

"Yes," I said. "It's less than thirty minutes away. Sorry if that doesn't fit into your schedule of how I should be spending my time."

"You just have to screw everything up, don't you?" His face flushed, and I was almost relieved by the anger that flooded through me.

"Don't be getting all indignant on me," I said.

"Don't you tell me how to act. You just can't

stand it when we're getting along. You have to do something to screw it up."

"Like disagreeing with you, maybe? Just because you helped me out doesn't mean I'm going to jump every time you snap your fingers."

"That's not the real reason." He shoved his face in mine. "The real reason is that you're afraid of getting close to me again. Admit it."

"That's the most ridiculous thing I ever heard. Of course I don't want to be close to you. You took everything I ever loved."

"No, Reebie." He grabbed my shoulders. "You *left* everything you ever loved. You're the one who threw it all away."

"That's a lie." I whipped the words out, my heart racing.

He turned abruptly, and without a word, he stalked out into the vineyards. I watched him go and felt tears fill my eyes. Standing there, as the golden light began to fade, leaving the vines in shadow, I wrapped my arms around myself and wondered if he could be right. It was a hell of a lot easier to get married than to get divorced. I needed to remember that.

I stomped off, too, past the crush pad with its stainless-steel tanks. I headed into the little white house that contained the small kitchen and lab equipment and offices for the cellar master and, once, for me. This was where I'd crushed the first grapes to be tested for my 2003 cab. I touched the counter where I had pressed the heel of my hand into the plastic

Baggie. We'd picked them at just the right moment that year. Now I felt removed, a part of it, but not.

It was no better in the tasting room, with its stone floors and large windows overlooking the grove. Along the window, the three pots of violets I'd saved from my wedding reception seemed to have quadrupled in size, flourishing long after the love was dead.

I leaned on the granite counter and looked at a poster on the wall, a poster Geoff had given me when we first started dating. A couple in a passionate kiss, Paris in the background, paled by their passion. Her long, dark skirt stopped above the ankle. His umbrella was poised on the ground as he leaned into her.

I heard movement behind me, turned, although I knew it was Geoff.

"Remember?" he asked, looking up at the poster.

"Yes," I said. Then I walked out the back door.

In spite of what I'd said to Geoff, I decided to wait until the next day to drive over to my dad's. Instead, I went back to the room that had been my office, the room in which I now slept on a futon, a guest in the house I had once thought of as mine. Better than in our old bedroom, though. I didn't know how Geoff did it.

I lay on the cool sheets staring at the ceiling, listening to the early-evening sounds that used to lull me. I wondered what they hid. The man who was after me would be back. There was no way I could hide from him. I could only keep moving.

At least I knew what he was after now. A photo of what or whom?

I phoned Daph, only half expecting her to be home.

"What, no hot date?" I asked when she answered the phone.

"Not even a cool one." I could hear music, voices.

"I'm sorry to bother you," I said. "Sounds like you have company."

"Just a few people from work. We're barbecuing. My old boyfriend's in town, and I thought I'd give him a break."

"I thought he lived in Singapore." I knew it was silly, but I felt left out, good old Temp Lady, here today, gone tomorrow.

"He's just here on business," she said. "What's going on with you? Have you and Geoffrey killed each other yet?"

"Just about," I said. "I miss you, and Chico, of course. I'm calling to see if you know how I could get in touch with Gaylene. I need to ask her something about Jeanette."

Her pause was so brief that I wouldn't have noticed it if I didn't know her so well. "Your timing couldn't be better," she said. "Gaylene's here, actually."

I didn't need to ask with whom. Still my throat tightened and made it difficult to speak. "Could I talk to her for a minute?"

Gaylene sounded breathless. I could picture her in something elegant, could see that hair, those Shangri-la-la Lilac nails.

"Did Jeanette have any important photographs?" I asked. "Something that she might have kept hidden?"

"If she hid them, I didn't know anything about it," she said. "She kept some images on her computer. The only other photos I know of are the ones she used for her paintings."

"Where did she keep them?"

"She usually stuck them on the backs of the paintings. Then, after she sold a painting, she had some kind of crazy filing system at the gallery where she kept the receipts. I think she filed the photos there, too. Why?"

"I'd like to see some of the photos," I said. "Is that possible?"

"It's okay with me, but I guess you didn't hear. There was a fire at the gallery. Everything's gone."

"No. Was anyone hurt?"

"Lucky for me, I was on a date." She paused ever so slightly. "I have great insurance. Most of the damage was in Jeanette's gallery, anyway."

"What about the paintings at your home?"

"Gone," she said, "but it's a good thing. They were all purchased, the ones that didn't burn up in the fire that is."

"You sold Jeanette's paintings?"

"It's what she would have wanted. She sure as heck wouldn't have wanted them gathering dust in my old garage. This interior decorator is going to put them to good use."

"And the money? Jeanette didn't have a family."

"I was her partner, but the money isn't my issue,"

she said in a tone that suggested it was mine. "Maybe I'll just donate it to charity."

"Let me talk to Leo," I said.

She sighed. "Hang on."

"Listen," I said the minute he answered. "I don't give a damn if you date that bimbo, but why the hell did you let her sell Jeanette's paintings?"

"What?" he said. "I didn't know. It must have just happened."

"It's what they're looking for," I said. "A photograph that may be on one of those paintings. Tell genius girl there that she's got to get them back."

I could hear Gaylene's flurry of exclamations in the background. "When?" he demanded.

"Yesterday?" Gaylene said. "To a woman. An interior designer in Washington."

Washington. "Leo," I said. "That gardener guy who tried to kidnap me from my neighbor's house said he was taking me to Washington." I felt the chill of recognition, finally seeing a nightmarish shape beginning to take form out of the mass of questions and doubts I'd been grappling with.

"I'm going there," Leo said.

"So am I."

The Widow

June knew she would die in this place. She wondered if others did that, if they finally realized it when they'd found the home they'd never leave. Rem had loved it, too, and she was glad they'd moved here for the last years of his life. She could still catch a trace of his scent in the air now and again, or perhaps it was only her imagination. Either way, she felt his presence more than not, and she didn't feel alone here. She knew that he was with her, and that she must do what he would want her to, whatever the cost.

She had scheduled the appointment early in the morning, because she didn't want to walk around with it in her mind all day. The sun on her face calmed her, reminding her that Rem was not that far away.

She smelled the unmistakable sachet scent before Darla joined her on the balcony. "Sit down." She nodded at the chair across from hers. No movement, then hesitant steps.

"I did as you asked," Darla said, standing before her. "Seventeen paintings. The only other ones I could trace are in a hotel in Las Vegas. If you're interested, I can contact them on your behalf."

"Sit, please. Tell me when I can have them."

"Tomorrow. I'll unpack them in the morning." The chair legs scraped the balcony as Darla sat. "But it's not that simple."

June caught her breath, poised on the edge of her chair. She had to be strong. "Whatever do you mean?"

The chair legs scratched again, closer to her. "We need to talk," Darla said.

Twenty-Nine

Reebie

My dad had never tried to pressure me about how much time I did or didn't spend with him, which had been not much since Geoff and I had split nine months ago. He'd never tried to make me feel guilty about either my mother's desertion of us or my responsibilities as an only child, so I'm not sure why I shouldered the burden of both.

The front of the house was hidden by lavender growing wild in untamed clumps. I could never smell it without thinking of him. I drove up the hill to his house, wishing I didn't have to do this, but unable to leave before trying to assuage the concerns Geoff had created.

A sign I didn't remember announced Mahoney's Greens and displayed the stylized leaf logo familiar to anyone who buys fresh herbs at the supermarket.

Not bad for an old pot farmer with a degree from Davis. I found him out on his knees, harvesting basil. He jumped up, and in his sturdy hug, I inhaled the licorice scent of herbs.

If I'd gotten to pick a father for myself, he would have come pretty close. I would have made the reddish beard a little shorter with less gray in it. But I liked his blue eyes, his brogue, barely discernable until the second Guinness. Growing up as a weird kid with no mom, I was pleased that he didn't dress in the three-piece monkey suits like the dads of my friends, yet was always the one to pick up the tab, to treat us to weekends in Mendocino and San Francisco. I wasn't ever going to be able to pass myself off as a run-of-the-mill kid from a run-of-the-mill family, so to have a father who made being different admirable, maybe even enviable, got me through childhood with a minimum of scars.

I could see that although he was still muscular, he'd gotten more barrel-chested and red faced in the past three months, and I wondered if he was hitting the Guinness too hard. I hoped my divorce wasn't the reason.

"It's so good to see you," he said. "You're too skinny, of course. Let's go to the house, and I'll fix you something to eat, while you tell me what's happening."

"I'm not going to be here that long," I said. "I'm flying to Washington today."

"Reeb." He put his arm around my shoulder. "Geoff told me what's been going on."

"As usual, he's going for the drama," I said. "He's

just trying to make you think that the only safe place for me is here."

I tried to shake off his arm, but he gripped me tighter. "It's true I don't know much about what's happened to you since you guys split, and I want to hear it from you, not Geoff. Come on. Sit down and tell me."

He returned to the basil, and I settled on the wooden bench. "He told you about Jeanette?" I asked.

"He said someone was trying to kill you." He searched my face for a response.

"If they wanted to kill me, I'd be dead," I told him. "They think Jeanette gave me something, a photograph of some kind. She's supposed to have had an affair with President Remington, so maybe it's a photo of them. They can't kill me because they're not sure what I did with it. The problem, of course, is that I don't have the photo."

"Do you know where it is?" he asked.

"Maybe," I said. "That's why I'm going to Washington."

"Geoff seems to think you'd be safer here."

"Geoff just wants me back."

"And you?" he asked. "What do you want?"

I couldn't lie to those eyes. "I don't know. But I can't go through any more of those shouting matches."

He nodded. "I can relate to that."

He'd been honest with me about the problems he'd had with my mother. I didn't feel like going through them again. But he was already on a roll.

"We fought like cats and dogs. When you were born, it was better, then I'd do something that would piss her off. She'd say something that pissed me off. But bottom line, we loved the hell out of each other. Maybe you and Geoff—maybe it will calm down."

"You'd better believe it," I said. "We're divorced. And we're going to stay that way. He proved the kind of person he was when he wouldn't let me have even part of the winery. It was his legal right, but not his moral right, and he knew it."

"He did that only because he wanted you to come back." He got up and sat beside me on the bench. "He knew how much you loved the winery, and he hoped you'd stay for it. I think he's still hoping."

"But how could I ever trust him?" I asked.

He put his arm around me. "I don't have any answers, baby. I do think this is a safe place for you right now."

"I'm not going to be safe anyplace until they find out who killed Jeanette Sheldon," I said. "I just wanted to see you before I left. I'm sorry I haven't come sooner. It's just tough for me to be here right now."

"I know. Stay for dinner, though. Pam brought over some vegetarian tamales that will make you faint."

"I can't, Dad." I got up and dusted off my jeans. "Walk me to the car."

We crunched through the lavender field. "Fighting doesn't mean you don't love each other," he said, and I knew he wasn't talking only about Geoff and me.

"If she'd loved you," I said. "If she'd loved us…" My trembling voice made me realize how angry I still was.

"We loved the hell out of each other, Reeb. No one else has even come close."

I stopped between several clumps of lavender. "Not even Pam?"

He looked down, then at me. "She's a good woman."

"She settles for much too little from you."

"Hey, now." He tapped the air as if to soften what he heard, but I couldn't stop.

"I mean it. I'd dump you on your sorry ass. I'll bet my mother would, too."

"She already did." His eyes glistened. "She'll never come back. I know that now, but it took a lot of years."

"You're using Pam, using a woman who trusts you when you tell her you're healing. How many frigging decades can you tell her that, Dad?"

"What is it about you and trust?"

The words—too gentle, too painful—shot through me. My lip began to quiver. Shit. *Never trust a man with an Irish brogue.*

"Come here, baby." Beefy arms extended, and I caved into them, sobbing, as he patted my back, repeating, "It's all right, it's all right," like a lullabye.

The Widow

June saw fire. It was the first thing she'd seen since that night, and she saw it in detail, raging yellow flames, burning into red. David was right. She was in control now.

She leaned toward the scrape of Darla's chair and

said, "I may appear vulnerable here. We chose this place, in part, because of the need for reduced security. One word from me, however, and Secret Service personnel will join us out here."

"I'm on your side." Darla's voice sounded thinner, more strident. "I purchased the paintings, just as you asked. If you want to decorate your homes with seventeen nude abstracts by this Nora McFarland, that's your business. I do read the newspapers, though."

"As long as you're getting paid, what do you care about the newspapers?" The fire in June's brain grew brighter.

"I don't care. I do know who Nora McFarland's supposed to have been, and if that's true, I know you wouldn't hang her art in any of your homes. But I bought it for you, anyway. My concern isn't the art. It's Nicholas."

"You care about him?" June's heart ached. The flames in her head ignited her cheeks. She pressed her cool hands over them.

"He's in trouble." Darla reached out and took June's hands. "We've got to help him."

"Nita? They just got in from Europe. They're both exhausted and jet-legged."

"Worse than Nita. Is it safe to talk here?"

Was it safe? This was something June had never considered while living within these walls. "The beach would be better," she said. "I'll meet you there after dinner."

"Just you?" Darla squeezed her fingers.

"Of course. We'll talk tonight. Then, tomorrow, I want to pick up the paintings."

She stared into the blaze before her eyes. Yes, she would take care of the paintings, but she also needed to take care of her son.

The Mobster

I still run, Jeanette, early mornings like this, wind biting my face. It's what I did after my old man died, after you and I split the first time, after that night back in seventy-six. Much as I like to run alone, I asked the bastard to meet me this morning. Pisses me off to share the air with him, but here we are, this old man and that younger one, who looks so much the way I used to when I was starting out. He made a big deal about it, saying he had a plane to catch, like he was doing me a favor.

"You're in great shape, Eddie P, but not as fast as you used to be," he huffs at me as we dart through the back of my place, up toward the hills. He's trying to hide his growing gut with a tank top, but I can see more by what he's covering than by what he's revealing.

"Talk to me," I say. "What's going on since you worked for me, Phil?"

"Not much, man."

We run farther, then I stop. "I was there that night, in the hotel elevator with that chick," I say.

He screeches to a stop, Jeanette, as if someone has slammed on the brakes. "What chick?"

"Her name was Sunny Perry," I say. "Pretty girl, a little bit flirty. She and I were the only ones getting off on the top floor that night."

"I don't know any Sunny." He's ready to fly away again. I reach out for him, pull him up to my face like I'm going to kiss him, but he knows better. "Keep your ass out of this, Phil."

"My ass isn't into it," he says. "And you're breathing a little hard for such a short run, man. You sure you're okay?"

"Never felt better." I release him and take a deep breath to prove it. "Just remember where you started and leave my people alone."

"I didn't know that chick was your people," he says.

"She wasn't. Reebie Mahoney is."

He wipes his forehead and squints up at me as if I'd just given him a headache. "No one wants to hurt her, Eddie P."

"No one better *anything* her," I say. "It's an old war that goes way back before your time. No reason for you to get involved."

"I already am involved, more than I can tell you."

"You think you can get uninvolved?"

He acts like he's thinking it over, and I can tell he likes being the one with the power now. "I'd do anything for you, Eddie P. You know that."

I stare up at the sun. I'm going to miss the best part of the morning, Jeanette, and I don't have many left. "So?" I start to look at my watch to urge him on, but I realize I'm not wearing one. "It's not the money, is it?" Make him feel small. That always worked with Phil.

He shakes his head. "It's the people I'm playing with. I've come pretty far."

"I know the people," I say. "I know what they want. The girl doesn't have it. You won't be hurting them if you back off, and you'll be helping me."

He nods, claps me on the back like we're old buddies. "You really think she doesn't have it?"

"I can smell a lie. You know that."

He steps back, and a grin starts to creep across the face that used to be handsome. "And you taught me to do the same," he says. "What's wrong with you, man? Heart?"

"You wish." I know trying to explain would just make it worse. I look up at the sun, spreading too fast across the sky. "All this bullshitting is costing me the best part of the morning. That might not matter to a man your age, but I'm going to finish this run."

"My plane doesn't leave until late. Still feel like company?" Phil asks, but he's figured out he hasn't been invited here because I miss seeing him.

"No. You have some decisions to make, and you need to think about them. And you can pass along a message to your boss."

"What kind of message?"

"The son," I say.

"What son?"

The stupid bastard. "They'll know," I say.

Now, he's gone, and it's just me, the morning and the memories.

I'm terminal, Jeanette. I've been terminal all my life, and my odds of beating this, slim as they are, are a whole lot better than surviving those first crazy years. Not that I believe anything could kill me. But I swear to you, no fucked-up cancer, pardon my French, is going to take me out until I keep my promise to you.

Thirty

Reebie

I landed in Seattle about four and was picked up by one of the island people to take me across on the ferry. He had long, gray hair and a sixties brown corduroy jacket that my dad would approve of, and he told me he was a Spanish teacher and a minister. I digested all of this in silence, until it started to rain, the windshield fogged up, and I realized the reason for the squeegee on his dashboard.

The window continued to mist and fog over. The penetrating wind shooting in from below went straight to my bones.

"Are you cold?" he asked.

"Yes," I stuttered, hugging myself.

He reached down between his space and mine and handed me a thin blanket, its edges whip-stitched.

"You don't have a defroster or a heater?" I asked.

"Sorry," he said in that laid-back way of his. "I just bought the car two years ago. I'm going to get one as soon as I have time."

I'd heard Whidbey Island was relaxed, but this was ridiculous.

The rain stopped as gently and with as little warning as it had started, and we drove onto the ferry, while he gave me tour-guide talk about the island statistics—seventy miles long, people sleeping with their doors unlocked, a great place to raise kids.

"Do you know Darla Ames?" I asked, repeating the name of the woman Gaylene said had bought the paintings.

"Darla's good people," he said, doing a double take. "Are you staying at that place she built?"

"Considering it." I looked out the window at the churning water. "For a honeymoon."

In a few minutes, he dropped me off in front of one of the most striking homes I'd ever seen. My first thought was that no one who'd built a home with the kind of love that infused The Tuscan Lady would ever be able to allow anyone else to stay there, whatever the price. It looked like a puzzle piece fitted into the lush green and purple landscape, the woods beyond, the flowers dripping from every surface.

"It's a bed-and-breakfast," my charming driver said. "Costs more than my monthly salary to stay here one night."

"And has anyone stayed here?" I asked. It was too

perfect, too much a part of the larger home beside it. No, this was a baby who had not been let go yet.

"I don't know. It's way out of my price range."

I gave him more tip than I could afford and said, "Get yourself some windshield wipers." He drove away in a rush, promising to return for me in an hour. What was it about me that I was always in need of a driver? Wasn't I up to steering my own way through this life?

I don't know what I expected Darla Ames to be, but I hadn't expected her to be beautiful. The woman who stepped out through the glass doors of The Tuscan Lady was indeed beautiful. She was also small, yet as vivid as the surroundings in her violet sweater and baggy black jeans. Her short hair, almost hidden by a thick headband, was black, as well. I tried to guess her age and couldn't—forty, maybe—fifty—maybe even older.

She held a hammer with one hand, shielded her eyes with the other, then motioned for me to come forward. "It's about time you got here. I was starting to worry." Her voice was girlish and light as chiffon.

"I'm lucky I got here at all," I said. "The driver doesn't have windshield wipers or heat in that car of his."

"He's working on it," she said, "and he's a great guy. Don't you love this island?"

"What I've seen of it." In spite of my exhaustion and frozen body, I tried to fake enthusiasm. I was supposed to be a potential client, after all.

"I'm thrilled that you're interested in my Tuscan Lady. When's the wedding?"

Not even I could handle a lie that blatant. "It's my sister's wedding," I stammered. "Still a year away. We're starting early."

"A year isn't early." She looked down at the wide black band around the wrist of the hand holding the hammer. I realized it was a watch. "I have an appointment right now, but you want to see the place, right?" Few women her age could make a dimple work, but she did it. I felt bad about lying to her.

"I don't want to make you late. I could come back tomorrow."

"Don't be silly. Come on. I'm just putting on the finishing touches. She led the way in through the open glass doors of the deck.

There, leaning against the staircase, was an unframed canvas of overlapping nudes, only their lips vivid purple against the smoke that seemed to strangle them. One glance at the oddly layered faces, and I knew this was a distorted self-portrait of Jeanette Sheldon.

"Do you like it?" Darla asked, then without waiting for an answer, "I thought I'd try it in here, but it just doesn't go with the room. Too, what? Moody, I guess."

She was right. It didn't go with the room. I was almost distracted when I saw what she had created within these walls, most of them glass. I tried to take in the soaring ceilings and warm, fragrant presence, from the fireplace to the tiled kitchen, to the white willow strung with twinkling lights and reaching to the loft above. Darla watched my face with an impish grin, like a little kid trying to stifle an outburst.

"Well, what do you think?"

"I've never seen greater design in a space this size," I said. "You're very good at what you do."

"Thank you." She ducked her head. "May I show you the rest of it?"

"The painting," I began, not sure how to continue.

"The artist is Nora McFarland. Ever hear of her?"

I shook my head.

"Neither had I. But I have a client who loves her work. I picked up as many as I could. Seventeen, in all." She gave me another dimpled smile. "I haven't even unpacked them yet. Come on, let me show you around before I leave. Of course, you can stay here tonight, as my guest."

I couldn't take advantage of the offer she made only because she thought I was a potential client. "The driver's coming back for me," I said. "I'm going to get a room in Langley tonight."

"No, you're not." She moved closer to me, and I could tell that her scent was the same romantic floral one as this home's. "The house isn't ready for paying customers yet. Besides, you'll fall in love with it and tell all your friends, I know. I already put the bed warmer out for you. Please say you'll spend the night."

"I couldn't," I said. "I can't."

"But I want you to. To be honest, I can't quite give

it up yet. Having you here will help me get used to the idea."

"I had that feeling," I told her. "Maybe you should rent out that big house over there and move in here. It feels like you. It looks like you. It even smells like you."

Her embarrassed grin told me all I needed to know. "I've thought about it."

"It's so serene," I said. "There's nothing in California like it."

"The whole island's like that. You'd be surprised how many people live here," she said. "Richard Bach, who wrote *Jonathan Livingston Seagull*. June Remington and her son have homes on the other side of my complex."

I felt a fluttering in my chest. "Do you know them?"

Her expression was open, unguarded. "I know everyone on the island. We all respect each other's privacy."

The fluttering settled into an ache. It was no coincidence that President Remington's widow lived near the woman who had just purchased Jeanette's paintings.

Darla motioned with her hammer toward the ladder. "I just need to secure that birch tree," she said. "Will you hold it against the wall for me?"

So, there I was, holding the soaring white birch, while Darla perched on the ladder, hammering the tree to the beam. She'd not only bought my story, but she'd invited me to stay at her guest house. It was more than I'd hoped for, but that didn't make me feel any better about taking advantage of her.

As she took off to her meeting, I found myself becoming part of The Tuscan Lady. From no windshield wipers to this soft taupe sofa, from Squeegee Man to Darla. This had been a day of large leaps. Through the glass windows, I watched the sun drop, saw the variegated rainbows in the sky. Then I looked back into the hazy, haunted faces of the nudes. Somewhere in this home were the paintings Darla had purchased for her client.

The Mistress

Jeanette stepped back from the painting and waved away the smoke from her bundle of smoldering sage.

Sharing a secret was like handing over a burden. The sharer was lighter, the receiver heavier. She'd borne two secrets for too many years, one hers, one Rem's. The longer she lived, the more her life shrank around her, and the larger and heavier the lies became.

The phone found its way into her left hand. She knew her number would announce itself on Marcus's caller ID. Private as he was, he would always take her calls.

"Jeannette, honey. You okay?"

"Not exactly." She turned away from the painting she'd done in the wide, cold room, its high ceilings promising freedom she'd never been able to find here. "He's dead," she said.

"I know."

"Even after all this time, it hurts."

"You'll get through it. You've gotten through worse."

She hadn't called him for logic. She'd called him for comfort. "You never believed he loved me."

"Quite the contrary. I knew he did."

She bit her lip, looked up at the expansive space between her and the top of this deceptive container she called her studio. "I made a promise to him a long time ago."

"No." His response was fierce, almost angry, and she regretted causing him concern.

"Not that," she said. "He told me something, something that will eat me alive if I don't tell it. How long are you committed to a secret? Past death?"

He paused, then said, "You need to get away, honey. Why not come out, spend the summer with Deborah and me?"

The thought was so appealing that she wanted to shriek her response, but the burden she carried held her back. "What I know, I haven't even told you. I can't live with it haunting me. And, damn, I don't want to die with it."

"We'll talk when you get here," he said. "Please come tomorrow. Can you come tomorrow?"

Could she? Could Marcus and Deborah pull her back as they always did? Could she escape the bad dreams, the fear of more to come? She turned back, stared at her painting—the Scheherazade Pose—

curls of smoke hiding the face of the overlapped, double-exposed woman, everything blended to gray except those lips that seemed to say, *Speak.*

"I want you to know that I'm going to do something you won't approve of. I'm going to get in touch with Reebie Mahoney. I know where she is."

"Please don't open that can of worms."

"It's not a can of worms, Marcus. It's my conscience. I have to talk to her."

"Why? Why now?" Even his actor voice couldn't hide the fact that she was trying his patience. "That's all in the past."

"No, it's not. It's part of me, and of you." She felt the tears and didn't care. Tears for her, for Rem, for all of the lost hopes, all of the years she'd had to hide from everyone, including herself.

"You can't do it."

"I have to. It will kill me if I don't."

"It will kill you if you do," he said.

Thirty-One

The Widow

She shouldn't be out alone like this in the dark. That's what Nicholas would say, not realizing, of course, the irony of that thought. She knew every pebble, every bird cry on this beach, and she wasn't afraid. Not of the night. Not of this woman. She felt her there already, felt the waiting in the air, the expectation.

And she had the gun in her bag, not that she would use it. She carried it only to make herself feel better.

She stopped on the path, damp air, too cool for this night, chilling her hot face. *Sometimes discomfort is good for you,* Rem used to say. *Makes you stronger.*

Darla would be standing, her back to the water, about ten feet away, maybe less.

June addressed the silence. "You arrived ahead of me."

"Not by much." There was an edge to her voice that June bet she was trying to cover with a glossy little smile. "It grew cold so suddenly. Are you sure you're warm enough?"

"I'm not here by choice," she said. "I'm here, as you know, because you thought we should talk about the paintings."

"The paintings?" Darla sounded caught off guard. "I did what you hired me to do, and the rest is your business. I hope you don't destroy them, though. There's a kind of disturbing loveliness to them."

"Unfortunately, I won't be able to appreciate that," June said. She shouldn't have been so quick to mention the paintings. She needed to calm down and speak slowly in the haughty, in-charge way that had caused Rem to call her Queen June. "You have concerns about my son, as well?"

"You've got to help him." Darla's voice caught.

"I support my son's choices, even if I don't understand them," she said. "However, if you feel there's something I should know…"

"His wife abuses him," she said.

June tried to push the word away from her. *Abuse.* It was such a nasty word, and it didn't belong to this family, not to her son. "Nita can be caustic, I'll admit."

"That's not what I'm saying." Darla was strident, refusing to be quieted. "She abuses him, with words, with her fists."

"No." June tried to shut out the words. In spite of the cold, she felt her skin turn to fire. She'd wanted Nicholas to marry. She'd wanted to have a grandchild, grandchildren, a legacy for Rem and her. That was only normal. It was normal to yearn for a legacy.

"He's a sensitive, loving man." Darla lowered her voice almost to a whisper, but June could feel her moving closer. She could smell that floral scent, no longer pleasant, trying to suffocate her. Perhaps she wasn't safe, after all. She clutched the bag to her side. "A *simple* man," Darla said.

"There's nothing wrong with my son."

"No, there's not. He's charming and sweet, but he's not the eccentric genius you passed him off as, either. He's trying to play a role that isn't anything close to who he is, and it's destroying him."

No one dared to address her in such a fashion. No one. She would do anything to stop the words, the now-strident voice. She reached into the handbag, found the solid handle. "You can't talk to me like this. I won't let you."

"What about your son?" Darla blasted back. "Are you going to let her batter him? It's driving him crazy. He's starting to have the dreams again."

No, she couldn't take any more of this. She was frightened, horrified by the fiery images that danced before her. Her hand was too limp for the gun, too indecisive. "What dreams?" she asked.

"Don't lie to me," Darla said, gripping her wrist. "You know *what dreams*."

Reebie

There I was, alone in Darla's fragrant, multicolored guest house. Alone with Jeanette's paintings, at least one of them. I walked past the white birch that shot up to the loft and picked up the remote control for the fireplace.

It burst into orange light that settled into well-groomed little flames. I settled on the taupe sofa facing it, the huge Italian windows beside me, and wondered what the hell I was doing here.

Darla had to have ordered the paintings for June Remington. And what would June do with them? Or maybe Darla wasn't what she appeared. Maybe she'd ordered the paintings to have something to hold against June Remington. I needed to look at them, needed to find out what Darla knew that I didn't.

Leaving the fire was difficult. Leaving Darla's comforting colors and textures wasn't any easier. I had to find the rest of the paintings, and I knew they were here, somewhere.

I took the stairs to the loft. Elaborate screens separated three double beds and one daybed. A long closet lined one wall. I opened the sliding door, but found only an apricot-colored bathrobe that looked as if it had never been worn. I chided myself for not asking Darla where she'd left the paintings. They had to be downstairs or perhaps in the garage outside. I returned to the first floor, checking the master bedroom where I would sleep tonight. It held only a writing desk, two antique chests of drawers and a fairy-talelike bed with a billowing floral comforter. I saw a small cord leading to it, reached under the covers and found the bed warmer in a matching floral pillowcase. The bathroom held baskets of soaps and towels and a sunken tub with spa jets. Not even a closet. Perhaps they were outside. I didn't relish the possibility.

The kitchen was divided from the living room only by the beam on which we'd attached the willow branch, giving it an airy, open feeling. The dining table overlooked the curtainless glass windows facing the path to the house. The gas range looked untouched, as if it had just been installed.

On the wall opposite the windows was a rustic wrought-iron gate. Just a couple of feet behind it, someone had painted a mural. A trompe l'oeil niche held a pot of dangling ivy so real-looking that it took me a moment to realize it was the result of skillful faux finishing that created the illusion of three-dimensional space. I almost turned away, but stepped inside the gate, anyway. To my left, a long, narrow pantry ran the length of the bedroom. Leave it to Darla to figure out a clever way to hide her storage space. The shelves held only a package of herb tea and an eight-pack of bottled water.

On the other side were Darla's tools—screwdrivers, saws, a yardstick. Farther inside, three large packages leaned against the shelves. My breathing quickened. I went inside, grabbed the first one and dragged it closer to the light cast from the bulb above the painted-on niche. The return address was Gaylene's.

These had to be the paintings. I stumbled over the box and hurried into the kitchen, where Darla had left her hammer. With the claw end, I pried open the cardboard, dizzy and shaking. I dragged out three large paintings and two smaller ones, all unframed. Then, uncertain what to do next, I leaned them against the shelves of the pantry. In the dim light, the faces seemed twisted, the vivid mouths frozen into screams. Jeanette was a haunted woman; she had to have been.

I leaned the first one forward and felt behind it. My fingers connected to something slick. I tugged hard. It came free, and I was holding an envelope. Inside were photographs of the model, nude in varying poses, smoking a cigarette. Jeanette must have blown up the photos and painted over them, coloring in the lips. I didn't know enough about art to know if they were good, but I did know that they evoked an emotion—terror.

Each painting had a similar envelope on its backside, but I couldn't understand the meaning. They were all women I'd never seen before, nude and posing in stark dread in a room of smoke. The Scheherazade Pose.

With the help of the hammer, I removed the casing from the second box and pulled out more paintings, placing them over the first ones. One appeared to be a self-portrait and, like the others, had an envelope of photographs attached.

The second one was different. At first I thought it was her usual double-exposure technique, but these were different faces overlapped, expressions so tortured I could almost hear the cries of anguish. Yet, their lips were twisted into smiles. This was the most terrifying of the lot.

I tilted it forward, toward me, feeling for an envelope, glad I didn't have to look at it another moment. The envelope wasn't in the upper corner as the others had been. I turned the painting over. Nothing. There was no envelope, no photograph. Nothing.

I couldn't calm my racing heart. Someone had removed the photograph for this painting. Or there had never been one. I leaned it back against the shelf, crouching in front of it, gazing eye-to-eye into the tormented faces. Then, I realized. I was not staring into the eyes of women as with the other paintings. No, the subjects of this one were men.

Still crouching, I began to tremble, knowing I was beginning to uncover the reason for Jeanette's murder. This was not the double exposure of a single model. It was five, no six, different men, overlapping in what seemed like a never-ending circular pattern. Around their necks were loops of rope or crudely shaped necklaces—I wasn't sure which.

The light dimmed. I looked up with a jerk. On the other side of the gate, a large shape blocked out the glow from the lamp in the kitchen. I held my breath.

Someone waited just outside. My mind raced with possible ways of escape, and I fought the urge to scream. Maybe he didn't know I was here. And it was a he; the figure loomed larger, moving closer. He seemed to pause, then the gate began to swing slowly outward.

I pressed myself flat against the wall and grabbed the only weapon I had—the hammer.

The Widow

She hadn't been able to answer, couldn't face the truth of Darla's words. A roar like that of a storm filled her ears. She reached out to support herself on Darla's arm. There was no longer anywhere to hide. "You're right," she said. "I know the dreams. I just don't know what they mean."

She wanted to cry, wanted to hide, but it was too late. Darla knew what she hadn't wanted to know, and now they must talk if they were to help Nicholas.

"Has he told you about it?" Darla asked.

She shook her head. "Not directly, but on more than one occasion when he slept, I heard him cry out." It was almost a relief to be able to speak those horrifying words.

From far away, she heard the steady pattern of footsteps along the path, something a person who could see probably wouldn't pick up.

"Someone's coming," she told Darla.

"Are you sure?"

"Yes, on the path. Please, tell me what you see."
She reached for her bag again.

"No one," Darla said, at first. Then, in a low voice.
"My God, you're right. It's Nita."

Thirty-Two

The Mistress

"Look at you, all haunchy and naked." From where Jeanette lay on the chaise, her head resting on Eddie's ankles, the lines of his body were as taut as they had been thirty-five years before.

"Kind of surprised myself." He reached down and patted her flank. "And in your gallery. After everything I've gotten away with in this screwed-up life of mine, it would serve me right to get arrested for something like outraging the public decency."

"Not in California," she said. From her vantage point, she could see only her paintings, images she'd made peace with, the way you make your peace with a recurring nightmare, images she'd have to live with until she died. She squeezed his hand. "Maybe it's wrong. I mean, he just died this morning."

"And I know you're hurting. But this isn't wrong. It's never been wrong with us."

"I love you, Eddie."

"I love you, too. There was never anyone like you."

"Well, I do recall a certain fluff-ball actress who gave me a run for my money."

He chuckled, shifted his body around, so that they were head to head, with him behind her. "She was a sweet girl, but she wasn't Jeanette Sheldon." He kissed the back of her neck. "Not even close."

"I'm an old lady, Eddie."

"No way."

This was the time to say it, with his warm breath on the back of her neck, his arms around her. "I talked to Marcus this morning."

"I know. He called me."

Damn Marcus. Didn't he know Eddie would tell her? "Did he tell you what I'm going to do?" she asked.

"Yeah, and I'm not sure how smart it is. Why drag the kid into it?"

"Because she has a right to know."

He shifted again and pulled her up, so that they were side to side on the chaise, paintings staring at them from every direction.

"Suddenly, I feel naked," she said, then stood and bent down to retrieve her clothes. He reached out for her arm and pulled her next to him, as if she were on a leash.

"Question. Why tell the kid anything?"

"I already told you that. Put yourself in her place. Wouldn't you wonder?"

"So, are you the Red Cross? If you tell her who you are, they'll know you're still alive. And what would happen next? Remember the last time?"

She'd never forget that night—the fear, the blood, the long, terrifying days after. Eddie was trying to remind her of the price tag for contacting Reebie. She pressed her cheek against his chest. "I don't know what I'd do without you."

He wrapped his arms around her, pressed his face into her hair. "We had a good thing once. We still do. I know you loved Rem more, but I got over that a long time ago."

"I didn't love him more, just different." She felt the heat surge to her cheeks and was glad he couldn't see her face.

He chuckled into her hair. "Doesn't matter, babe. He screwed up, and I'm the one who got to keep you."

"You've been good to me, Eddie."

"I'm the one who got to keep you," he repeated, pulling her to him. "Don't talk to that little girl. Let's just do what we've been doing. You painting. Us spending time together, going to see Marcus and Deborah. And when I get real lucky, making love in a frigging high-class art gallery."

"A frigging high-class art gallery that you pay for," she said.

"Why the hell not? I pay for two ex-wives and their fucked-up lifestyles, pardon my French. I pay for one cokehead daughter who's so screwed up she doesn't even know who I am most of the time."

"And you pay for me."

He pressed his lips onto her shoulder. "I'd marry you if I could. Right this minute."

The words broke her heart. That's what she should have done all those years ago—married Ed Palacios instead of throwing herself into that crazy, no-win, head-over-heels thing with Rem.

"You're thinking about him, aren't you?"

"Only how stupid I was to do it. Only that."

"I always kind of blamed myself. We'd been fighting a lot."

She laughed. "Over said fluff-ball actress, as I recall. It probably would have happened, anyway."

"No, it wouldn't have, because if I hadn't been fluff-balling it, you wouldn't have been out there driving a golf cart in nothing but a bikini that day, and you wouldn't have had a chance to meet him."

"We would have met, one way or the other." She stood up, naked as the nudes that lined this room. "You know I've always told you everything. But there's something I haven't dared to talk about with you or Marcus, something I have to tell you now."

"About him?" he asked.

She couldn't look at him. She just needed to say it. "About something he did. I swore to keep it secret, but now that he's gone, I can't keep it to myself anymore."

He got up and took both of her hands in his. "Sounds serious."

"A nightmare, literally." She closed her eyes, still remembering every moment of that night after they'd drunk too much champagne and passed out in her bed, Secret Service men on guard outside. She could still hear the moaning in his sleep, still feel his clammy, wet skin when she wakened him. Remembered how they sat on the bed, partially asleep, partially awake, her arms wrapped around him as he told her.

"It's okay, baby." Ed led her back to the sofa and settled her silk jacket over her shoulders, but she was no longer cold. "He had an old negative," she said. "I wouldn't believe it if I hadn't seen it for myself. I told him he had to get rid of it, that it was too damning. Then I took it in my darkroom, said I was burning it, but I couldn't do it. I burned another negative instead. Later, I told him the truth."

What had she been thinking? That it would get him back? That it would force him into a commitment? "I was the only person he ever told," she said. "Not even June. I know he loved me."

"Jeanette." His voice was low and soft as one of his love songs. "He tried to have you killed while you were carrying his child. What kind of monster would do that?"

"I should have known." She couldn't fight the tears any longer, could no longer hold on to her belief in Rem. "He was a murderer."

"I know," he whispered. "Because of him, Kim is dead."

"That's not what I'm talking about." She looked up at him. Through her tears, his face blurred like an image in one of her paintings. "Michael Remington was a murderer, Eddie, a cold-blooded killer."

The Widow

"So what, pray tell, have I interrupted here?" Nita's demand faded into the wind, and June could pick up a slur. She couldn't be drinking, not pregnant.

"Welcome back," Darla said. "Where's Nicholas?"

"That's what I'd like to know. You're the two women he loves the most. And you just happen to be together out here. Don't tell me he hasn't come whining to you." Yes, it was a definite slur.

June's throat tightened. She reached for Darla's arm again. "Whatever's happened?" she asked, trying to stay calm. "I didn't want to disturb you while you were sleeping off your jet lag."

"We weren't sleeping," Nita said. "We had a disagreement, actually, and it kind of got out of control."

Darla sucked in her breath. "What have you done to him?"

"He's my husband. I can do whatever I want."

"No, you can't." June's shawl slipped from her shoulders, and she didn't bother to retrieve it. The cold pierced her skin, but she saw only consuming flames again. "I've tried to pretend that I didn't know what was going on, but I cannot any longer. I'm holding you accountable for your actions. I demand that you tell me what you've done to my son."

"Cut your fake First Lady crap." Her voice grew closer, more blatant, and June could smell the sour alcohol on it. "I know your family secrets, and it's going to take a lot for me to keep my mouth shut." She laughed. "There's a good-looking California newspaper reporter asking questions around the island."

"That's true," Darla said. "A Leo somebody. He was by this morning. I refused to talk to him."

"Well, I just might. I have his number. What do you think an exclusive interview with me would be worth?"

"Don't listen to her." Darla squeezed June's arm. "Nicholas is probably at my house. That's where he comes when he's afraid."

Oh, God. Her own son couldn't come to her, couldn't trust her. She moved toward Nita, tried one last appeal. "How could you do this to our family? We're your family, too, now, and your baby's. If you ruin us, what will your child have left?"

"What child?" The words blew into June's face on the cold, pungent wind, washed over her in harsh waves.

"You bitch," Darla whispered. "Is that what you fought with Nicholas about?"

"One of the things. Women have been faking pregnancy for years to get what they want. Only once I got it, I realized I couldn't stand looking at the poor, pathetic bastard. And on this little European trip you were so kind as to finance, I got enough information out of him to realize there was a better way."

June couldn't speak. The one reason she'd tolerated this woman, the only reason she'd allowed Nicholas to suffer—and it had all been a lie. She thought about the gun in her purse. Only that would burn the smug, spiteful voice from her mind. Did she really have the courage to use it on herself? To put it to her own head and pull the trigger? And if she did, what would happen to Nicholas?

No. She had to do what she'd refused to do her entire life. She had to face the truth, whatever that was. She squeezed Darla's hand, too weak to trust her senses to find her way back. "Let's go," she said. "We've got to find my son."

"What about me?" Nita stumbled behind them, her voice trailing into a whine. "I meant what I said. I'll talk to that reporter. I'll tell him everything."

June whirled in the direction of her voice. "If you've hurt my son, I'll have you arrested. That's how much I care about that reporter."

"Oh, really?" As June turned away, she heard the electronic dialing of a cell phone. She couldn't care anymore. She had to walk through this unending cold night, to Darla's. She had to help her son.

"Mr. Kersikovski?" Nita enunciated carefully into the phone, keeping up with them as she spoke. "I'm

Nita Remington, soon-to-be ex-wife of Nicholas Remington."

"Good riddance," Darla whispered to June. "Be glad he's free of her."

"The reason?" Nita's voice rose. "That's why I'm calling you. You know that Jeanette Sheldon, President Remington's old girlfriend, the one who was murdered?"

June stopped with a shudder, unable to take another step.

"No," Darla said with a moan.

"Do I know who killed her?" Nita chimed out in a singsong rhythm. "Of course, I do. I'm married to him."

June's knees buckled. She sank to them, shaking her head, shaking out the noises. But still Nita's malicious little-girl voice persisted. "That's right. My husband, Nicholas, murdered Jeanette Sheldon. He told me all about it."

Thirty-Three

Reebie

The man stepped into the pantry, stopping before the faux niche, as if wondering, as I had not long before, if that's all there was to this part of the house. Pressed against the shelves, gripping the hammer, I could see his lower profile—his muscular left leg, and his arm with its long-sleeved white shirt and cuff links that caught even this dim light. Ed Palacios.

He stepped into view and stopped. It was as if he sensed me before he saw me. "Just what I thought," he said. "Do you even know what you're looking for?"

"No." I grasped the hammer tighter, and out of nowhere, I remembered my struggle with the man posing as Jeanette's doorman. I'd had one chance then, and I'd have one chance now, if I were lucky enough to get that.

"Maybe I can help." He moved neither forward

nor back, speaking in the love-song voice, trying to coax me out. "I know what it is," he said. "And I think it's here."

"I don't want any part of this. I never did."

"I know that." Soft and slow, he almost sang the words, trying to lull me into trusting him.

The air in the pantry felt heavy with the cardboard packages. I strained to breathe. "Then why did she call me? Why did she have to take that photograph of me?"

"She took the photo for a damn good reason." As if propelled by his own anger, he sailed forward, grabbed me by the arm and jerked me to my feet. He looked down at my makeshift weapon, then shook his head with a dry laugh that bore no resemblance to the real thing. "A hammer? Do you have any idea who you're dealing with, missy?"

I tried to answer, tried to scream, to jerk away.

Without a sound, the house went dead and dark— not just the lights—everything, the way the power goes in a storm, so suddenly that the silence itself is like an explosion. Palacios dropped my arm.

"Son of a bitch."

I swung the hammer in the direction of his voice, smashing it, with all of my force into solid, screaming flesh.

Nicholas

White roses. That's the surprise she'd promised him. While he and Nita had been gone, her rosebushes had bloomed, all twenty or so of them, pure white. He sat on the stone bench. He knew already how she'd look here, with her hair the color of the eggplant she grew and those white petals shining silver even in this little bit of light.

He touched his hand to his face. The pain came in waves now. He was used to Nita losing her temper, but this was the first time she'd hit him with her shoe. It was the rest of it, though, what she said about the baby, that made him know he had to run.

He could run away from Nita, but not the dreams. He didn't even have to be asleep anymore. They were with him all the time.

His twenty-first birthday, and he'd been out with his buddies way past last call at an after-hours place, right before Christmas. Topless dancers, bubble-gum-smelling disinfectant in the restroom, a jukebox that could waltz across Texas. Backslaps. Buddies. Girls kissing him. Picking up the tab, trying to order coffee, the words coming out, "C-C-C-Coors."

They'd taken their guns, just for fun. They shot them into hay barrels, and yeah, a couple of tires, but the cars were parked at curbs, not moving or anything.

His mother approved of his friends because they were from good families, like theirs. She hadn't paid that much attention to his friends or anything at home after the car accident that made her blind. Then, his friends went back to their good families, leaving him so drunk he couldn't find his ass with both hands.

* * *

Can't let anybody see him. Can't let anybody know. His dad can be mean, really mean, president or not, if he screws up. Coming home drunk is a screwup. If a newspaper printed the story, it would shame the family.

He sees the sofa in his father's office, black leather, the TV on, some doctor show. No one will find him here, huddling on the cool floor, praying he won't puke. No one will hurt him.

"What the hell is that supposed to mean?"

His father. Shit. At first, he thinks he's caught. He puts his hand over his face, just in case.

He hears a clicking, like dice in a cup, then Uncle David's voice. "I learned it from the Buddhists. They just shift possessions from one hand to the other like this to remind themselves to never be attached to anything. You might want to give it a try, Rem. It can be damned freeing."

"Spare me fucking Buddhism." Ice rattles in a glass. His father's voice sounds as wet as Nicholas's was earlier. "I don't care what you say or how many car keys you jiggle from hand to hand," he said. "I'm not going to allow anyone to harm Jeanette. I'm in love with her."

The clicking continues, like a clock, or like that thing by his mother's piano, that metronome that counts off the time.

"What about June? What about Nicholas? What about the fucking history books?"

"Stop it."

Even in this safe hidey-hole, Nicholas cringes and tries to pull his knees up to keep his father's anger away. Jeanette Sheldon. That must be who they mean, that beautiful blond lady who's been nice to him at parties.

"It's already scheduled, Rem," Uncle David says. "She's going to a Christmas party with that fag Marcus Olson and a couple of loose wannabe actresses he's collected. She's at his place on Sherman Drive. If we don't act now, it will be too late."

More ice. More anger. "I'm going there, too," his dad says. "No one is going to hurt Jeanette. I mean that. No one is going to hurt my woman, and no one is going to take my child from me."

He's calling someone else his woman, calling someone else his child.

"Settle down, Rem." The sound reminds Nicholas of how it felt when his buddies slapped him on the back when he picked up their tab. A slap is almost always false, he thinks. It's pain pretending to be friendly.

"Besides, that's not the real reason you're so worried about her, is it?" his dad says, lowering his voice.

"What the hell are you talking about, Rem?"

"You know what I told her, but she swore to me that she destroyed the negative. Chas Sullivan in the psych ward is the only one left. Chas is incapable of telling what happened, or even remembering. I know. I checked him out."

"So did I," Uncle David says. "Jeanette is the only problem. She could bring you down, my friend."

"She doesn't want to. It's the last thing she wants."

"She could do it, anyway."

"I had to tell someone, had to show someone, and I trust her."

"You trust her with history, Rem? With how you'll be remembered? Are you that fucking stupid?"

"That's about enough." He hasn't heard his father use that gruff voice very often, and never on him. He's glad of that. "I'm not proud of what happened, but it's behind me, and I've served my country well since then."

"And I've served you well." He can tell by the way he says it that Uncle David doesn't like his father's gruff voice, either.

"You have," his dad says. "You're a fine adviser. Let's never discuss this subject again."

"You're going to let her have the child, in spite of the risk? You're going to jeopardize your whole family?"

"I said never again. The conversation is over."

"You're the boss, Mr. President," Uncle David says.

"Yes, I am."

"Sleep well, then."

Don't go, Uncle David. Make him stop that woman. But no. The door clicks shut. His father rattles more

ice in a glass and says something soft and whispered
under his breath that sounds like swearwords.

Tears fill Nicholas's eyes. He no longer feels sick.
He no longer feels drunk. After a while his dad
leaves the room, and Nicholas is alone with the darkness and his own breathing.

Arms enfolded him. "Thank goodness you're
okay." Yes, it really was Darla, holding him, tears
wet on his forehead. "What did she do to you?
There's a gash on your face."

"A shoe," he said, "but it's okay."

"It is not okay." His mother's voice. He got up
from the bench, turned away from the rosebushes.
"What are you doing here?"

"Looking for you," Darla said. "We saw Nita on
the beach. She was terrible."

"She lied about the baby." He felt too bad to say
more.

"We'll fix it," his mother said. "You don't have
to go on living like that."

"I killed her," he said.

His mother gulped as if she'd just taken a big
drink of water. Her eyes always made him nervous,
anyway, but he could never look away, not then and
for sure not now. They blazed, even in the dim light.

"Of course you didn't kill anyone," Darla said.
She touched his head where it hurt. "Let me fix this
for you."

"I killed her," he said again, "and it's not something I made up. I never touched a gun after that."

"What are you talking about?" His mother's eyes burned through him. "Whom do you think you killed, Nicholas?"

"Jeanette Sheldon." He looked down at the black ground, then up at his mother. "She and her baby were going to destroy our family."

He let Darla hold him and listened to his mother's sobbing, knowing he was the reason.

"Nita's not going to hurt you anymore," Darla said.

"But I killed her. It was my fault she died."

"We'll work that out later. For now, just calm down."

Before he could explain that he'd never been calm, just quiet—before he could say anything, Darla's house went dark.

"The house," his mother shouted. "Who's in there?"

"Only a client in the guest house," Darla said.

Then, before she could say anything else, Nicholas heard the crashing of glass, followed by a sound he knew too well, the sound of a gun being fired.

Thirty-Four

Reebie

Eddie Palacios dove into the darkness. I stayed, breathing in short, labored gasps, still holding the hammer. I didn't dare touch the head of it, afraid of what I'd feel if I did.

"Reebie? Where are you, Reebie?" A new voice, one I didn't know. "It's okay now."

I wanted to call out, to ask if this new person in the house was a cop, an associate of Kersikovski's, maybe. But cops and reporters don't shut off the lights before they question you.

"Stay where you are, Reebie." Palacios sounded as if someone had tried to strangle him, his voice a raspy imitation of the one that had tried to soothe me into trust moments before.

"He's a mobster, Reebie. He wants you dead."

"Fucking liar."

Glass crashed from somewhere nearby, and then a gun fired. Only silence followed. Although I'd first thought this narrow pantry was dark, I now knew that I would be easy to spot to anyone who stepped through the door. Of course, Palacios knew where I was, but he couldn't get back here as long as the other man was in the house.

"Reebie, are you still there?" The new voice again. No answer from me.

"Ed Palacios has never severed his mob connections. He's the one who fired that shot, although he wouldn't admit it to you."

"Hell, yes, I'll admit it." Palacios shouted. "I'll kill you before this is over, you rotten bastard."

"The way you threatened to kill the president's son? He threatened Nicholas Remington's life, Reebie. Did he tell you that when he was trying to come across like the respectable philanthropist?"

"Yeah, I threatened the kid. I was trying to protect you." Palacios was getting back his voice. I fought to keep from screaming. "Don't believe him. I know you, Reebie. I knew your mother. You look just like her."

A second gun blast followed his words, but all I heard was *your mother.*

The Widow

This was the end, the end of all of the secrets. Her only regret was how she had pushed Nicholas away.

How could she have just cut her baby adrift so that she could devote herself to protecting Rem's image?

A second shot was followed by the sound of breaking glass.

"God, no," Darla cried. "What are they doing to my home?"

"We can't go."

"But they'll destroy my guest house, all of that work."

"They could destroy us if we do."

"You stay here. I'm going."

"No way, Darla." Nicholas sounded stronger, calmer than before. "I'm the one who has to go, and that's it. Mother can't see, and you need to be here with her."

"You can't go without a gun," Darla said. "You shouldn't go at all."

"I'll go with a gun. I carry it for protection, like you do, Mother." He touched June. With a start, she felt his cold hands on her hot cheeks. "I could shoot once, and I haven't forgotten how," he said. "Where's yours? In your bag again?"

Again? "How did you know?"

"You don't have to be a genius to figure out if your mother carries a gun. My dad did, too, even when he played golf."

She wanted to tell him that sometimes the Secret Service isn't enough, wanted to try to explain the fear that creeps into even the most protected rooms after about three in the morning, when every thought is a

regret, and every noise a threat, a potential punishment.

She squeezed his hand and tried to picture his face,
the way he must look now, but she saw only her once
twenty-one-year-old son, the challenge in his eyes.
"Nita called a reporter who's probably contacted the
police," she said. "Please wait just a little longer."

"Yes." She felt Darla move from her to him. "Wait,
baby. I care about you. We can still make this all right."

He stood facing both of them, and June felt his
scrutiny as much as his presence. Even though she
could not see him, she turned away.

"I can't wait," he said in a voice she barely recognized. "I can't."

Reebie

Your mother.

I couldn't think beyond the words, couldn't react
to the shots. *What about my mother?* That's what I
should cry out, but maybe he hadn't known my
mother, at all. Maybe this was just a trick to bring
me out in the open, where I would be an easier target for whomever of the two wanted to kill me.

"She was a class-act lady, Reebie, and loyal. Not
even Nicholas Remington knows the truth about what
happened, and he's the one who pulled the trigger."

"You're the one who pulled the trigger," the other
man said, speaking with so much certainty that his
modulated voice might as well have been shouting.

"You were obsessed with her. You couldn't believe Jeanette would dump a full-time thing with the illustrious Eddie P for a part-time fling with the president. When she confided to you that she was pregnant, you made the one desperate act that's as natural for people like you as breathing. You tried to kill her. You just got the wrong person."

I cringed, expecting another shot from Eddie P's gun.

Instead, only itchy silence.

I glanced over at the shelf I'd memorized by now. The small, pointed saw grinned up at me. Was this what fear did to people? Did it get you considering whether you'd like to ram into your enemies with a saw, a hammer, an ice pick, perhaps? I gingerly put down the hammer, picked up the saw, ran its sharp little teeth along my finger.

"Reebie." Palacios again, his voice coming from somewhere closer. He'd worked his away around the living room and returned to the kitchen, dangerously close to my hiding place. "They think you're Jeanette's daughter. They're convinced that's the reason she contacted you, why she wanted you protected, and why she told you the other stuff."

But she didn't tell me anything.

For one moment, I wondered—could I be Jeanette Sheldon's daughter? The love child from the brief union of Jeanette Sheldon and President Michael Remington? No. It couldn't be. I had photographs of my mother, a few early memories. I looked like her, not Jeanette. I knew who my mother was. I just didn't know why she'd deserted me.

"They thought they shot Jeanette, but it was Kim, your mother, who was killed. We let them think Jeanette was dead. It was the only way." His voice came closer. Why was he coming back here if he didn't want to hurt me, if he was telling the truth about my mother? I inched farther down the length of the pantry past one still-unwrapped package of paintings.

At the back of the pantry was a faint rectangle of light I hadn't noticed before. With a jolt of hope, I realized that it might be a door. I stumbled to it, felt with my hands.

"Jeanette couldn't live with the guilt," Palacios continued. "She wanted you to know the truth. That's what got her killed. They knew she was coming forward, and they were afraid she'd give you the tools to destroy them."

I gripped a knob. Oh, yes, it was a door and a simple dead bolt. I flipped the lock with a snap, threw open the door and ran into the night.

I didn't slow down or look behind me. The woods beyond Darla's house looked black and impenetrable. Still I dashed in, breathing the scent of the trees and the night, biting back the scream that had been lodged into my throat. I couldn't trust either of these men, not Palacios, not the stranger. I couldn't even trust what Palacios said about my mother. My lip quivered. I hadn't realized how much it still bothered me, how I'd lived with the wound of desertion still raw beneath the surface of my life.

The trees were so close together I could barely get between them. I wasn't sure how I'd find my way back. This little saw was not going to be much help. I heard a scraping noise, then flattened myself against the tree. A deer, bounding into the woods. I wondered what other creatures this darkness held. Whatever they were, being out here with them was better than being closed in the narrow pantry with Palacios and the stranger trying to talk me out.

I tried to get my bearings. I had run in a straight line, at least I thought I had. If I could retrace my steps, I could still remain hidden, but be close enough to hear what was going on. I began to work my way back, but the trees overlapped, like the figures in Jeanette Sheldon's paintings. I began to slow down. I was lost.

My flesh prickled. This was no time to panic. I hadn't come that far. I could find my way back, if I just moved slowly and stayed in control of my emotions. Don't think about the men in the house. Don't think about my mother.

A second branch cracked, to my right, this time. Another deer, that was all, but I couldn't see anything in the blackness. Another crack. The prickle turned to a shudder. I looked frantically for a hiding place. The tree behind me was wide enough.

"Don't move." The voice was surprisingly close. It came from the tree. Someone had circled behind me, someone who knew these woods.

I couldn't run now. It was too late. "Who are you?" I asked.

A man stepped out from behind the tree. He held a gun pointed at me.

"Tell me the truth," he said. "Are you Jeanette Sheldon's daughter?"

Thirty-Five

The Widow

Nicholas left them there together, Darla's arm around June. She'd never seen him like this, not even that one night. Nita had pushed him too far, how far she wasn't sure.

"He couldn't hurt anyone," June said.

Darla was silent. The cold wind grew harsher. June's flesh felt as it were frozen to her bones, and she wondered if she could take another step.

"Are we safe out here? Should we go in? Should I call someone?"

"No one can see us. We're bordered by woods," Darla said. "I'm worried about Reebie, though."

"Reebie?" The word hit her with such a jolt that June's hand flew to her chest. "Reebie Mahoney?"

"Yes, of course."

"What's going on? What's she doing here?"

"She's a client. I invited her to spend the night."

June backed away, holding her handbag close to her quaking body. Was Darla involved in this, as well? "You really don't know who she is?" A second thought hit her. "What about the paintings? Are they in there, as well?"

"Of course they are. What does that have to do with anything?"

"Did she see them?" She was shaking now. At one time she had only wanted to talk to Reebie, to question her about her mother, see if she could discern the truth she dreaded most. But once Ed Palacios had threatened Nicholas's life, she agreed with David that they were best leaving Reebie alone and simply destroying as many of Jeanette's paintings as they could.

Darla didn't answer.

"I asked you if she saw the paintings."

"Yes, she saw them, or one of them. But that's not our problem right now. Can you stay here by yourself?"

She still no longer trusted Darla completely. "Why?"

"Because a vehicle has just pulled into my back driveway. Two people are getting out, and—oh, my God, it's Nita. Nita and some man."

"Do you recognize him?" she asked. At this moment when she needed vision most, she cursed her lack of it.

"The same guy who came by the morning. The newspaper reporter. He's driving an old VW bus."

"What's Nita done now?"

"I'm going to find out." Darla rushed away from June in the direction of her home. "Hey, you guys, over here. And be careful. Someone's been shooting up a storm in there."

The Mistress

The doorbell. Reebie was right on time. Jeanette checked her face in the mirror. What would Reebie say when she heard the truth? She could handle it. Jeanette had figured that out after the day at the cosmetics counter.

Reebie was a tough little chick, just like her mother. She could take the truth that had been waiting all these years to be told. And the rest of it?

Why?

What good could it possibly do?

Jeanette looked down at the diamond Rem had given her—on her right hand now, only because she knew Eddie wanted one of his rings on her left.

She wasn't sure at first how she'd feel about the secret after Rem was gone, but she knew now. The love was what lasted, the loyalty. Rem's secret might haunt her the rest of her life, but it would die with her.

She got to the door before that god-awful doorbell Eddie had bought for her stopped chiming.

But it wasn't Reebie waiting on the other side of

the door. It was him. Before she could reason, he'd
pushed his way inside and pressed the door shut,
leaning against it in his too-tight gray suit. God, he'd
been handsome once. Now, he looked like a carica-
ture of himself.

"I'm expecting visitors," she said.

"You don't really think I believe that, do you? You
have no social life. You can't even live under your
own name."

"How long have you known where I live?" She
took a couple of steps back. She'd always been able
to calm him. Rem had taught her how. He was all
bluster, all confrontation, but like a true bully, easy to
back down. "Has that been your job since the White
House? Checking up on me, maybe, hoping you could
catch me coming out of the shower all wet and naked?"

"You were always a tramp, Jeanette."

The words stung, until she remembered who was
speaking them. "Not everyone would agree with
that. Rem wouldn't."

"Rem was a fool when it came to you." He
stomped away from the door as she had hoped. She
could run past him in a moment, have the doorman
call the police. If it got ugly, so be it.

"I might say the same about you, David."

"I served Rem well. I'm still serving him." He
glanced up at the paintings, his eyes wide and
expressionless. She'd captured that look, all right.
He'd never gotten all the way back from Vietnam,
had only pretended to. "I want that negative."

"I destroyed it," she said. "And I don't think Rem told you it would be okay to come harass me for it just because he's dead."

"Now!" His voice rose. If he as much as touched her, she'd scream her lungs out. "Rem thought you got rid of the negative, but I knew you didn't, any more than you got rid of—"

"Rem's child?" There was the one thing she had to know, and the only way to find out was to fake it. Since the last time she'd seen him, David had turned into a toad. She felt no fear. "I always thought it odd that Rem would want me murdered when he found out I was pregnant, especially considering that his only child with June was Nicholas."

"Rem didn't okay it," he said. "Nicholas did."

She wanted to weep. That was what she had to find out. Deep down she'd known, in spite of what Marcus and Eddie believed, that Rem would never have wanted her killed. He'd wanted their child, as she had.

"Did you back Nicholas?" she asked.

The toad crept closer. "Nicholas was the boss."

"And now?"

"The First Lady's the boss now. I'll do whatever she wants me to." He reached out for her, the flat, dead glow in his eyes as much about sex as it was preserving the legend. He'd always looked at her that way. It was just more obvious now.

She shoved him back. "Touch me, and I'll have your balls, little man. Do you have any idea what Eddie Palacios will do to you if you try to hurt me?"

"I'm not trying to hurt you. I just want the negative, and I want it fucking now."

Before she could respond, he slapped her across the face, knocking her to the sofa. Tears filled her eyes. Pain chimed through her head. She touched her face, looked at her wet finger, saw blood.

"You idiot." She struggled to find her feet. "I'm expecting a visitor any minute. Her name is Reebie Mahoney. Perhaps you've heard of her?"

"Your daughter." His lips twisted as if he could barely speak the words.

She couldn't say, didn't dare let him wonder. At least she had taken the photo for Eddie. He'd protect Reebie—and her.

She wiped her face and steadied herself. "I can't believe you let Nicholas Remington dictate my murder."

"He was the boss."

"No," she said. "Rem was the boss. I know he told you not to touch me."

"That's not the issue now." His face was blotched and purple, and he moved like an old man, straining to catch his breath. "You have the negative, and you're going to give it to Reebie. The two of you are going to ruin Rem's legacy as payback for what happened all those years ago."

One of her easels stood by the window. She could hit him with it and probably flatten him. She could phone the new doorman and demand that he get up here and help her.

"What makes you think I would come forward now?" She moved along the sofa, making her way toward the telephone and the easel behind it.

"Because you contacted the Mahoney girl. You never did that before."

"You've been watching me all of these years?"

"Only someone like you could live this close to your own daughter and not contact her. Rem insisted that I keep track of you."

"Until his death?" She fought the tightness in her throat. He was wrong, but she couldn't let him know that, not even to protect Reebie.

"That's correct."

"And he didn't tell you to come here? To try to get the negative?"

"I told you I'm working for the First Lady now."

"And she knows? She knows what was on that film?"

His gaze shifted from hers. Not as good at lying as he had once been. "She knows it's incriminating. A sexual indiscretion, perhaps."

"And of course she got that idea from you." That was it. She was throwing him out. But first she had to ask. "Why did Rem ever take that picture, anyway? Why would he want such a memento?"

He sagged, and if he hadn't just manhandled her, she would have felt sorry for his caved-in body, his tortured expression, so like the one in the painting. "We took worse ones. They were terrible times. We didn't think we'd live past that moment. Until you've been in a situation like that, you don't know what you'd do."

Yet there had been glee in their eyes, crazy glee. He hadn't noticed that she'd almost made it to the phone. "What happened to the others?" she asked.

"Chas Sullivan is in an institution." He closed his eyes as if saying a silent prayer. "Totally out of his mind. When I went to see him, he didn't recognize me. Just kept repeating The Lord's Prayer."

"And the others?"

"Dead."

How could they all be dead? His gleaming eyes met hers. God, he couldn't have done that, could he?

"And all to protect Rem's legacy?" she whispered. *The Emperor of Ice Cream,* the poem he loved. Things *were* not what they seemed, not to Rem, either.

"I'm not ashamed of that."

She saw David for what he really was, not what he had pretended to be all of these years. "You wanted me dead because I'd seen the photo, didn't you? The child was only a minor reason compared to that."

"I was only trying to protect—"

"Shut up."

"Don't raise your voice, or you'll have more trouble than you want," he said, but he was powerless. She knew that.

"Don't you come in here, slap me across the face and tell me not to raise my voice." She strode up to him, full of fury now, angry that this toad was the reason she'd had to live her life in secrecy under a nonexistent woman's name. "You weren't trying to protect the precious legacy, were you? You were trying to protect David Ritchey, trying to protect your own ass."

"That's ridiculous." He raised his hand as if trying to halt the words.

"It's ridiculous that I didn't figure it out sooner, that Rem or long-suffering June didn't." She stepped back from him, a baggy used-up man, his eyes not right, his only strength in the past. "Rem didn't kill those people alone. You were in that negative, too, David. You're in my painting with the rest of them. You and Rem and the others, displaying your trophies."

"What are you going to do?"

"For starters, I'm going to get you out of here before Reebie comes," she said. "Stay the hell out of my life, and I'll stay the hell out of yours."

"But you won't. You'll change your mind."

"That's your guilt speaking," she said. "You have the rest of your life to live with what you've done, David. The older you get, the more you become what you haven't resolved. I know I have. That's why I'm seeing Reebie tonight. And that's why I'm kicking your sorry ass out."

She picked up the phone, and when the doorman answered, said, "There's a gentleman in my home, a David Ritchey, former aide to President Reming-

ton. He's assaulted me, and I'd like some help re-
moving him, if you don't mind."

"Sure thing," the doorman said, and hung up.

"That's how it is," she said. "You don't run my
life anymore. Get out of here, or you'll have to deal
with more than your own ghosts. And believe me,
those babies are going to be enough for you."

"You won't be able to keep it to yourself now that
he's gone," he said. "To paraphrase another president, you don't have the moral fiber."

"And you do, you crazy bastard? Who instructed
you to kill your war buddies? Nicholas, maybe?
June? Where was your moral fiber when you let
Nicholas murder Kim?"

He reached for her throat, his expression dazed
as if he instead of she had been the one struck.

She jumped away from him, picked up the easel.
The doorman would be here any minute, Reebie right
behind him. She wasn't worried, only enraged that
she had let his paranoia dictate her life for too many
years.

He charged, head down. She knelt and shoved the
easel in the direction of his groin.

"Bitch."

Good. Maybe she'd hit something. "Get out of
here, right now, David. I'm not afraid of you anymore." And she wasn't. Perhaps she'd never been. "I
was afraid that Rem was part of it," she said, "that
he wanted to hurt me. I never gave you a second
thought, and I never will again. Go home now and

dream about those people you killed. Think about those trophies you collected."

He exhaled a profanity and charged her again. She rammed him again, but this time, he grabbed hold of the easel. They struggled, swinging it from side to side, two dogs with a bone.

Still, she felt no fear. David was used up, a husk. She yanked back the easel, and he fell to the floor. She laughed. "Better go, little man, while you still can."

He grabbed her ankle and bit. She kicked and screamed. She could feel his bite to the bone. He grinned up at her, blood shining on his teeth. He grabbed her leg, pulled her down next to him. Her head hit the carpet, and she blinked away the lights in her eyes.

"I'm not afraid of you," she sputtered. "You always wanted me. I wouldn't have spit on you."

He banged her head against the carpet. "You were a slut. I could have had any woman I wanted. Still could. Hell, I could have June."

"Big prize."

He slammed her head down again. She felt the reverberations in her shoulders, her neck. "Shut up about June."

She strained for breath. "You probably don't know this, little man, but Rem kept you only because of what you'd gone through in Vietnam, only because of that. He said you were a nutcase. That's what he called you, honey. A nutcase."

"Lying slut." He dragged her up onto the sofa, his breath heavy and heaving as a heart attack.

"Not afraid," she repeated.

"You'd better be, you bitch." He slammed her into the sofa again, but his own strength was draining, she could tell.

She kicked him where she knew he'd be weak. Kicked him hard and repeatedly. Somewhere in the contest, he gained strength, pushed his body down on hers.

"It will never happen," she said. "You'll never have what you wanted with me. And maybe I will rethink the situation. Maybe the country does need to know what you did in Vietnam."

"You'll never tell them."

Something hard and cold pressed against her head. No, not now, not before she got to talk to Reebie. Not yet, please not yet.

There had to be a way to let him know he couldn't do this. There had to be a way for her to live.

"The doorman," she gasped, looking up into his cold eyes.

He shoved the gun harder against her head. "The doorman works for me."

And then the shout, the smell, the fiery rush of pain, blowing out every light in her head.

Thirty-Six

Reebie

Nicholas Remington looked a decade younger than his fifty-something years. Part of it was his casual jeans and loose-fitting black sweater. The rest was his unlined face, handsome at first view, then less so the longer I stared at him.

"My name is Reebie Mahoney," I said, my voice thinner than I would have liked. "My mother's name was Kim Mahoney. I met Jeanette once. I can assure you she was not my mother."

He lowered the gun, and it was all I could to do keep from fleeing into the woods.

"They said she was still alive, but I don't believe it."

"Believe it," I said. "I saw her before she was killed. She looked just like the photos of her."

"Then, who was that other woman?"

For the first time in my life, I might have had an answer for him, one I could have never dreamed. But I wasn't about to say it. "What do you want?"

"There's trouble at Darla's." He said it calmly, without apparent fear. It was too dark to be sure about his eyes. "I'm not going to let anyone hurt her."

"Do you know the way back?" I asked.

He nodded. "I've spent most of my life in these woods."

"When you weren't jet-setting all over the world."

I'd meant it as a joke, but his reaction was an odd smile. "Those were just stories," he said finally. "We need to get to Darla's."

"Ed Palacios is in the guest house," I said. "Do you know him?"

Another nod, and the gun arm stiffened. "He's no good. What's he doing here? What's he doing at Darla's?"

I wasn't about to tell him about the paintings. "I don't know," I said. "There's another man with him, as well. They're shooting at each other."

"They don't belong in her house. We have to go."

I couldn't figure out what was wrong with him. He knew the woods, and seemed to be comfortable with the weapon, but something about him—the slow-paced speech, perhaps—made him resemble an actor who'd forgotten his lines.

I leaned against a tree to hide the saw I still carried. "I have a cell phone," I said. "Let's call the police."

"No police." He lifted the gun again.

"Why?" I asked, shrinking up against the tree.

"Because I killed someone, and I don't want to tell them. Killed someone a long time ago."

I remembered what Ed Palacios had shouted in the house: "Nicholas Remington—he's the one who pulled the trigger."

"Who'd you kill?"

He shrugged and looked at me as if I should have the answer. "I don't know anymore. I hate violence."

"Then, why?" My voice shook.

"Our family—" he began, then stopped. "We have to go to Darla's."

"Give me the gun." I put out my free hand.

He looked down at it then back at me. "I don't even know who you are, and until I do, I'm not giving you anything. Now, get going. I know a way we can come up behind them."

I squeezed the tears from my eyes. For one moment there, when I asked for the gun, I'm not sure what I would have done if he'd handed it to me, not sure if I wouldn't have used it on him. Was that how easily a person could flip the violence switch? Was that what had happened to him?

"Get going," he said. "It's right through those trees. They look too narrow to pass through, but once you do, you just go over a bridge and you're almost at Darla's back door."

I moved reluctantly from my shelter.

"Hurry up."

"I'm coming," I said.

"No." He turned. "Don't walk back there. Come on, get ahead of me. I'm not going to do anything to you. I just want to help Darla."

I did as he instructed, edging close to the wall of trees.

"What's that?" he asked. "A saw?"

"Yes."

"Why are you carrying it?" he asked, coming up on my right as I slowed down.

"Why are you carrying a gun?"

"For protection, not because I want to."

"Ditto," I said.

"You've got a smart mouth on you." He frowned, as though not sure what to do about it. "I think you'd better give me that."

"Sure thing." I grabbed the saw in both hands, and swung it at the gun, connected. It went off. He shouted and I ran into the trees.

"Get back out here," he shouted. "You can't hide from me in there! I know these woods like my living room."

I prayed that he'd decide, living room or no living room, that he'd better head for Darla's. He marched past me, stopped. Tangled in a bush, I didn't dare try to see what he was doing. "I know you're here," he said, almost directly in front of me. "I'll be back." Then he laughed. "If somebody else doesn't get you first."

The Widow

Darla returned with Nita and the newspaper reporter, who had a deep voice she would have once considered sexy.

"Could you drive June home?" Darla asked him. "She's chilled to the bone, and she doesn't need to be out here."

"I don't think any of us should go anywhere until the police get here," he said. "Where's your son, Mrs. Remington?"

"There was shooting. He took his gun and went to my place," Darla said. "God, I hope he's okay."

"I hope he's flattened."

June gasped at Nita's blatant disrespect. "Please, dear. Let family matters stay that way."

"Family, my ass." Her perfume was overwhelming even outdoors. "It's murder, and you know it." She heard a shuffling and a "damn" from Nita. "Hey, Mr. Reporter, is it okay if I hang on to you? These heels of mine aren't meant for the great outdoors." It was her seductress voice. June wondered if the reporter were going for it.

"You say your husband killed Jeanette Sheldon?" he asked.

"The woman they *thought* was Jeanette Sheldon,"

she said. "It's made him half-crazy, and when he told me, I thought I should go to the authorities."

"Were you aware of this, Mrs. Remington?" His husky voice was brusque but not unkind.

"It's untrue," she said. "My daughter-in-law is mistaken. I was with my son the night in question."

Before he could respond, there was another shot from within the guest house. Darla moaned as if she felt the bullet. "There's someone coming out," she said. "Finally."

"June. Sweetheart, are you all right?"

Without waiting for assistance, she threw herself in the direction of David Ritchey's voice. His arm wrapped around her. She could smell the sweat, the fear. "David, what's happening?"

"Ed Palacios," he said. "He broke in, tried to murder that girl, Reebie Mahoney. She got away. I shot him."

June's heart begin to calm down. "Is he alive?"

"I don't know. Let's all just wait out here until the police get here."

"Way to go, Uncle David." Nita emphasized the *uncle* in a way that made it sound lewd. "Kill Palacios so that he can't tell that it was really Nicholas who murdered that woman."

"I'm sure you'll have second thoughts once you sober up," he said. "And I'm sure our reporter friend here will try to spare Mrs. Remington any more grief."

"Our reporter friend would like to go inside that

house," the gruff voice replied. "If Palacios is alive, we have to try to help him."

"I realize you have no way of knowing this," David said, "but he sought me out in D.C. when Rem was still lying in state. When I met with him, he threatened Nicholas Remington's life. The man's a long-time enemy of the Remington family. Frankly, I hope he is dead."

"No." June leaned against him, trying to draw in warmth, strength, but it wasn't working. "Ed Palacios may use a gun to solve his problems, but we can't do that. Rem wouldn't want us to."

"I'm going in there," the reporter said.

"With all due respect, I can't let you do that."

"With all due respect, get your ass out of my way."

David jerked away from her. "Stop right there," he said.

Nita screamed.

"And you shut your mouth."

"David?" June reached out for him. She felt as if she were sinking in a pool of water, her breaths coming faster. Something acrid caught in her nostrils, her throat.

"It's all right, sweetheart. You just stay there. It will all be okay."

"No, it won't. I'm the boss now, David. This is the end of it, right here. Let the reporter go into the house. If Ed Palacios is alive, we can and will press charges."

"Sounds like a good idea to me," the reporter said. Finally, she'd spoken. They would be all right now. She reached out for David again, felt him move farther away.

"No one's going inside," he said.

"You're afraid of Palacios," Nita said. "That's why you want him dead. He knows what really went on that night. He knows what Nicholas did."

The gun fired. Nita shrieked. Another gunshot, and silence. June screamed. She couldn't stop screaming.

David grabbed her around the wrist. "You have to stop that now, sweetheart."

She jerked away from him. "I can't."

She could hear Darla's stifled whimpers, no sound from the reporter.

"Don't make me hurt you," he said.

This couldn't be David. "You were like family," she said.

"I still am. I'm still doing what's right for all of us."

From behind her, Darla began to sob. "My house. It's on fire."

Yes, that's what she smelled. The house was burning. Already the bitter smoke stung June's nostrils. David pushed past her, nearly knocking her down.

"All right, Mr. Reporter. You want to go in there so much? Let's just march on in, all of you."

Reebie

Nicholas Remington must have been some kind of idiot savant, or maybe I was. Once he left, I tried to remember the way out as he had described it and, after crossing the bridge, found myself just outside the back door to Darla's living room. Then, I saw the smoke.

I looked around to be sure Remington was nowhere in sight, then crept to the French doors in back. Someone had started a fire in the middle of the living room, using one of Darla's comforters for kindling. It had climbed the willow to the second floor, but it would spread down here in minutes. Ed Palacios lay sprawled in front of the fireplace. He struggled to rise, but something held him back. He saw me, or appeared to, and I saw the bloody hole in his shoulder. I forgot about fear. I forgot about trust. I ran to the door and pulled it open. He was close to me, so close. This was a man I feared would kill me not long before. Now, all I could think about was how to save his life.

"Got to get out of here." He grabbed for me. "Lost too much blood. Too weak." He doubled into a coughing fit. Smoke was twisting through the room. Together, we tumbled out the doors and fell to the cold grass. Air had never felt so good, so precious. I drank it in, then got up and knelt beside him.

"You're tough as your mother, kid," he gasped. "Tougher."

From this angle, I could see the strong boning and glinting eyes that had once made him one of the sexiest men in an America that had faded away before I was born. I felt the sting of unshed tears. Finally, I'd be able to cry for my mother, but not now. I had to trust this man, I must. I took off my sweater and bound it around his arm.

He winced. "David Ritchey's the one who did all this," he said, as if he understood my questions. "If I hadn't threatened Rem's kid, Ritchey would have had you killed the way he killed your friend."

"He murdered Sunny?"

"Guy who worked for him did it," he said. "Problem was, the guy used to work for me. We had a talk. He won't be bothering you."

"But he killed Sunny. We have to do something."

"The life will take care of him. David was the one paying him. He might as well have pulled the trigger."

David Ritchey, one of the most respected men in the country. "Remington's chief of staff?"

"And fellow war hero." He choked on his own words. "Only those two bastards were no heroes. They slaughtered a village." More choking. I wanted to tell him to stay quiet, but I had to know. "Slaughtered old men, women, children. They cut off their ears and strung them into necklaces. Took pictures of themselves. Madmen."

Now I understood all too vividly Jeanette's painting and what those haunted, hideous men had been wearing around their necks.

"And that's what she was going to come forward about?"

"That's just what they thought. All Jeanette wanted was to tell you about Kim, your mother, so you didn't live the rest of your life thinking Kim ran off on you. Marcus and I tried to talk her out of it, but Jeanette said she owed it to you."

I couldn't hold back the tears, for my mother, and, yes, for Jeanette, too.

He reached for his arm. "I think the bleeding's stopped. Help me up."

"You'd better keep still," I said.

"Can't." He tried to move, then moaned low as if fighting against great pain. "Got to get up. The bastard will be back for me, I know."

Suddenly there was movement in the house. Through the window we could see Ritchey forcing people in through the back door. The first was Leo Kersikovski. I don't know what kind of noise I made, but it was enough for Palacios to clap his hand over my mouth.

"Quiet."

I nodded to let him know I was okay.

He removed his hand. "That's better," he whispered. "He's got June Remington in there, too. That's a surprise. Come on. We've got to get out of here."

"Why does he have them in there?" I asked.

"Why do you think?" His look, riddled with shadows and moonlight, forced me to turn away from his eyes. "He's going to kill them."

"We have to do something," I whispered back.

He nodded. "You better believe we do."

Ritchey marched them over to the stairs, now lit

with flame. I wanted to jump him right there, seeing how he had ruined Darla's home. I remembered Jeanette's painting, the manic grin I knew now was his.

"Bastard." Palacios retrieved his gun from the ground. I clutched his arm. I hadn't trusted anyone in a long time, but I now trusted this old man with the bullet wound and the questionable past. With a start, I realized I'd bet my life on Ed Palacios, which was essentially what I was doing.

They stood there before him—Leo, Darla, even June Remington. How could he do this to the widow of the man he'd served? I couldn't hear what he was saying, but I could see his large form convulse in a coughing fit, his fleshy face glazed by the heat.

"What do we do?" I asked him.

"You run like hell. Get some help. I'm going in."

Thirty-Seven

Reebie

No way could I run with Leo inside that house. I watched Palacios creep toward the open door, the gun in his hand. Beyond him, I saw movement. Leo jumped the still-coughing Ritchey, who slammed his gun into Leo's face. Palacios shouted. Ritchey turned, and Palacios shot him.

He went down on all fours, picked up a fire poker and attacked Palacios. Now the struggle was man to man, the two of them on the floor. The two women held on to each other on the hearth, weeping. I couldn't see Leo any longer. Had he been shot, as well?

Palacios had said I was as tough as my mother, tougher. I grabbed the only weapon I had and charged into the room, and sank the sharp saw into Ritchey's back.

He let out a wail that horrified me as much as the terrible feeling of cutting into his flesh. I drove the saw deeper.

He stumbled to his feet, raging, the saw still hanging from his shirt like an odd, drooping wing of a prehistoric creature. In that moment, he became the madman from Jeanette's painting. All of the faces in the painting overlapped into his one hideous grimace.

He grabbed me by the neck, drove his fingers into my throat. The smoke filled the room, making it impossible to breathe. I tried to jerk away from him, but I couldn't gulp enough air to revive myself. I knew I was fading and tried to break free one more time.

He stumbled, and we fell to the floor. His grasp on me broke. I rolled away from him, into Leo's bloody face.

The Widow

June tried to watch the struggle on the floor in her mind. The reporter was young and strong, but David was David. She still couldn't believe he'd allow her in this room where the searing smoke was burning up her lungs. "Help me, David," she said.

"He doesn't care about you." She wondered where Eddie had managed to hide himself. His voice sounded as weak and defeated as hers.

"Where are you, David? Please let's get out of here. I don't care any longer about any of it. If Jeanette had Rem's child, so be it. Let's just leave here before the place burns up and takes us with it."

"It's not about Jeanette's child," David said, his voice close to her ear.

"What, then?"

"There's a negative, and now a painting of something only other men who went to war would understand."

"A massacre," Palacios shouted.

"Easy for you to say. Rem was fighting for his country while you were paying to have your enemies' legs broken."

"I never killed helpless old people. I never killed women and kids. I sure as hell never cut off their ears or wore them on a necklace."

June let the smoke take her breath. This couldn't be true. It couldn't. Not David, definitely not her husband.

"Rem did what he had to do," David said.

She collapsed on the hearth, unable to breathe, not caring. She had just enough voice for one question. "But you fought together, David. If Rem did those things, so did you."

"Exactly," Palacios said, in a voice as clear as one of his songs.

Reebie

I lay there, nudged against Leo's body. Something, someone had stopped Ritchey. Stopped but not finished.

"Ungrateful bastard." He slammed his hand on the floor and connected with the gun. I drew closer to Leo, my eyes burning with smoke. In moments there would be no escape from this place.

Ritchey began firing into the darkness. At what? And how soon would he turn on us?

The idea seemed to occur to him about the same time it did to me.

He whipped his head around, looked at me through the blood that cascaded down his forehead into his eye, and took aim. I cringed.

The shot was as loud as if it had been fired into my head, but it hadn't been. I wept against Leo and watched David Ritchey hit the ground.

"Who?" I asked.

Outside the door stood Nicholas Remington, his face as sad as a child's, his gun anything but child-like.

"I'm sorry," he said.

"I know." I stood and put out my hand. "You hate violence, right? So give me the gun."

To my amazement, he did just that.

Darla ran to him, and the two of them went outside. Into the air. Palacios and Leo tried to get Ritchey outside, but he was too heavy.

"He's dead," Leo said. "We have to get out of here." He reached for my hand, and we started out the door. Then, I saw June Remington. She'd moved to the burning stairs, her eyes raging, as if she could see the destruction.

"Come on," I shouted. A piece of timber crashed before me, separating her from us.

"June," Leo called. "Mrs. Remington." Another piece of timber, larger this time, showered sparks onto us. Smoke filled my nostrils, my lungs.

Sirens screamed from outside.

"Finally," I said. "Let's get help for her."

Even as we ran from the collapsing building, I doubted my own words. We wouldn't be able to help June Remington. She didn't want help.

The Widow

Her breath was gone. She could smell the singe of burning hair. The embers seared her flesh, melted her down onto the stairs. No longer could she remember the cause of her pain. No longer could she think.

Someone shouted, but their words seemed a lifetime away. Finally—her sight restored—she could see, as the flames consuming her mind and the ones consuming her flesh became one.

Reebie

I pressed my face against Leo's chest as a crackling chunk of the house crashed down.

Somewhere, I heard Nicholas's voice consoling Darla. "We'll rebuild," he said. "We'll rebuild." Such an optimistic word for the destruction that surrounded us.

Police officers scrambled down to us. "Anyone hurt?" one of them shouted.

"Yes," I said, and the tears poured out of me.

"We're okay now." Leo hung on, put his lips against my hair. And I swore I heard him say, "I love you."

I couldn't remember the last time I had heard those words. Geoff had stopped saying them long before the end of our nightmare, even when we were still sleeping together, trying to get back what we had so completely lost. When they stopped saying "I love you," that was the first sign.

Never trust a man who doesn't say "I love you."

Never trust a man who does.

Never trust a man.

I pulled myself from Leo's arms and looked up into his eyes. "I want to go home," I said.

The Mobster

So, it's over, Jeanette, not the way we wanted, but it's done. Yesterday was my first one out of the hospital. I went to June Remington's memorial service, and surprised myself when I felt tears in my eyes. Going soft, maybe. That's what age will do to you.

I'm back in the city, the restaurant, watching that fog outside my window, watching it drift closer like maybe it got braver while I was gone. My desk is piled with newspapers, and someone—one of the girls—has spread one out, opened to a story about what happened. There's a photo of me I don't remember having taken that night, my shirt torn, blood running down my face. Looks like I'm going to go out a hero. Who could be less likely? The only decent thing I ever did was love you.

The cops are looking for Phil, to charge him with murder. They may catch him, too, thanks to an anonymous tip they're going to get today, something I never thought I'd do. I never ratted out anyone in my life. Hell, I must be believing my own press.

There's also a story in the paper about the Remington kid. I don't read it. Can't. Poor bastard told the cops everything about that night Kim was killed. How he blamed himself for waking his mother, telling her you were going to ruin their family. He'd even driven her there, against his father's wishes, something not even that lowlife Ritchey would've had the nerve to do. He thought he'd killed Jeanette because he was the one who'd told her, but June was the one who pulled the trigger.

And all because she was afraid Rem was going to leave her for you. Maybe he would have, Jeanette. Maybe he would have. Maybe you were right about him all the time.

I pick up the phone. It feels heavy as a boulder in my hand. Time to make that call.

Thirty-Eight

Reebie

When I told Leo I wanted to go home that night with the fire still consuming the bodies of June Remington and David Ritchey, I wasn't sure what I meant. After that, I realized I just meant I wanted to get away. Away from what had happened, away from the fear and the death. And yes, away from him. I could already feel him writing the story in his mind, even as we stood there in the ashes. I didn't want to be his source or his anything else.

As soon as the police finished with me, I took the next plane back. Only then did I call my dad and tell him what I knew he'd soon be hearing on the news. His sobs made me realize how much pain we'd both lived with when I was growing up and how well he'd managed to hide it from me.

I talked to Darla after I got home. She and Nicholas were rebuilding her guest house on the lot adjacent from the original, she said. She invited me to visit, but I knew I couldn't.

Before I left, we unpacked and went through the paintings. Except for minimal smoke damage, they were unharmed. One portrait bore such a striking resemblance to me that Darla gasped and demanded to know when it was painted. We looked at the date—1976—and I knew the model had to have been my mother. The photographs attached to the back confirmed it. I brought the painting back with me, and suddenly I had a possession I cared about.

I also had unfinished business.

The plane landed in Palm Springs around noon. I took a taxi to Marcus Olson's home.

He received me in the living room, uncomfortable but polite. We talked about what happened, and he made it clear that he'd been in contact with Palacios.

"Ed suggested I give this to you," I said, handing him an envelope. "It's the money for Jeanette's paintings. She had no next of kin."

He nodded. "I'll find a good cause for it." He still had those remarkable eyes, but they weren't happy eyes.

"I'm so sorry about what happened to Hal," I said. "The police believe it was the same man who killed my friend. I hope they find him."

"I'm sorry about what happened to Hal, too." The

pain in his eyes deepened, and I wondered if he would weep. "I'm sorry for a lot."

I stood to leave, and a young woman in tennis clothes bounded into the room. She planted a kiss on Olson's cheek, and he introduced me to her.

"My daughter, Deborah."

She had a generous mouth and hair the color of taffy. What struck me most about her was how absolutely relaxed she was, how comfortable with herself.

Olson put his arm around her and said, "More of the paintings sold, Deb. Isn't that wonderful?"

She looked at the two on the wall by the odd-shaped fireplace and asked me, "Do you like them?"

"Very much."

"My mother painted them."

I glanced at Marcus Olson's pleading eyes, then back at her. "Your mother?" I asked. "I'm a big fan of Nora McFarland's work."

Her eyes grew wider, her voice softer. "Did you know her?"

"No," I said. "No, I didn't. I'm just a fan."

"It was so awful about what happened, so unfair. Even though she and Dad were separated, she came here all the time. We were best friends. I don't know how she got mistaken for that other woman."

"I'm sure it be cleared up soon," I said, eyeing Olson again. "And I know she'd be very proud of you."

"I hope so." She smiled and put her arm around

Olson, and I saw joy flood his expression. He'd given up everything for Jeanette and her daughter, and there was no regret in that love filling his face. "He and Mom both tried to talk me out of politics," Deborah said, "but it's what I love. Did he tell you? I'm going to go for the state Senate. I think I can make it, too."

My gaze shifted to Olson. His expression was wary, his eyes on me, wondering what I would or wouldn't say.

"So do I," I said. "So do I."

I flew in late that Thursday. Daphne said Geoff had been phoning around the clock, so I call him early this morning, knowing he will be up with his coffee and his paper. When he answers, I realize how glad I am to hear his voice.

"If anything had happened to you—" he begins.

"It didn't. I'm going to be okay." I still smell smoke in my sleep. My tongue feels as if it's been parboiled, but I'm going to be okay.

"Reeb, you can have the winery. I'll sign it over to you, give you half of it, whatever."

Those words would have once filled me with joy. "Are you serious?" I say. "Why? Just because I almost got myself killed, you're willing to let me have the winery?"

"I would have, anyway. You know I don't care about material possessions. The car was some kind of midlife thing. I'm getting rid of it. I just held on to the winery because I thought it would get you back."

I remember how it had felt being back there in the little white house that holds the kitchen, lab and offices. How I had to fight the memories that cornered me in the tasting room with its large windows and that poster on the wall—the umbrella, the embrace. It was never my winery; it was ours. I can't go back there. It was a different time, a different life, and it will always be an us place, not a me place.

Geoff says to think it over, that maybe I'll change my mind. As usual, he doesn't give me credit for knowing what I want. There are other wineries. I'm good at what I do. I'd like a medium-size family operation, maybe a hundred thousand cases a year. I'll find it, too. I'll find a place for me to do what I love.

Chico is starting to look like a shepherd, his stomach sprouting white and brown shag. I remind myself to make an appointment to have him groomed. I give him his breakfast and go into the living room to see if the newspaper has come. Daph's bags cover the floor. She comes out of the bathroom in jeans and a black T-shirt, cut off the shoulder and frayed around the edges. I remember that it's been about a month since her last trip to London.

"Another haircut?" I ask.

"Edward."

"Who?"

"That's his name, my old boyfriend. Edward. I didn't want to say anything after all you've been through. But he was here for a few days while you were gone. We talked, and well, I'm going back to Singapore to be with him."

I throw my arms around her. "Oh, Daph, that's wonderful. Are you going to get married?"

"I'm not sure of anything. I just have to find out."

I understand what she's doing. The computer dates never made that much sense to me. How do you do that once you've loved someone, had a life with them? I wonder. How do you layer one person over another, blurring out one set of memories, trying to create another?

"I'm glad for you," I say, "really glad."

"Can you drive me to the airport tomorrow?"

"Sure." I look down at Chico, spaniel eyes staring back at me, as if he knows already. "What about him?"

"I talked to my dad. It will cost a little, but we can get him through quarantine."

"Good," I say, and crouch down next to him, fluff the curly hair on his ears. "Bet you'd like a treat, wouldn't you, boy?" I retrieve one of the jerky strips from the container on the counter. He sits, then leaps and chomps it out of my hands.

"He'll be one of the indoor dogs. I made sure of that."

I pat his side. "I'll miss him." Tears prick at my eyes. Not now, I think.

She reaches down to pick up the new toy I bought for him, a squeaking, velour Frisbee of purple and green. "He'll have his own maid. They'll call him Uncle Chico. That's a sign of respect."

"He'll like that." I can't take any more of this. "I'll check in with you a little later," I say, my throat closing around pain so quick and unexpected it makes it difficult for me to breathe. "I'm going to check out a possible job."

"Back at the department store?"

"At a winery in Oakland." I say it as if I seek employment in wineries every day, and she nods accordingly.

"I'm doing the right thing about Edward," she says.

"I know you are, regardless of what happens. See you later."

I am almost to the door when she calls out, in a choked voice, "Reebie?"

I turn. Tears run down her cheeks.

"He's not my dog," she says, with a sob. "He's yours."

"Are you serious?"

"You're the one who walks him. You're the one who feeds him, the one he sleeps with. I love him, but I can't just take him away from you. It's not fair."

I hug Daph. I hug Chico. Daph hugs Chico, and Daph and I shed tears we probably needed to even if we hadn't been exchanging ownership of an animal. Then, I realize what I have to do.

"I have one more favor," I say.

"Don't tell me you want my Johnny Cash poster, too?"

"I'd never ask you for that. This is a biggie, though."

She wipes a tear from her eye and says, "Shoot, partner."

On the radio, I hear that in the East Bay some maniac is still killing cabdrivers. I'm glad Pargat has found another home, and I'm grateful for Geoff's help. Gratitude—what an odd emotion for the embers of what we had to cool into. At least gratitude can't consume you.

It's almost five-thirty. I sit in the parking lot of the newspaper and dial Leo on my cell phone.

"What time do you get off?" I ask.

"About now." His voice is neutral, the way it was the first time he interviewed me. "Why?"

"I'm in the parking lot. I have something I want to give you."

His face is even more cut and bruised than mine, and he's wearing long sleeves. I wonder if the burns on his arms are worse than he said. As I lean against his VW, I'm not sure I can read the expression on his face.

I can't tell him about Palm Springs. That secret belongs to Marcus, Jeanette and Ed Palacios. They paid dearly for it. I will keep it to myself, as I know my mother would if she were here.

"Where've you been?" he asks.

"Trying to make sense out of what happened," I say.

"And not answering your phone." His eyes are cold, analytical.

"Here. I brought you a present."

He looks down at the record album, its funky cover of four longhairs, naked from the waist up, as if they are blooming within a bouquet of pine branches.

"Green Tambourine," he reads. *"The Best of the Lemon Pipers."*

"Your dad probably owned one just like it," I say. It's the only way to let him know the feelings I can't find the words to express. "You'll notice there are also such hits as 'Love Beads' and 'Meditation' and the surely unforgettable 'Jelly Jungle.'"

Still holding the record album, he crushes me into a kiss, right here, in this very public parking lot right outside his place of employment.

"I love you," he says. "You know that."

How easy to hear it. How easy, after all this, to finally say it. "Oh, Leo, I love you, too."

Another kiss. I marvel that his body can fit so perfectly to mine, that I can melt into him with not just passion but something that feels like hope.

"I can't believe it," he says. "Just when I was ready to give up on us, here we are—no bullshit, no baggage."

"Oh, there's baggage," I say, looking up at his battered, beautiful face. "And he's addicted to flank steak."

"Chico?"

"Daph gave him to me."

He breaks into a grin and shakes his head. Then he opens the car door. I scramble in, snuggling against him, twisting around the gearshift. "How did people ever celebrate free love in these vehicles?" I ask.

"I have a feeling we'll find out." He pulls me to him, and my face presses against that safe place on his chest. "Why?" he asks, breathing the question into my ear.

Why did I come back? Why did I ever leave? I'm not sure what he's asking, and I don't have an answer for either. I don't know where we're heading, or if I'll ever be able to blot out the past, but I saw what happened to people who didn't try, and I don't want to be left someday with nothing but regrets.

"Why, Reebie?" he asks again.

"Because," I say. "Because."

New York Times Bestselling Author

SUSAN WIGGS

Before an estranged couple is killed in an unthinkable tragedy, they designate two guardians for their children—Lily Robinson and Sean McGuire. Brought together by tragedy, the two strangers are joined in grief and their mutual love for these orphaned children. Sean and Lily are about to embark on the journey of ups and downs, and love and hope that makes a family.

"Wiggs has done an excellent job of depicting what lies beneath the surface of relationships…"
—*Booklist*

Available April 2005,
wherever books are sold!

table for five

MSW2167

International Bestselling Sensation

Melanie Starks and her son have been running petty con jobs for as long as they can remember. But just as Melanie is ready to go straight and settle down, her brother—recently released from prison—reenters their lives with a ballsy plan for the ultimate bank heist. Melanie reluctantly agrees, but when the day comes to pull off the robbery, everything goes wrong. Now they're on the run, and they're one false move away from getting caught....

ONE FALSE MOVE

"[An] explosive climax."
—*Publisher's Weekly* on *One False Move*

Available April 2005
wherever paperbacks are sold!

The first novel in the
Cleo North trilogy from
USA TODAY bestselling author

MERLINE
LOVELACE

Ten years ago, former special
agent Cleo North ignored her
gut instinct—and a young
sergeant wound up brutally
murdered. Now, more than a
decade later, Cleo finds new
evidence that proves the
official story—a murder-suicide—
is false. With OSI agent Major
Jack Donovan assigned to watch
her investigative tactics, the two
of them uncover the events that
led to that first deadly mistake.

THE
FIRST
MISTAKE

"Strong, action-packed stuff
from Lovelace, an ex–Air Force
officer herself."
—*Publishers Weekly* on *Line of Duty*

*Available April 2005,
wherever paperbacks are sold!*

BONNIE HEARN HILL

32127 KILLER BODY   ___ $6.99 U.S.   ___ $8.50 CAN.
32001 INTERN   ___ $6.50 U.S.   ___ $7.99 CAN.

(limited quantities available)

TOTAL AMOUNT	$_____
POSTAGE & HANDLING	$_____
($1.00 for one book; 50¢ for each additional)	
APPLICABLE TAXES*	$_____
<u>TOTAL PAYABLE</u>	$_____

(check or money order—please do not send cash)

To order, complete this form and send it, along with a check or
money order for the total above, payable to MIRA Books, to:
In the U.S.: 3010 Walden Avenue, P.O. Box 9077, Buffalo, NY
14269-9077; **In Canada:** P.O. Box 636, Fort Erie, Ontario L2A 5X3.

Name:_____
Address:_____ City:_____
State/Prov.:_____ Zip/Postal Code:_____
Account Number (if applicable):_____
075 CSAS

  *New York residents remit applicable sales taxes.
   Canadian residents remit applicable GST and provincial taxes.

MIRA®

       MBHH0405BL